THE
BRACELET

OTHER BOOKS AND AUDIO BOOKS
BY JENNIE HANSEN:

Abandoned

All I Hold Dear

Beyond Summer Dreams

Breaking Point

Chance Encounter

Code Red

Coming Home

High Stakes

Journey Home

Macady

The River Path

Run Away Home

Some Sweet Day

When Tomorrow Comes

THE BRACELET

a novel by

Jennie Hansen

Covenant Communications, Inc.

Covenant

Published by Covenant Communications, Inc.
American Fork, Utah

Printed in Canada
First Printing: August 2005

11 10 09 08 07 06 05   10 9 8 7 6 5 4 3 2 1

ISBN 1-59156-911-7

This book is dedicated to the "goosies," who stood by me with their wisdom and encouragement through a difficult time and who constantly encourage me to spread my wings.

1

Brushing aside a low-hanging branch, Georgiana was rewarded with a splatter of raindrops that had been hiding in the thick leaves since the morning's early shower. She paid them no mind and hurried on. Sydney was waiting, and he was always impatient when she was late. Of course, he of all people should know she couldn't just leave Burton House whenever she chose.

Lady Burton had been most demanding today, insisting Georgiana try four different hairstyles on her before she was satisfied, not that Lady Burton was ever truly satisfied. Though far more attractive than most women in their early forties, Caroline Burton exerted a great deal of time and expense to maintain an illusion of being younger than her actual years. Georgiana had been Lady Burton's hairdresser for two seasons, and before that, she had served in several other notable houses, so she knew a great deal about ladies' fashions. She also pored over the fashion pattern books to which all of her wealthy employers subscribed to keep up with the latest trends.

Sidestepping a puddle, Georgiana frowned for a just a moment. She was an excellent hairdresser and should still be in London or accompanying a titled lady to the various European capitals, instead of being stuck in the country. Unlike many servants in England's great houses who had fled domestic service for the textile mills of the north and independence, Georgiana had clung to a lifestyle that promised greater access to her dreams. Her mood darkened as she remembered her previous employer, the Marchioness of Stanhope. She'd promised to take Georgiana to Paris. Instead, she'd dismissed Georgiana when she discovered her loathsome son, the heir to the Stanhope fortune, attempting to steal a kiss from her in the music room. *As if it were any of my doing! I wouldn't ally myself with that fat toad even for all of the Stanhope fortune.*

Georgiana turned down a familiar shortcut through the woods that separated the manor house from the village, her thoughts still on the events that had resulted in her meeting and falling in love with Sydney Burton. At first, she'd been happy to leave Stanhope House and had considered herself fortunate she wasn't turned away without a recommendation, as this wasn't the first time her beauty had brought her trouble. Being blessed with wide green eyes, long, dark curls, and a shapely form often seemed more like a curse than a blessing for a woman in service.

Georgiana had long since made up her mind to use her beauty to aid her ambition to wed favorably, but she'd had no idea escaping unfavorable attention would be so difficult. Thank goodness Sydney was more enlightened than his parents and most of their contemporaries. He was not only rich, handsome, and charming, but he frequently told her that class and the artificial divisions of society it created were no longer pertinent to the modern world. *It is no wonder I love him.* She sighed and increased her pace.

She resented being considered unworthy of the attentions of the young men in elite households and of being the one punished when husbands or sons assumed she welcomed their flirtations. None of her several employers had been dissatisfied with her work, but more than once she had been discreetly recommended to another lady as a means of removing her from a gentleman-of-the-household's notice. Nothing had been said to her, but in two cases, Georgiana knew her mistresses had agreed to her change of service because their husbands paid her too much attention. Her first position had come to an end when her young mistress had married an older man who was too clutch-fisted to pay for a hairdresser in addition to a lady's maid, so she had served as both—until the husband had attempted to add a third duty to her responsibilities.

Georgiana brushed back her tiered skirt before it could make contact with the droppings left on the footpath by some careless gentleman's steed.

Lady Burton had appeared at first to be the answer to Georgiana's prayers. It had been a pleasant surprise to discover a mistress so assured of her own beauty that she didn't seem to notice Georgiana's appearance. But Lady Burton, she had learned, was no different from many others of her class. She not only didn't notice that Georgiana was beautiful, she didn't notice that Georgiana—or any of her other servants—were even people. To her, there was the elite class to which she belonged, and everyone else simply existed as nameless, faceless hands to make life smooth and comfortable. Caroline had been a debutante during the time of the Prince Regent. She seemed to think she still lived in that time when servants were little more than slaves.

Georgiana resented too that Lady Burton paid her substantially less since their arrival in the country than she had while they were in town. She couldn't blame those servants who had left the Burtons' employ to try their fortunes in the mills up north where it was rumored some workers earned as much as thirty pounds a year. She'd even considered doing so herself, though she couldn't see being tied to the long hours and tedious tasks required of factory workers. She wanted more than drudgery in her life, and Sydney had promised her travel, beautiful gowns, and security. Of course, it helped that Sydney was handsome, charming, and educated. He was all she had dreamed of in a future husband.

For some inexplicable reason, Lady Burton had retired to the country before the season ended last spring, taking her second son, Sydney, her personal maid, Gwen, and Georgiana with her. Georgiana was well aware "the season" wasn't the grand social event it had once been, but it still held a great deal of glamour and was highly valued by Lady Burton and her social set.

What had first appeared to be a disastrous train of events that landed her in the country, she now saw as incredible luck. Crossing a small footbridge, she smiled at her reflection in the water below, seeing the happiness on her own face. It was all because of Sydney. She'd scarcely been aware of him in London. He'd spent little time at the Burton townhouse on Grosvenor Street. He had rooms of his own near his favorite club and had only put in brief courtesy appearances at his mother's entertainments.

The sudden flight of birds in front of Georgiana reminded her of the recent rash of muggings and thefts in the neighborhood. She looked around nervously, noting the thick woods on all sides of her. Young Lord Haven had been discovered in just such a place in the next county a fortnight ago with his throat slashed and his purse missing. Even with the hefty reward his grandfather, a magistrate of the royal court, had posted, no one had come forward with any information leading to an arrest. She turned quickly down the path leading to the village, and her mind filled almost at once with her preoccupation with Sydney.

Georgiana recalled how Sydney had spent the first few weeks recovering from a slight wound to his throat that he'd received during a scrape he and a couple of his rowdier friends had gotten into in London. She hadn't learned the details, and when she'd asked, he'd dismissed the wound as trivial. After the first few weeks spent in the country, he'd become bored. The young man claimed the Burton stables didn't provide much of a challenge, which left him without amusement or companionship other than that which he found at the village pub or in pursuing "the prettiest girl in all England."

With few entertainments requiring elaborate hairstyles for her mistress, Georgiana, too, found the country limiting. At first, boredom had been both the reason

Sydney began flirting with her and the reason she had responded. But as they became better acquainted, flirtation had blossomed into romance.

Georgiana's feet flew down the faint path. It was a fair day, and she had only a few precious hours to enjoy the summer festivities with Sydney before Lady Burton would awaken from her nap, expecting Georgiana to be there to help her dress and do her hair all over again for that evening's ball. Her mistress was in a dither over the ball. She was as excited as if this were her first ball, which it certainly was not. Nearly thirty years had passed since Lady Burton, the youngest daughter of the Earl of Middleton, was presented to the queen and her papa had almost immediately betrothed her to wealthy Viscount Burton, a man considerably her elder.

Lord Burton spent most of his time in town and only visited his estate on rare occasions. Unlike her previous employers' husbands, Lord Burton paid her no attention, so she didn't dread his visits. But his arrival the previous week had thrown the staff into a flurry of activity and sent the viscountess scurrying to arrange a ball. The older country servants were almost as excited as their mistress and spent countless hours running about and whispering behind their hands as though the town servants weren't meant to be privy to the plans for the ball.

Far fewer guests had arrived to stay at the manor the past few days than Georgiana had expected, leaving her with more free time than many of the other staff members, whose ranks hadn't been increased to meet the demands placed on the servants by preparations for the ball. When her last employer had entertained at his country estate, the house had been filled with house-guests, and extra maids were employed to ensure that all went smoothly. And there had been a bonfire and supper for the servants with dancing afterward.

Once she and Sydney were married, she hoped to spend most of her time in town. She'd had enough of dull country pursuits. Being a second son, Sydney wasn't required to learn estate management, and life in the country bored him as surely as it did her. She shivered in delightful anticipation of becoming Sydney's bride and wondered at her own audacity in presuming to wed a member of the aristocracy, even if he was only the second son of a viscount. There would be a terrible scandal at first, but she didn't doubt for a minute she would eventually win over even the highest sticklers. Society wasn't as stiff as it had been prior to the commencement of Queen Victoria's reign. Georgiana's time at Lord Burton's country estate had proved advantageous, but she longed for the elopement Sydney had promised and their return to the city.

Music reached her ears and her excitement grew. Would Sydney dance with her? It had been almost two years since a handsome man had held her in his arms as they swayed to music. She had a fondness for music but had found little in the way of musical entertainment on the Burton estate.

"Psst! Georgiana! Over here." A whisper came from behind a tree just before the path ended in a break in the hedge that almost surrounded the village.

"Sydney!" She recognized his voice and came to a halt. He sat behind a tree, almost hidden from the path. Stepping around the tree, she knelt beside him. Before taking her hands, he shoved two small silver pistols into his coat pocket.

"You're looking lovely." He grinned in appreciation of her long, dark curls, heart-shaped face, and winsome form. His mouth angled toward her full lips, but she backed up, giving him a slight, but calculated pout.

"Playing with toys?" She arched a teasing eyebrow.

"You mean these?" He pulled the silver guns from his pocket. "They're not toys, my dear." He grinned mischievously. "They're very real, as more than one cheater at cards has discovered. I got them from a friend who acquired the matched pair on his recent visit to America, where they've become quite popular since they can easily be hid up a sleeve or inside a boot." He returned the pistols to his pocket, then caught her off guard with a sudden lunge, grabbing her around the shoulders and pulling her closer.

"You promised we'd visit the fair." She pouted.

"And we shall, my sweet. I only wished a taste."

Georgiana hesitated. It was important that she and Sydney be seen together in public, and giving into him now could spoil all her plans. If the villagers knew Sidney was squiring her about, it would be far more difficult for Lord Burton to have their marriage set aside when they returned from their elopement. Then, too, she hoped that when Sydney realized that the inevitable gossip which would follow their being seen together would certainly reach his parents, it would spur him to run away with her before Lady Burton could dismiss her and Lord Burton could send him abroad. Sydney was already in his father's poor graces for some boyish prank he'd involved himself in during the recent social season in London. Thus far they'd been discreet and circumspect, seeing each other only in darkened hallways, the woods, and at the summer pavilion late at night when everyone else was asleep, but Sydney was growing more and more demanding. If they didn't soon visit the parson Sydney had told her would wed them with only a special license and no posting of banns, she feared she would yield to his coaxing and her own desires.

She didn't mean to be just another dalliance, easily dismissed when Sydney spied another pretty face. He'd promised to wed her, and she meant to hold him to that promise. She loved him, but she wasn't a fool. Of course, there was the possibility that since Sydney was merely a second son, Lord Burton would show his displeasure by purchasing a commission for Sydney, and she would find herself following the drum. Even that would be preferable to the dull life she now led, and, at least, they would be together.

"Just one dance, my love." She pitched her voice to a throaty purr and let one hand slide slowly up his arm. She leaned forward, giving his cheek a fluttering kiss. When he sought more, she clasped his hand to lead him toward the couples dancing just beyond the hedge. He seemed about to draw back, then with a shrug of his shoulders, burst through the hedge a step behind her dancing figure.

He clasped her waist and held her close as they spun about the dirt-packed floor. His fingers toyed with her curls, then strayed to the ribbons of her bodice. The fiddle sounded a faster beat, and she twirled away, then back. She'd never felt so alive and happy before in the whole of her life.

Following a couple of country-dances, they paused to catch their breaths. Georgiana smiled happily at the couples surrounding them. There were few faces from the manor, though she did spy a dark-haired young man she thought was a gypsy from the camp she'd heard was nearby. She knew his name was Raul and that he was often in Sydney's company. He appeared to be watching her, his dark eyes seeming to mock her. She turned her back, refusing to let him dampen her gaiety and was surprised to catch a shared conspiratorial wink passing between Sydney and the gypsy.

Sydney greeted a few of the young men they encountered on the dance floor by name. They grinned and clapped him on the back in a friendly fashion, and she had to stifle her annoyance when he didn't offer to introduce her. She comforted herself with the reminder that they would soon meet again under far different circumstances.

She didn't protest when Sydney took her hand, leading her away from the makeshift dance floor. They paused at a booth where he bought her a small lemon custard. A short time later, he hesitated in front of a table heaped with an odd assortment of items. A toothless old woman beckoned him closer, and he leaned toward her. The hag whispered in his ear, and they both laughed. As Georgiana grew impatient, the old woman handed Sydney a paper, which he dropped into his pocket before slipping a silver coin in her palm. Moments later, he whisked Georgiana back through the hedge. His arm encircled her waist as he led her deep into the wood that separated the manor from the village.

Sydney stopped in a quiet glen. Large trees formed a bowery with their branches, allowing only an occasional dapple of light to penetrate to the grassy floor. To one side, she caught a glimpse of a roof through the thick foliage and heard the shuffle of a heavy animal's hooves accompanied by its blustery blowing of air. For a brief moment, she wondered why a horse was stabled in the woods, then she forgot everything except Sydney.

Taking Georgiana with him, Sydney sank to his knees. She was vaguely aware of a blanket spread across the grass, but before she could consider its implication, Sydney kissed her and pulled her closer.

"Sydney." Her protest was feeble as she felt his hands stroke her back and begin to stray.

"Don't worry, my love," he murmured in her ear. "Tomorrow we will fly to our own destiny. Special license or Gretna Green, it doesn't matter to me as long as you are mine."

"We should wait."

"Perhaps this should wait too." His voice was soft in her ear as he dangled a piece of jewelry before her eyes. "I bought it as a symbol of all the many facets of my love for you."

A silver chain swayed slightly before Georgiana's face, and she gasped at the sight of five large jewels, each one different from the others, set in the length of twisted shining strands. There was something ostentatious about the large gems and their varied hues that lent the bracelet a gaudy appearance. It both offended Georgiana's sense of aesthetics and drew her hypnotically. Never in her life, before capturing Sydney's heart, had she owned anything of monetary value or great beauty. She stretched out her hand and lightly touched the glittering object.

"This is where it belongs. Precious jewels for my precious jewel." Sydney captured her hand and fastened the bracelet around her wrist. She held up her arm, allowing the slanting rays of the late-summer sun to reflect the varied hues of the bracelet, sending a prism of color to dance before her eyes.

"It's beautiful." Tears dimmed Georgiana's eyes, and her heart beat faster with the thrill of being loved by handsome, generous Sydney.

"You're beautiful," Sydney whispered. With one hand, he drew her mouth to his. The bracelet pressed deeply against her skin, weakening her will to resist. Softly her fingers brushed the red welt at the base of his throat.

"Sydney!" The peremptory voice of Sydney's brother, the Honorable Gerald Burton, drifted toward them. The call was repeated, sounding closer. Sydney removed his hand from where, Georgiana realized with a burst of heat suffusing her face, she shouldn't have permitted it to stray. Sydney scrambled to his feet while Georgiana struggled to straighten her dress.

"Your mother will be expecting me," she mumbled, her face downcast.

"Look, luv," Sydney's hands cupped her cheeks, drawing her close for a final kiss. "We have to go, but tonight, after Mother's ball, meet me here. She keeps the Middleton betrothal ring, which is my bride's right, locked away. Until I can persuade her to give it to me, this bracelet will serve as a symbol of our betrothal, and before dawn, you shall be my bride."

2

Georgiana ignored the glare Lady Burton gave her when she walked into the lady's dressing room. She didn't apologize for being late, nor for the fact that her mistress had sent a maid and two pages to summon her. The silly woman maintained an icy silence as Georgiana twisted and curled her hair into the elaborate style Lady Burton had chosen for the evening. As a final touch, Georgiana wove three pale pink rosebuds into the coiffure around the base of a long feather dyed to match Lady Burton's deep rose, multiflounced gown.

Her mistress examined the flowers with a critical eye, then preened into the glass as they met her approval.

"Ah, they were worth the search." Georgiana let her voice convey an insinuation that her tardiness was due to searching every bush in the garden for the perfect buds to adorn her mistress's hair.

When Lady Burton was satisfied with the elegance of her appearance, she rose to her feet and made her way to the door of her chamber. She paused once to tap her closed fan across her left palm, a sign Georgiana had learned was an indication her ladyship was up to something.

"You are to assist Gwen in preparing our young guests for this evening's entertainment. After they have gone downstairs, you may straighten my suite and set their rooms in order. You will not be needed after that and may retire to your bed." With a swirl of the flounced layers of her skirt, she turned sideways to the door to accommodate her wide hoops and was gone.

Georgiana crept after her, just to where she could glimpse the musicians warming up their instruments. She watched Lady Burton descend the grand staircase to join her husband, who waited impatiently in the hall. Georgiana flung one longing look toward Sydney, standing beside his parents, prepared to greet their guests. He was attired in a lemon-colored waistcoat, buff pantaloons, shining boots, and his cravat was knotted in the latest fashion. She noted that Sydney's older brother, Gerald, and his mousy wife had also arrived in the hall and joined the receiving line. Elizabeth's hoops were narrower than Caroline's, revealing she wasn't nearly as particular about fashion as was her mother-in-law.

Gerald and Elizabeth had been married four years without producing an heir to secure the family name and fortune, though not from a failure of trying. Elizabeth had suffered two miscarriages and delivered a stillborn son. Georgiana's lip curved up in the faintest hint of a smile. There was a good possibility her own children would eventually be heirs to the manor, the Burton fortune, and the hereditary title since it didn't appear likely that Elizabeth would manage to produce an heir.

"Georgiana!" she heard Gwen's impatient voice. "Lady Burton said we should assist the Wellington ladies in their dress. Come at once!"

Georgiana turned back, doing her best to hide her reluctance. She should be standing beside Sydney, not dressing his mother's guests' hair. The fingers of her right hand slipped beneath the left cuff of the unfashionable gown she wore. Dreamily, they ran across the five jewels set in the bracelet Sydney had given her as a token of his love. Only his reluctance to anger his parents by skipping his mother's ball had delayed their running away before the wee hours of the morning. The touch of the bracelet served to brighten her mood, and she turned away to follow Gwen to the guest wing.

All four of the Wellington offspring were dressed in shimmering white satin and lace gowns adorned with different hues of ribbon on each gown. They, with their mother, were gathered in the oldest daughter's room. Their mother, a large, loud, pasty-faced woman, obviously considered them incomparables and had spared no expense for their shoes and gowns, though with their pale hair, the white made them look insipid. The countess fluttered about her darlings, smiling and showering them with compliments and generally making a nuisance of herself.

Georgiana ignored the younger girls' giggles and whispered conversation as she set about curling and braiding their hair. She'd become adept at blocking out silly chatter in favor of her own thoughts as she worked. Georgiana felt a tug of sympathy for the eldest daughter, who appeared almost ill with her pasty face and pinched lips. This was Lady Daphne's third season, and the only suitors she'd managed to attract thus far were younger sons with pockets to let and crass fortune hunters.

Daphne didn't join her sisters' gay chatter, but she occasionally sighed as though greatly troubled. Thinking a ribbon in the older girl's hair might give her a bit more color, she wove a bit of pink satin into the elaborate braids she'd used to give the girl an illusion of height.

"Oh, this won't do!" Lady Daphne stared at her image in the glass when Georgiana finished. She looked as if she might burst into tears.

"But Lady Daphne . . . the color—" Georgiana began, only to be cut off by the countess.

"She'll be wearing the Wellington rubies tonight." The Countess huffed proudly and set a small casket on the dressing table, then slipped a key into the lock. After the tiniest click, it opened to reveal a magnificent tiara of bloodred rubies the size of robins' eggs sitting atop a glittering rainbow of jewels.

Georgiana barely managed to suppress the gasp that arose to her lips. Even a lowly hairdresser such as herself had heard of the fortune in rubies that was part of the Wellington heiress's dowry. Georgiana's right hand went unconsciously to her left wrist, fingering the slight ridges she could feel with her fingertips. She had never expected to own even a small fortune in jewels. Now, thanks to Sydney, five beautiful gems were hers, including one that was an almost identical match to the amazing stone at the center of the ring Lady Wellington returned to the case that held the glittering array of jewels.

"Yes, I see, madam." Georgiana returned to business, stripping the offending ribbons from the girl's hair and beginning to build a style worthy of the tiara. Only to herself did she complain that a great deal of time and irritation could have been saved if she'd been informed of the tiara to begin with. *And what does Lady Wellington expect to accomplish by allowing Lady Daphne to wear the famous rubies tonight? And to a country ball no less!*

When Georgiana finished Lady Daphne's hair, she noticed the brilliant stones did bring out some color in the girl's cheeks, making her look almost pretty. Turning to the girl's sisters, she asked if any of them were planning to wear jewelry or any sort of ornamentation in their hair. They giggled, and Lady Wellington announced that ribbons would do for them. Though they would, of course, wear jewelry, there would be no more tiaras.

The stout, horsey-looking woman tossed her head, and Georgiana noticed the sparkling sapphires encircling her thick neck. They were likely as valuable as the rubies, and she had heard it said that just one of the Wellington rubies would feed the British navy for a full year. It was no wonder Lady Daphne was plagued by fortune hunters.

Georgiana stifled a groan when she saw the heavy necklaces, ear bobs, and bracelets the countess draped on her younger daughters. The ornate ruby pieces at Daphne's throat and dangling from her ear lobes came close to being too much for the girl, though they did improve her color, but the glitter of jewels on her younger sisters looked absurdly ostentatious. At last the girls were ready for the ball, and their mother shepherded them from the room. Georgiana was glad to see them go.

A sound behind her reminded her she wasn't alone. Gwen, too, seemed to be relieved to see the fluttering young women depart. Lady Burton's maid had been the only other female servant to accompany her mistress to the country. She was much older than Georgiana and had been with Caroline's mother before becoming Caroline's personal maid. Though Georgiana and Gwen shared a peaceful coexistence, they'd never become close friends.

Giving a sigh, Gwen arched her back, revealing the toll age and arthritis had inflicted on her. She looked around the room, now cluttered with discarded clothing and toiletries. "We'll have to straighten it before they return," she said with a noticeable lack of enthusiasm. Georgiana felt a twinge of sympathy for the woman who had served Lady Burton for more than thirty years with little to show for her hard work and loyalty. She'd been granted few privileges for her many years of service. Though she must have been pretty as a young woman, she had no husband, children, or life of her own. Georgiana touched the bracelet beneath her sleeve. Thankfully, she wouldn't share the older maid's fate.

"I'm not a maid," Georgiana protested even as she bent to pick up a discarded stocking. She wasn't really complaining; she was too happy for that. Besides, there was something about Gwen that reminded Georgiana of her own mother's struggle with declining health before her death.

"Lord Wellington's man and her ladyship's maid will do their rooms. The housemaids have all been pressed into service to help with the refreshments and other guests, which leaves only the two of us to set the young ladies' and Lady Burton's rooms to rights. On a night like this, everything must be just right." She cast a glance that seemed almost sympathetic toward Georgiana.

Doubtless, Georgiana guessed, Gwen thought Georgiana was feeling left out because she hadn't been included among the servants given assignments that would bring them in contact with the beautifully decorated ballroom, orchestra, and glittering guests. She did feel a tinge of resentment, but for an entirely different reason. Except for Lady Burton's silly ball, this would be her wedding night. Keeping her thoughts to herself, she bent to the task, whisking discarded items into their appropriate places. She closed the jewel casket, noticing again that the spectacular ruby ring was the only piece of the set Lady Daphne hadn't worn. She looked around for a place to leave the jewel casket, then tucked it out of sight in a drawer.

"I'll finish in here," she told Gwen. "Go ahead to Lady Burton's suite."

Gwen smiled to be granted this small consideration and left, closing the door behind her. Georgiana finished straightening the Wellington misses' rooms, and instead of joining Gwen, she made her way to the gallery where she could hide behind thick curtains to watch the ball below. She was much too excited to return to the room she shared with the other female household help. Smiling a secret smile, she remembering how once Sydney had caught her in the upper hallway and had pulled her into the gallery for an impromptu kiss. He'd told her how he and his brother had been allowed to go there with their nanny when they were small boys to watch their mother's parties. A cloud of

dust arose, leaving her struggling to suppress a sneeze as she
slid behind the long velvet draperies. She supposed that
with no children in the house and a smaller staff than was
once employed to keep the mansion spotless, this part of
the house had become neglected.

Peering through the curtains, she found the ballroom
ablaze with candles, and the dancers were a swirl of color.
Music drifted to her ears, and she couldn't help swaying to
the rhythm, imagining herself dancing in Sydney's arms
around the grand room. How she loved to dance.

It took several minutes before she found Sydney's
elegant form moving among the dancers. She didn't
recognize his partner, a tall, auburn-haired beauty who
coquettishly tossed her curls and laughed each time the
country-dance brought them together. It seemed to
Georgiana that the young lady was allowing each touch to
linger longer than was called for by the steps of the dance.

When the music ended, she watched Sydney escort
the young lady to a chair next to her chaperone, bow
deeply, then turn away. Moments later, he presented
himself to Lady Daphne. Georgiana tried not to mind. It
would be expected of him to dance with the daughter of
his mother's houseguests. The girl's slipper caught on the
hem of her gown, and she stumbled a bit as she rose to her
feet. Georgiana smiled ruefully, knowing the matrons
would cluck and the poor girl would only be saved from
their scorn by her father's fortune.

The musicians struck up a waltz, and Georgiana
watched jealously as Sydney held Lady Daphne close and
glided with her across the floor. The poor thing appeared

almost graceful in Sydney's arms. When the music stopped this time, everyone stayed in place. Viscount Burton stepped to the dais and held up his arms. He then beckoned for Sydney to join him.

Georgiana didn't know what was happening, but she felt a nervous tremor in the pit of her stomach. She watched Sydney extend his arm to Lady Daphne and saw the encouraging smile he gave her as she placed her hand above his. Even from the distance of the balcony, Georgiana could see the glitter of a huge diamond on the girl's left hand. A ripple of approving noises emanated from the assembled crowd, then as Sydney and Daphne made their way toward Lord Burton, Georgiana clapped her hands over her ears. She didn't want to hear Lord Burton's speech. Nausea was now threatening, and she doubled over in pain.

In spite of her efforts, Lord Burton's deep voice penetrated her senses, piercing her heart. ". . . announce betrothal . . . Sydney . . . Daphne Wellington, daughter of . . . banns to be posted . . . a toast . . ." Georgiana took a stunned step forward, disbelieving, and totally oblivious to the swarm of servants balancing trays of fluted glasses moving through the crowd. Her mind conjured up her last glimpse of the jewel casket the Countess of Wellington had carried to Lady Daphne's room. She'd draped the entire ruby collection on her daughter, save one piece. Daphne's fingers had been left bare because the countess knew her daughter's hand would be adorned that night with the Middleton diamond betrothal ring that had come to Lady Burton from her mother and hence to Sydney.

Georgiana's hand clawed at the bracelet on her wrist. Tears ran down her cheeks and dropped on the bright stones. Sydney had promised her the Middleton diamond would be hers after they wed. It came from his mother's side of the family since the Burton betrothal ring had gone to Gerald's wife. Because Sydney couldn't access the ring without his mother's approval, he'd chosen a bracelet of bright jewels to pledge his love. Had it all been a lie? Was Sydney going to marry Lady Daphne? Or was he simply taking part in a charade while planning secretly to elope with her? The answer was more than she could bear. The candles grew dim, and Georgiana felt herself falling. It didn't matter. She would rather fall to her death at Sydney's feet than live seeing him wed to Lady Daphne.

Groggily, she came awake. For a moment, she wasn't certain of her whereabouts, then she realized she was lying on the floor of the gallery balcony. And she was very much alive. Sitting up slowly, she noted that the ball was continuing. The sounds that reached her were those of a celebration. Then she remembered.

No! This is Lord and Lady Burton's doing. Somehow they learned their son had fallen in love with a woman in service. The betrothal means nothing. In a few hours, Sydney will take me away just as we planned! He's only going along with the betrothal to avoid suspicion.

Crouching low, she hurried from her exposed position to the safety of the thick velvet drapes. She was shivering with cold and paused to wrap the heavy folds of fabric around herself to stave off the chill while she attempted to gain control of her emotions. She couldn't let any of the other servants see her in this state.

Voices caught her attention, freezing her to the spot where she stood wrapped in the deepest folds of the velvet curtains.

"Put that toy away and get back to Lady Wellington." It was Gerald's grating voice.

"I assure you this is no toy. At close range, it is as deadly as a full-size pistol. I have to . . ." She recognized Sydney's voice and longed to throw herself into his arms, but Gerald cut his brother off.

"What? Make certain your mistress doesn't cause a scene? If you had any sense at all, you would have paid her off and made certain she was nowhere near here tonight. If Wellington even begins to suspect you gambled away your inheritance from Grandmother Middleton's estate and are now penniless except for the allowance you receive from Father, he'll call off the betrothal. He won't allow his precious daughter to be the means of repairing your fortune."

"I'm not that much of a fool. I gave the chit a bracelet and made arrangements," Sydney responded in an indifferent voice. Georgiana's hand went once more to the jewel-laden chain encircling her wrist.

"And if I know you, the bracelet is nothing but brass with a few bits of glass." Gerald's voice was scathing. "And why is your little hairdresser still here? She should have been gone before the Ladies Wellington arrived."

"The time wasn't right." Sydney's voice was sullen. "And Mother had need of her skills."

"It's a good thing I caught a glimpse of her on the balcony. Wellington will cut up if he catches wind of this. It was your plan to restore your fortune with Lady

Daphne's dowry. And you know perfectly well that you stand to inherit the Wellington fortune since there is no male heir. You're finally in Father's good graces because he sees you might produce the heir Elizabeth and I have thus far failed to give him, but you stand to lose it all if you don't get your paramour out of here."

"It's taken care of!" Sydney snapped back in a voice Georgiana had never heard before. "I've made arrangements. She'll be gone before first light. Raul assures me she will fetch a tidy sum." Why Georgiana's memory flew to the exchange between Sydney and the old gypsy woman at the fair, she didn't know, but she was suddenly afraid. She scarcely dared breathe until the brothers moved on.

"Get back to Lady Daphne!" Gerald ordered. "I'll look for the wench."

She didn't hear Sydney's response, but she stayed hidden for some time. Slowly the shock receded to be replaced by anger. Sydney had lied to her. He had no intention of marrying her. His proposal had been a sham calculated to get past her guard. She curled her fingers into her palms, forming fists in her fury. Far greater than the blow to her heart was the pain of being made a fool. She wanted to make Sydney pay for her smashed dreams. She thought of sneaking into the ballroom and making her own announcement. It would serve him right to lose Lady Daphne's dowry—and the Wellington fortune!

Before she could act, another voice reached her ears. "Georgiana?" She recognized Gwen's voice. She was afraid to answer. What if Gerald had sent Gwen after her?

He was determined to get her out of the house, and she wasn't sure what lengths he'd go to to accomplish that feat. She'd been a fool to assume the other servants hadn't noticed Sydney's attention to her. And what did Sydney have in mind? What did he mean, "Fetch a tidy sum"?

"Georgiana, you must come with me now." The curtain moved, and Gwen clasped her hand. "Hurry—and be quiet."

"Gerald . . ." she stammered.

"He won't look in my room. Now be quick." Georgiana had to trust someone, and Gwen had always been kind to her. She ran down the darkened hall behind the older maid until they came to the small room off Lady Burton's dressing room. Once they were inside, Gwen guided Georgiana to a chair before demanding the whole story. By the time Georgiana finished, she was in tears again.

"Shush," Gwen demanded. "We need to think, and we mustn't risk any sound that will alert the Burtons or the other servants. The local staff are a clannish lot, and they've been snickering over your infatuation with young Sydney." Gwen ratified Georgiana's own belated conclusion concerning their fellow servants. "I've known the Burton fortune was faltering for some time," Gwen admitted. "Lord Burton and young Sydney both gamble extensively. Gerald's marriage to an earl's daughter bolstered the family resources for some time, but apparently it needs another financial infusion. Sydney has never had an ounce of scruples, and it was his gambling losses, coupled with fear that his latest escapade would endanger the Wellington arrangement, that drove Lady Burton to retire to the country with him until the formal betrothal was announced." Gwen paced the floor, taking short, agitated steps.

"I thought he loved me." Georgiana covered her face with her hands, but already snatches of memory were painting a different picture of Sydney than the one with whom she'd fallen in love. "He gave me this bracelet as a token of his love. He said the stones were precious jewels." She unclasped the chain and thrust it toward Gwen, her heart twisting at the sight of green marks left by the cheap metal on her wrist.

Gwen took the bracelet from Georgiana's hand and studied it carefully. "Hmft! Precious jewels all right," she snorted. "Ten years ago, the village church burned down. The heat exploded the stained glass windows, which depicted Jesus with a group of children gathered around Him. It was entitled *Precious Jewels*. The ground was covered for some distance with pieces of bright, colored glass, some rather large. Children collected the pretty lumps of glass to play with, and Sydney came home from exploring the ruins with his pockets full of the brightly colored bits. He must have had some of them specially cut for jewelry."

Georgiana sat up straight, suddenly recognizing the extent of his betrayal. "He plans to send me away tomorrow without a referral. Without any money and only a worthless piece of jewelry, what will become of me?"

"I fear his plans are worse than that." Gwen folded her arms and looked greatly troubled. "I heard him send word by the kitchen boy to Raul over at the gypsy camp, telling him to come at once. That's how I knew something was afoot. I don't like to speak harshly of my mistress's son, but Sydney has had a cruel, selfish side since he was a boy, and he has always resented not being the heir. His mother excused the drowned kittens, servants' accidents, and times he was sent down from school as childish pranks, but I've had my suspicions about Sydney since he sent for Raul the day Elizabeth began labor while he was the only other family member at home."

"Sent for Raul? Why? Was there no midwife?"

"Raul brought some strange woman here who claimed she was a midwife. The old hag insisted Elizabeth drink some vile mixture that put the poor girl to sleep. Raul and the woman were gone, and I couldn't awaken Elizabeth when the real midwife and Gerald arrived. Her wee babe never drew breath, and that poor girl hovered at death's door for nigh a week. When she was able to sit up and speak again, she had no memory of her ordeal, and I thought it best to keep my lips sealed."

"What?" Georgiana jumped to her feet, and Gwen had to remind her to be quiet. Her heart pounded with fear. The enormity of Gwen's words sank in. Gwen had accused Sydney of murdering his own nephew. If Gerald and Elizabeth's baby had meant nothing to Sydney, certainly her own life would have no value.

"Why didn't you warn me? Though Sydney and I took care not to draw attention to our meetings, surely some of the staff must have talked among themselves. I've seen you have tea with the housekeeper and know the staff hasn't shunned you as they have me."

"Oh, my dear." Tears came to Gwen's eyes. "After Sydney got in trouble over that actress, Lady Burton was frantic to keep him out of London until his betrothal was made public. She expected she couldn't keep him here once his throat healed without a distraction. That is why she brought you here. I assumed you had agreed to . . . entertain Sydney and keep him from rushing back to London and that actress with whom he is obsessed."

"She knew . . . Lady Burton expected . . . She had no right to think that I . . ." Rage and mortification churned inside Georgiana, rendering her nearly incapable of rational speech. "I've got to get away. Now! Tonight!" Georgiana paced across the small room.

"I have a little money," Gwen told her, reaching out to touch her arm. "It isn't much, but I've been saving for the time when I will no longer be able to earn my keep. It will get you away from here."

"I can't take—"

"You must." Gwen was suddenly fierce. "I was much like you when I was a girl. I too loved unwisely. My mistress, who was just a girl herself, discovered my feelings for her brother and that her parents were dismissing me without a reference. She made some quiet plans of her own. She convinced Lord Middleton to hire me to care for his new bride and whisked me out of the house. Without her, I would have starved or been forced to turn to an unsavory life. I vowed if I could ever be of service to another young woman in a like situation, I would."

"But—"

"No, you mustn't argue. Just stay here until I return. I'll pack a few clothes for you and get the money. Do you have any keepsakes in your room you especially value?"

Georgiana shook her head. She had nothing—nothing but a useless bracelet. She watched Gwen check the hall then move soundlessly toward the servant's wing before closing the door that led to the hall.

By the light of the moon streaming through the window, Georgiana examined the bracelet she'd believed was a token of Sydney's true love. It glittered brightly, and she contemplated throwing it from the tiny window in Gwen's room to the paved driveway below. *With my luck, it will land on some dutiful servant's head who will take it to Gerald.* She let the bracelet drop to the floor.

With Gwen gone from the room, she was again assailed by doubts. Could she trust Gwen? Even if Gwen were being honest with her, how could she take the older woman's money, and how could Gwen have saved enough to be of use on her meager salary? She hung her head, wondering where she should go and how she would get there. Her eyes caught the bright array of colors in the bracelet she'd flung to the floor. If only the bits of glass were real jewels! A picture of the ruby ring Lady Daphne's mother had left behind in the little jewel casket flashed into her mind. A piece of red glass seemed to wink at her from the bracelet at her feet. Her knees bent and her hand reached out for the bracelet, almost as if it had a will of its own.

3

Georgiana opened the door a crack. The hall appeared long and dark with only one wall sconce lit, another sign the Burton fortune was faltering and household servants were not as readily available as they once were. The single lamp was near the grand staircase that led to the drawing rooms and beyond to the ballroom below. Its light didn't reach the doorway where she stood.

Leaving the door open a crack, she hurried toward the dim hall used by the servants. Something caused her to pause. If Gerald and some of the servants were searching for her, they would expect her to use the servants' passages. She listened for footsteps before darting into the hall where the guest rooms were located.

When she reached Lady Daphne's room, she turned the door handle and slipped soundlessly inside. It was just as she'd left it. She went straight to the jewel casket she'd tucked inside the dressing table. Opening the lid, she hesitated a moment before lifting the ring from its resting place. Holding it high, she considered the jewel set in a band of gold. The faint light coming through the windows gave it an ominous glow, like a forgotten ember buried deep within the lumps of charcoal left behind by fire. The stone, along with the others in the set, were rumored to have been a wedding gift from an Indian rajah to his bride and had been stolen by an English soldier who defeated the rajah in battle, then claimed the jewels when the bride joined her prince on his royal funeral pyre. Georgiana shuddered and almost returned the ring to the jewel casket.

No, I have need of it. With the Wellingtons' vast wealth, the stone won't be missed, she reasoned. She didn't attempt to justify her action by dwelling on the fact that the gem was first stolen by a Wellington ancestor. Or even by claiming it was fair since Lady Daphne had taken Sydney from her. Not revenge, but only survival led her to steal the ruby, she told herself. Still, she'd never taken anything that belonged to another. Then she reminded herself that Sydney would soon be the legal owner of this gem, and surely he owed her this much. She felt no animosity toward the girl who would be Sydney's wife. In a way, she felt pity for the girl.

She was going to need more light. Before lighting a candle, she closed the drapes, then felt her way back to the dressing table where she lit a candle. Reaching for a fingernail file, she pried the prongs holding the large, red stone away from the gem. The soft gold released its prize much more easily than she'd expected. It was a simple task to loosen the stone in her own bracelet and make the switch. She checked the ring to be certain there were no scratches on the setting and was pleased that without close inspection, the glass appeared identical to the ruby.

Footsteps reached her ears and her heart began to pound. She blew out the candle and pinched the wick to prevent it from smoking. Taking care to make no sound, she closed the jewel casket before dropping to her knees and creeping behind the chair where she had earlier draped Daphne's dressing gown.

She heard the sitting room door open. After a moment she heard someone whisper her name.

"Georgiana? Georgiana, are you in here?" She almost responded before common sense told her that the only reason one of the undermaids would be seeking her would be if Gerald or Sydney had enlisted the girl's help in searching for her. She had no friends among the long-entrenched country staff. She held still, scarcely daring to breathe, until the maid's steps receded and she heard the closing of the sitting room door.

She remained in her hidden position for several minutes more on the chance the closing door was a trick, though an inner alarm was screaming for her to flee. Reason told her the maid would be checking all of the rooms in the guest wing, and she must give the girl time to complete her assigned task. As she huddled behind the chair, she heard the opening and closing of doors farther along the hall, and her thoughts returned to Sydney. She replayed his courtship and promises along with his cruel words in the gallery until self-pity gave way to anger. He'd made a fool of her. He'd manipulated her, while planning to use her body then discard her. Perhaps the arrangement was to have Raul kill her! No, she'd overheard enough to suspect that a living death was what Sydney, with Raul's help, had in mind.

At last, all seemed quiet again. With her heart beating so fast she feared someone might hear it, she crept back to Gwen's room. Once inside the small room, she found the older woman hadn't yet returned. She might have been caught trying to smuggle Georgiana's few possessions from her room. Instead of waiting, Georgiana should probably be finding a way out of the house. But where could she go? She couldn't survive in the woods, and she had no family to whom she could flee. If she went north, she might find work in the mills, but that was most likely where Sydney would expect her to run. He might post watchers along the routes leading north. She had to find her way to London. The city's familiar streets were the only place she could hide.

But she had no money. Even if she managed to get away, how could she pay coach fare? She was certain the coachman wouldn't accept the ruby for fare. Lady Burton owed her wages. Perhaps she kept household money in her room, which was just through the dressing room. Would it be stealing to take her wages? Georgiana clasped her head between her hands. *I've never stolen anything before . . . I took the ruby, that was stealing . . . There is no difference between taking a jewel and taking money . . . Without money, I won't be able to escape the fate Sydney has planned for me. Anyway the viscountess owes me a quarter's salary.* She lowered her hands and moved toward Lady Burton's suite of rooms.

A lamp had been left burning on a low table, awaiting the mistress's return. Its glow enabled Georgiana to see, but after five minutes of fruitless searching, the only thing

of value she'd found was a sapphire brooch won by Lord
Burton during one of his rare winning streaks at cards.
Lady Burton had carelessly left it lying beneath the scarf
she'd worn earlier that day. Georgiana couldn't help
noticing how easily it would fit into her bracelet. Lady
Burton owed her! It was a simple matter to trade the large
center stone for its blue glass counterpart in her bracelet,
but it didn't change her need for cash.

She tiptoed to the far side of Lady Burton's bedroom,
where she pressed her ear against the door. Hearing
nothing, she tried the door that led to Lord Burton's
bedroom. It opened soundlessly. Again she listened. This
time she caught the faint sounds of slumber, not from the
bedroom she faced, but from the dressing room on the far
side of the master bedchamber. Luck was with her! Lord
Burton's man had fallen asleep, waiting for his master's
return. Turning her attention to the jumble of objects
that came to her hand as she skimmed it across a table,
she found what she was seeking. Quickly snatching a
handful of notes and coins, she retreated to Lady Burton's
bedroom, softly closing the door behind her.

Taking a deep breath and ordering her heart to slow its
beat, she opened her hand. A quick calculation in her
head told her the notes and coins were less than the
wages she had coming, but they were enough to get to
London and purchase a meal or two on her way. She
might even be able to rent a small room. She folded the
paper notes and tucked them in her bodice.

As she dropped the coins in her pocket, a flash of
bright gold caught her eye. Pushing a couple of coins aside

she found a cuff link hidden among them. She recognized it at once. Lord Burton often wore a flashy set of gold topaz gems on his cuffs. They had been in the Burton family for centuries, since the first Lord Burton, a knight of the realm, returned from the Crusades. She was surprised and pleased to realize the gem was a close match for the tawny glass in her bracelet.

She carried the jeweled cuff link to Lady Burton's dressing table where she again picked up the small knife that the lady often used for peeling the fresh fruit she loved to gorge herself on. Switching the stones was second nature to her now. When she finished with the topaz, she crossed once more to Lord Burton's door. She didn't open it this time, but pushed the doctored cuff link beneath it, where, hopefully, the servant finding it would assume it had merely fallen to the floor. Her only regret was that the jewel hadn't been Sydney's. She considered searching his room, then decided such an action would be foolhardy.

Creeping back to Gwen's room, she hesitated. Should she continue to wait? Might it be better to find her way out the back door and be gone before the ball ended or someone found her hiding in Lady Burton's personal maid's room?

A slight sound startled her, and before she could hide, the door leading to the hall opened, and Gwen slipped inside. Georgiana collapsed back against the bed, her heart pounding.

"I'm sorry I was gone so long." Gwen sounded agitated. "Gerald pressed me into searching the servants' hall for you. He has enlisted everyone who isn't needed in the ballroom." She drew a thin bundle from beneath her apron and extended it toward Georgiana. "I didn't dare take clothing that might be missed from your room." The bundle was composed of only a kerchief that had been Georgiana's mother's, a five-pence piece, a brush, two combs, and an extra petticoat.

"I don't own much more than that," Georgiana said as she accepted the few items the maid had brought her.

"The entrances are all being watched." Gwen wrung her hands. "I studied on the problem all while appearing to search the servants' quarters. You'll think me mad . . . I'm quite convinced it is the only way . . . Oh . . . It is dangerous, and I would never have the courage . . . But you . . ."

"I'll do anything, just tell me . . ."

Gwen hurried toward a small cupboard. She removed a box, which she placed on her narrow bed. Georgiana moved closer. The older woman opened the box and drew from it a gray gown trimmed with black velvet, not the sort a maid would wear, but one a lady, almost through her year of mourning, might don during her first weeks back in society. A matching pelisse with a lined hood would cover its wearer from head to toe.

"It's not too out of style, even though it has been more than forty years since I wore it." Gwen brushed the gown with a work-worn hand. "After Papa died, a distant cousin inherited . . ." She brushed at her eyes, then became businesslike. "Put it on. I'll borrow another petticoat from Lady Burton. She'll never miss one of the older ones . . .

And there's that hairpiece you made for her to wear to the Stirlingham's rout two years ago, right after her last hair-dresser singed her hair."

Georgiana knew what Gwen was suggesting. If she couldn't leave as herself through one of the exits ordinarily used by the servants, she'd have to boldly walk through the front door, disguised as a guest. If she left with a departing party in the wee hours of the morning, her presence might go unnoted. Her fingers trembled as she reached for the dress, pulling it over her dark serge gown. It was a chance she had to take.

Minutes later, she clung to the shadows in her borrowed dress with a cascade of blonde curls piled high on her head and just peeking beneath her gray hood, waiting for a signal from Gwen. She couldn't be seen carrying a bundle of clothing, so the gown she had been wearing was pinned in such a way that it wouldn't show beneath her layers of petticoats. A change of smallclothes served to pad her waist, making it appear thicker. From her wrist dangled a tiny, silk reticule Gwen produced, which matched the gown. The coins inside it were securely knotted inside a handkerchief to keep them from jangling together. She touched her bodice where the bank notes were hidden. Gwen would discover her own cache of coins returned to her, hidden beneath her pillow, long after Georgiana was safely away.

The minutes seemed to drag, and she felt certain she would be found out, but finally Gwen signaled, and Georgiana moved swiftly down the grand staircase to mingle with a bevy of young misses and their guardians, readying themselves for their journeys back to their respective country homes. Taking care to keep her face turned away from the family still in the ballroom, she swept through the front door with the vicar's daughters. As a footman handed the eldest daughter into a waiting carriage, Georgiana stepped into the shadow of a yew tree. From there, she stealthily followed the hedge to where a footpath led into the woods.

Expecting to feel a heavy hand on her shoulder with every step she took, she hurried her steps, putting as much distance as possible between herself and Burton Manor. She hadn't been entirely comfortable in the woods with daylight around her, but now in the dark, each rustle of sound in the woods added to her fear. At last her heart slowed its pounding, and she began to wonder where to go. She didn't dare go to the nearby village. That would be the first place Sydney and his brother would send someone to watch for her. They would expect her to take the coach from the village to the first rail station and make her way to Birmingham or Manchester to find work in the textile mills, so she must plan a different destination. The sky was getting lighter, and she wasn't certain which path she should take to find a more distant village. Her eyes were growing heavy, and she needed to find a place to rest.

Her steps slowed as she plodded on, and at first, the splashing sound of water flowing over stones failed to gain her attention, but somewhere deep inside, her brain told her she was thirsty, and she veered off the path to seek a drink. Not more than a dozen steps from the path she'd been following, she discovered a tiny pool fed by a trickle of water that plunged from rocks several feet higher. Kneeling, she filled her hands and let the cool water trickle down her throat, both easing her thirst and making her more alert, which also increased her awareness of her surroundings.

When she'd drunk her fill, she looked around at the small glen where she found herself. It seemed as good as any other place to rest for a few hours before continuing her journey. But just in case someone else should happen on the hidden spot, she spread her pelisse on the ground beneath a tangle of thick tree branches where she was unlikely to be seen should anyone else seek out the pool of water. She lay down and, despite being unaccustomed to sleeping outdoors, was soon fast asleep.

She awoke feeling confused. It took a few moments to remember how she'd come to be sleeping on the ground. She looked around with great trepidation until she was certain she was still alone. Once she was satisfied no one had discovered her hiding place, she refreshed herself at the small pool and determined to make some definite plans. While applying the brush she'd tucked in her reticule, she considered her options. She had no idea how much distance she'd put between herself and the manor or even in which direction she should go to find a village where she might purchase food and passage on a London-bound coach. She couldn't approach any of the peasants who might use the woods as a shortcut, and she must also take care to not stumble into the gypsy camp.

After considerable contemplation of her problem, she determined to continue in the direction she'd been traveling, since presumably it took her away from Burton Manor and whatever fate Sydney had planned for her. Tucking her hairbrush back into the reticule, she rose to her feet. She was about to step back onto the path when a sound reached her ears, causing her to shrink back into the shelter of the thick hedge that separated the pool from the path.

From behind the hedge, she watched two men draw near. They had swarthy skin and were ill dressed. She couldn't see their faces clearly, but one seemed slightly familiar. Fortunately for her, they were deep in conversation and paid little attention to their surroundings. They also appeared to be in a great hurry. As they passed the spot where she hid, she caught snatches of their conversation, enough to know they were planning to meet the London coach near some place they called "the bend." She grinned. *What luck!* All she needed to do was follow the peasants, taking care to stay out of sight, and they would lead her to the coach stop.

Once the men were some distance past the place where she hid, she stepped onto the path and hurried after them. Her stomach made a rumbling sound, and she slowed her steps, fearing the men might hear. She hoped there would be time after arranging her fare to purchase a meat pie before she boarded the coach.

She was so intent on following the two peasants, she almost missed the sound of a horse approaching at a rapid pace behind her. There was barely time to conceal herself behind a tree before the horse galloped past and she caught a glimpse of a black-clad rider, leaning low over a gray horse's neck, urging the animal to greater speed. She waited several minutes for her pounding pulse to return to normal before venturing out of concealment again.

Regaining the path, she listened intently but could no longer hear the peasants' voices. The sound of the horse's hooves had died away as well, leaving only silence and the occasional chirp of a bird. Swallowing her disappointment, she vowed to be more careful and set out in the direction the men she had been following had disappeared. She walked quickly in spite of a growing blister on one heel, but she kept her senses tuned to detect any sound or threat. The path seemed to rise gradually, and several times, she thought she heard the sound of a brook. Hearing water made her thirsty. If she didn't come to a village soon, she'd be forced to leave the path in search of the stream to ease her parched throat.

She was not only thirsty, but her stomach was making decidedly unladylike sounds. She needed food, and she was beginning to despair of ever finding the coach stop. She might have to spend another night in the forest. In fact, she couldn't keep at bay the rising suspicion she was helplessly lost and doomed to perish in the woods.

4

An explosion rent the air, and Georgiana dove for cover behind the trees and shrubs growing beside the path. To her amazement, she found she was no longer in the woods, and the only trees in the immediate area were those shading the path she had been following. Looking around, she could see that she was at the top of a grassy knoll overlooking a stream that wandered through a broad meadow. A road paralleled the stream, and a short distance ahead, it curved toward a bridge that spanned the water. A coach was halted just before the bridge.

She considered running, but she knew it would be useless. She couldn't possibly make her way down the hill before the coach resumed its journey. She was too late to claim a seat, and there was no way of knowing how many days would go by until the next coach would pass through.

She was about to give in to despair when she noticed a man, who looked like one of the men she'd been following in the woods, standing at the coach horses' heads, and another man, who appeared to be the second man she had followed, the one she thought looked a bit familiar, sitting on top of the coach, tossing the passengers' baggage to the ground. The man on horseback who had charged past her a short time earlier was there as well. He was pointing something at the small group of passengers who were gathered beside the coach.

Before she could assimilate the scene in front of her, she noticed something that brought the picture into focus and a scream bubbling up in her throat. The coachman lay unmoving in the dust. She'd stumbled onto a holdup! The explosion she'd heard was gunfire, magnified in volume by the stillness of a placid summer day in the country. She clapped her hands over her mouth and fought an urge to scream.

Burrowing deeper into the grass and shrubs separating the path from the open, grassy hillside, she endeavored to stay out of sight. Any movement might draw the thieves' attention. While lying still, she studied the outlaws carefully until she was certain she could identify the two footpads. She was positive the one who had looked familiar was Raul, the gypsy, and the other was one of the louts she'd seen with him at the village fair. The mounted outlaw was dressed in black from head to toe and wore a mask that concealed his face. He seemed to be in charge, and she regretted that she wouldn't be able to describe him to a magistrate. What was she thinking? She couldn't go to a magistrate; if she did, he would return her to the Burtons.

The rider moved closer to the passengers. Whatever he said, the lone male passenger took exception to. He took a threatening step closer to the black-clad rider. A shot rang out, and the passenger crumpled to the ground as squeals and screams arose from the bevy of women. One of the footpads, who was seemingly following the mounted thief's orders, stepped toward the women. He said something, and amid a torrent of shrieks and sobs, they began stripping rings, brooches, and necklaces from their persons to drop into the bag the rider's accomplice extended toward them. Following the mounted thief's orders, the two men on the ground turned toward the luggage spread across the ground. When one uncovered a small jewel casket, he carried it to the man on horseback. Taking the box, the black-clad thief dumped its contents into a pouch and tossed the box to the ground.

Moments later, the rider tucked the pouch inside his shirt. He then leaned forward, pointing the pistol toward the man lying on the ground. The women huddled together as the rider watched his friends fill two bags, which they swung over their shoulders. At last the thieves seemed to be finished.

The thunder of hooves ascending the hill behind Georgiana was her first indication the horseman had left the scene of the robbery. Drawing herself into a ball, she worried she may have been discovered, but the horse ran past her hiding place without a pause. When the sound of its passing faded, she lifted her head once more. There was no sign of the footpads, but hysterical weeping could be heard coming from below.

She hesitated several minutes, waiting for sounds of the footpads' retreat to pass her by. She didn't have to wait long before their heavy steps and harsh breathing were heard coming from the steep path. She remained hidden until after their passing. Fearing she might attract their attention, she didn't even breathe until they were gone. But after only a few minutes, concern for the coach's passengers had her leaving her hiding place to slip down the path to the weeping ladies.

She was about to announce herself to prevent startling the frightened women further when she made the discovery that the coach was not a public coach, but one belonging to a titled gentleman. A coat of arms was blazoned on the door, and the women were none other than Lady Wellington and her daughters. Fearing they might recognize her, she considered rushing back up the hill, but one of the young ladies spotted her and ran toward her crying for help.

"Help us, Miss! They've killed Papa!"

"Footpads attacked the coach," the Countess of Wellington shouted. "They've taken our jewelry and killed poor Wellington." Georgiana noted the coachman didn't rate a mention, and the lady, instead of rushing to her husband's aid, was attempting to calm the frightened horses, which were lunging and kicking, trying to free themselves from the coach, which was held stationary by a good-sized tree branch lodged between the spokes of two wheels.

None of the party showed any sign of having recognized her, so Georgiana knelt beside poor Wellington, who lay face down on the grassy verge of the road. She attempted to turn him over to examine his wound, but he was a heavy man, and she only succeeded in turning him to his side. Blood was flowing quite freely from a wound beneath his shirt. She leaned forward to check the wound and caught the faint rasp of breathing.

"He's alive," she called. "Help me turn him to his back, and bring me something to stanch the blood." No one moved. They stared at her blankly while she flipped up the hem of her skirt and ripped off a strip from Lady Caroline Burton's petticoat. Folding the cloth into a thick pad, she pressed it against the wound in the man's shoulder. As she did so, her eyes were drawn to a green stone shining brilliantly amid the folds of the man's cravat. It was just the size of the green glass in her bracelet.

"Fetch me some water." She turned to the ladies, who were no longer screaming, but were still maintaining their distance from her and Lord Wellington, though they were watching her closely. In exasperation, she began to rise. She'd have to fetch the water herself.

Her patient groaned, and the sound brought the women tiptoeing closer. Georgiana sank back down. Spying a flask lying near the man on the ground, she picked it up and shook it to assure herself it wasn't empty. She then removed the blood-soaked cloth from the wound and upended the flask over the wound. Wellington sputtered and appeared about to awaken, then lapsed back into his comatose state. She bandaged the wound with a fresh strip from her petticoat, holding it in place with the hem she tore from the man's own shirt.

"Lord Wellington!" Georgiana mustered her most commanding voice in an attempt to gain a response. "Lord Wellington, wake up!"

"Is he really alive?" the countess ventured to ask, tiptoeing closer. When Georgiana nodded her head, the frightened woman squared her shoulders, and her nostrils flared as she transformed herself into a field marshal. She ordered her daughters to fetch water while she renewed the task of calming the frightened horses. Lady Daphne and her sisters fled toward the stream. Sheepishly, Daphne returned moments later to collect her father's now-empty flask in which to carry the water.

Georgiana found herself quite alone with the earl. She had no quarrel with him, but someday, most of his possessions, including the emerald cravat pin, would likely fall to Sydney. Quick as a flash, she produced Lady Burton's tiny knife from the pocket of her gown where she had stashed it with vague thoughts of using it as a weapon should she be discovered. The soft gold prongs holding the emerald in place succumbed to her deft hands, and the green stone disappeared into her pocket. She pried loose the green glass from her bracelet and fastened the bit of window glass in the cravat pin. She closed the earl's shirt and vest to keep the wound from collecting dirt and grass, then she let the unconscious man roll back on his face.

Upon finishing her bit of rudimentary care, she left the earl's side to check on the coachman. He was beginning to stir, and she quickly ascertained that his greatest injury was a lump on his head. Doubtless, he would do well with a cold rag on his noggin once the Wellington ladies returned with water. She reported her findings to Lady Wellington.

"Hold on, Charlie," the countess called in a commanding voice to the coachman, though most of her attention was given to calming the horses and untangling their trailing lines. Georgiana was surprised to discover the lady was a dab hand with Wellington's cattle and soon had them placidly standing in their traces.

"Do you have smelling salts?" Georgiana called to Lady Wellington upon returning to that woman's husband.

"In my reticule," she shouted back. "Never use them myself, but one never knows when one of the young ladies might need them. I tucked my reticule beneath the carriage seat as a precaution when I discovered we had been accosted by highwaymen. I must stay with Wellington's pair until Charlie Coachman is right in his head, but you have my permission to fetch the salts, if you think they will help."

"Very well," Georgiana muttered. It seemed to her Lady Wellington was far more concerned with the horses than her husband. Rising to her feet, she shook the dust from her skirt and hurried to the carriage. Hoisting her skirt high, she climbed aboard.

Looking around inside the well-appointed carriage, she felt a moment's hesitation. What was she doing aiding the family of the young lady who had supplanted her in Sydney's affections? Before she could succumb to melancholy tears, common sense reminded her that Sydney hadn't exactly exhibited any affection for her or Daphne when he told Gerald of his plans to be rid of Georgiana and marry Daphne for her family's fortune. The whole mess really wasn't the young miss's fault.

Spying a basket tipped on its side, spilling across the carriage seat an array of fruit and rolls the party had intended as a repast for their journey, she took time to stuff a bun in her mouth and another in her pocket before beginning her search for the smelling salts. Her fingers probed under the seat cushions, and touching something hard, she withdrew the object to stare at a pistol. Had Wellington stashed it there, thinking to avoid bloodshed when he saw he was outnumbered? She considered keeping the firearm. One of her previous employers had taught her to shoot as a ploy to lure her into his bed, a scheme his wife took exception to, but not before Georgiana mastered the basics of handling a weapon. She carefully set the gun atop a plush cushion and continued her search for the smelling salts. Once she had them in hand, she took a moment to insert the emerald she had appropriated from the earl's cravat pin into her bracelet and to eat another bun. She was about to return to Wellington when she heard the thunder of a rapidly approaching horse.

Ducking below the window as a precaution, she pushed the carriage curtain aside just enough to catch a glimpse of the approaching horse and rider. To her horror, she saw that the highwayman had returned. This time he appeared to be alone. From the squeals of terror reaching her ears, she guessed Daphne and her sisters had also returned and they feared the highwayman would kill them all. She watched as the black-clad figure dismounted, his gun hand pointing a weapon toward the unconscious earl. He walked toward Lord Wellington and with the toe of his boot turned the earl face up.

The action stirred a great deal of annoyance in Georgiana. The lout would doubtless undo her efforts to save the earl's life. She felt a measure of satisfaction when the thief ripped the faux green jewel from Wellington's cravat before it occurred to her that the thief had known the jewel was there. He had come back specifically for it! Then he annoyed her further when he pulled matching studs from the injured man's shirt cuffs before allowing Wellington to roll back to his former supine position. The thief took his time pulling the strings of a fat bag he produced from inside his shirt, then dropping the jewelry inside before turning back to mount his horse. His arrogant assumption that the women weren't worth wasting his attention irritated her further.

From the corner of her eye, she caught movement from an unexpected source. Lady Wellington had somehow retrieved the coachman's whip and was drawing it back in a motion that indicated she knew what she was doing. Unfortunately, before Georgiana could take time to appreciate the woman's audacity, the thief noted the movement as well. He raised his gun, aiming it toward Lady Wellington. Without taking time to consider her action, Georgiana grasped the gun from the coach seat, aimed, and fired.

The thief staggered backward, clutching for his horse's reins with one hand while attempting to return fire. Their eyes met, and Georgiana saw recognition flash in his eyes at the same time his identity registered to her frightened senses. He lifted his gun with a trembling hand, pointing it toward her, and fired a shot. It crashed into the frame of the coach just above her head. At the same time, a glint of silver hit the ground. While Georgiana tried to steady the shaking pistol in her hand, the highwayman struggled to pull himself upright in the saddle. He leaned forward, clutching at his horse's mane, and Georgiana saw the small leather pouch fall to the grass unnoticed by the rider, whose full attention was now taken in remaining upright in the saddle as he urged his horse to run. She considered firing again but couldn't bring herself to do so. Shock held her immobile. It wasn't the bag of stolen jewels that held her attention and kept her from firing while the rider disappeared from sight or the knowledge that Sydney had not only robbed and shot his soon-to-be father-in-law. He had tried to kill her.

The coach lurched crazily for several minutes before Georgiana found the courage to jump free. She was glad the wheels were still blocked, or surely the horses would have run away. She considered running as fast and far as she possibly could, but the sight of the young Wellington ladies huddled in a frightened circle while their mother once more struggled to calm the frightened horses lent her courage. Georgiana saw the coachman attempting to sit up and ran to assist him. She was needed here, and Sydney was too badly injured to return anytime soon.

"Bring the water," she demanded, and one of the girls sidled closer with the flask. She poured a small amount onto the lump on Charlie's head, then offered him a small sip. When he began to grumble concerning the contents of the flask, she knew he was going to be all right and withdrew to see if anything could be done for the badly abused earl.

When she wafted the smelling salts under the earl's nose, he coughed and opened his eyes.

"Who are you?" he demanded suspiciously. Before she could respond, he was swarmed by his daughters.

"Papa!" they chorused. Suddenly they each had a version of the preceding events to tell him. He struggled to a sitting position, wincing at the tug to his shoulder. The girls fluttered around him, offering him cushions and a drink, which he spit out when he discovered the flask held water. After a few minutes, a series of demands that he find the thieves and regain their possessions replaced his daughters' solicitations.

Charlie Coachman stumbled his way to the horses, taking over for Lady Wellington, who flew at once to her husband's side to join her daughters' anxious cooing, interspersed with demands that the poor man do something.

Wellington looked downward to the source of the pain he felt in his shoulder, then at his family. Bewildered, he looked farther afield. His eyes met Georgiana's. "You bandaged me?" He paused. "And shot the thief?" *Had he not been unconscious all the time?*

She nodded her head slowly, uncomfortable with the man's scrutiny. "You must have a doctor remove the lead right away." She attempted to turn his attention to himself.

"My man will do it. Won't be the first time either," the stout earl said. Georgiana remembered the earl had been a military man before inheriting the title. She took a step away, then remembered the pouch the highwayman had dropped. She hurried to the spot where the black horse had stood. It only took a few minutes to discover the bag lying in the grass beside the highwayman's dropped pistol, a tiny silver derringer. The picture of a matched pair rose in her mind, bringing a shudder.

She reached for the leather bag, then after a moment's hesitation, picked up the gun as well and dropped them both in her pocket.

She looked up to see that the Wellington family members were all still occupied as was the coach driver. No one was paying her any attention. Turning her back to them, she withdrew the bag and wrenched it open. Just as she expected, it was filled with jewels. Next to the large green cravat pin was a ring she recognized—the Middleton betrothal ring, the ring double-dealing Sydney had promised to her. It was hers by right of promise! And she couldn't believe her luck—it was very like the last piece of glass in her bracelet.

She hesitated only a moment before making her way to the back of the coach where she made one last trade. She admired the bracelet on her wrist for only a moment before tucking it beneath her sleeve. It was no longer the worthless trinket Sydney had given her as a pledge of his equally worthless affection.

A long trumpet blast sounded from just over the hill, and Georgiana looked up to see the royal mail coach approaching at great speed. The coachman in his many-tiered greatcoat and tall hat stood on the brake as he pulled back on the reins and shouted for the horses to stop. He hallooed to the Wellington coachman to move aside so he could pass. Charlie approached the mail coach for a word with the coachman. Before he reached the other driver, they all heard another coach approaching from the other direction. It bore the Wellington coat of arms on its sides as well.

The earl's man stepped out of the second coach. "I ordered the coach turned around as soon as I discovered the earl and his ladies were not following closely behind." He rushed to his master. "Your coat is ruined, sir. I'll never get your coat clean again. And look at the splotches of blood on your britches." He knelt at once to see to the earl's wound.

Georgiana gasped when the valet removed her bandage, then withdrew a long narrow knife from his boot along with another flask. He poured the contents of the flask over his knife, which he then wiped a few times on the bandage she had applied earlier, before deftly inserting the knife into the wound. Fascinated, she watched him gently probe then slowly withdraw the blade with a tiny chunk of lead on it. He splashed a bit more of the flask's contents on the wound, then produced a fresh cravat from another pocket to rebind the wound before handing the flask to the earl, who downed a stiff belt. The entire procedure was finished in minutes with neither the earl's valet nor the earl appearing the least bit fazed by the procedure.

The ladies, who had retreated the moment Wellington's man began attending to the wound, rushed about the clearing, gathering up what remained of their luggage and bemoaning their fate. Lady Wellington's maid joined the fray, shushing the girls and taking charge of getting the party back on the road.

In the noise and confusion that ensued, Georgiana strolled to the spot where she'd picked up the bag of jewels and let it drop once more into the grass. Moments later she guided one of the Wellington daughters to the spot by hurrying her out of the way of Charlie Coachman's effort to free the blocked carriage wheels. Excitement mounted to a new level as the Wellington family reunited with their missing jewels. While they were occupied with rejoicing over their good fortune in regaining their valuables, Georgiana had a quiet word with the coachman driving the public coach. None of them noticed when she found a seat on the London-bound mail coach or watched as the large vehicle lumbered out of sight.

5

Georgiana hurried toward a London street that was home to seamstresses, small shops, and government workers. It was shabby and poor but superior to the teeming slums that occupied a good share of the city. She glanced over her shoulder frequently, fearing Sydney or Gerald, guessing she had made her way to London, might have sent someone to find her. Pickpockets were another danger. She breathed easier when she reached the shabby but respectable street where she had found lodging.

Climbing the stairs to a single room in the loft above a bakery brought her closer to a reprieve from worry. She'd been fortunate to find the room, though she'd had to give up more of her meager fundsthan she had expected. Reaching the top of the stairs, she looked around. It had become a habit to make a visual check of the small room each time she entered to satisfy herself that no intruder had entered during her absence. The room had little to recommend it beyond a lumpy bed, a sturdy lock on the door, and the promise she wouldn't have to share it with another tenant. It was barely large enough to accommodate the bed and a row of hooks for her meager wardrobe, and it shook and trembled each time a train rumbled past, two streets away, but she knew she was fortunate to find it. Vast numbers of people in the rapidly growing city were sleeping six to a bed in rooms no larger. Thousands more were sleeping under viaducts and in doorways in a city where housing for the poor was being torn out to provide space for the rail lines, and no provision was being made for the growing numbers of workers seeking employment in the city's expanding industry.

A glance through the one small window in the room revealed her landlady making her way to a shedlike structure tacked to the back of her shop. Mrs. White was a cheerful woman, who in appearance greatly resembled her wares. The room she rented to Georgiana had previously been her own, but as her lumpy figure had grown heavier, she'd had to forego climbing the narrow stairs and had moved her meager belongings to the shed. At first, Georgiana had hoped to find employment in the bakery, but Mrs. White had no need of an assistant. However, she supplied the addresses to her new tenant of a few businesses who might have need of a helper. It didn't take long to discover Georgiana's services were not needed by any of them.

She sank wearily onto her bed. She'd been searching for a position from sunup until dark for almost three weeks, but without a character reference or skills beyond waiting on wealthy women such as Lady Burton, she had begun to despair of finding employment. Deeming it prudent to steer clear of the fashionable society, she didn't dare seek work in any of the wealthy households.

Factories in London were smaller than those she'd heard of in Manchester and Liverpool and had an overabundance of applicants. They also paid smaller wages.

As her list of possible positions dwindled, Georgiana turned to studying her options—which were few—should she fail to find employment. She could apply for work at a public house, but waiting tables among London's courser elements held little appeal and a great deal of danger. Coming to London instead of traveling north had been a mistake, she feared, as far as finding employment. Now she lacked the necessary funds to make her way to the factories where she might find work.

Out of desperation, she'd spent all day seeking employment among the demimonde, not as some rich gentleman's mistress, but as a hairdresser or lady's maid. But she'd soon discovered that those who brokered such arrangements weren't interested in her skills, only in her face and figure. She'd received more than one offer of a protector. Remembering only deepened her gloom.

Her fingers touched the bracelet. It was all she had left between starvation and complete degradation. The time was rapidly approaching when she would be forced to sell one of the jewels.

She was never without her bracelet, deeming it her only security. It took on the aspects of a good-luck charm or talisman, and she touched it frequently for the reassurance it gave her. She was reluctant to have the stones appraised and sold, fearing that a jeweler might recognize the gems, especially if any of the substitutions had been spotted and reported. The almost priceless jewels were too well-known to be casually pawned. She didn't find the irony amusing that she possessed a great fortune in jewels but could only afford a stale roll for her supper—and soon not even that.

By avoiding contact with the servants who worked in the more affluent part of town, she'd hoped to remain safe, but the action had also cut her off from the gossip that might have either reassured her or warned of Sydney's whereabouts and informed her of whether or not the jewel substitutions had been noticed. Then there was the possibility that Sydney might have died from the gunshot wound she'd given him. That question weighed on her mind. Though his demise would prevent him from pursuing her to gain her silence, she didn't want his death on her conscience.

At last she ate the one small roll, which was all she had left from the half dozen she'd purchased from her landlady at the beginning of the week. She removed her gown and gave it a thorough brushing before lying down.

The next day, as she returned to her room following another fruitless search for employment, she thought of the few coins left in her reticule. Then she felt the bracelet on her left wrist through the long sleeve of the plain gown she'd worn beneath the gray when she fled Burton House. The fingers of her right hand ran across the now-familiar bumps. She'd had nothing to eat all day. She wondered how to go about selling one of the jewels. She didn't trust any of the fences who usually dealt with stolen wares. They would either far undervalue the jewels or outright steal them from her. And if she approached

one of the jewelers on Bond Street, they would suspect
the truth, that the gems were stolen.

On the journey to London, she'd developed a plan to
escape from the threat hanging over her, but it involved
finding a means of supporting herself while earning
passage to America. Leaving England was the only way to
be certain Sydney could not find her. Once she reached
the New World, she could sell the jewels and live
comfortably there. She could even change her name.
She'd heard the place was becoming quite civilized. If she
had to sell the jewels now, she'd never truly be safe.

Unable to rest, Georgiana left her room again. Only a
few blocks from her room, she noticed a small placard in a
window. It hadn't been there when she'd passed this way
earlier. She moved closer to read it, and her heart beat
faster when she discovered it was a notice for a position as
a seamstress. As a young girl, she'd trained as a lady's
maid, so of course she could sew, though it wasn't one of
her favorite activities. She'd moved swiftly from lady's
maid to hairdresser when it was discovered she had a
knack for arranging fashionable hairstyles. She could
learn just as quickly to be a seamstress, she assured herself.

Afraid the position might be taken by someone else if
she took the time to return to her room to change into
the gray dress, Georgiana pushed open the door leading to
the shop. She hurried inside and was pleased to see a
small but tidy shop where measurements could be taken
and gowns ordered. In cubicles to one side, two women
were being fitted for unusual gowns. A tall, blonde woman
was wearing a gown that draped elegantly from one

shoulder in smooth pleats that fell to the floor. The fitter beside her was winding a silver cord about her waist. The other woman was wearing a bright pink, diaphanous robe that revealed more of the dark-haired beauty than Georgiana considered proper. A lackluster seamstress with long, pale, limp hair was pinning swatches of lace to strategic places on the gauzy fabric.

"May I assist you?" Georgiana had been so absorbed in the fittings, she'd failed to see the elegant woman, who spoke with a slight accent, approach her. She started, then quickly recovering, told the woman she'd seen the advertisement and had come to apply for the seamstress opening in the shop.

"You have experience?" The woman had evidently once been a great beauty. Her gleaming black hair was piled high on her head, and even though Georgiana guessed she was beyond her prime, she had an elegance and style that warned Georgiana not to underestimate her.

Georgiana considered exaggerating her experience, but since the woman would be able to see for herself in a few minutes, if she accepted Georgiana's application, that her skills were rusty, she decided to tell the truth. Something about the shop and the woman who addressed her suggested she might understand Georgiana's plight.

"Only the experience I gained as a lady's maid," she answered. The woman frowned, then asked, "Your references, please?"

"I left in a hurry," she glanced down, accentuating her embarrassment. "My mistress's son was . . . uh, becoming too insistent."

"Was he too young—or with pockets to let?" The question came from behind her. She wasn't sure who had spoken, but she sensed the woman interviewing her disapproved of the question and they both chose to ignore it.

"Is your mother in London?" There was something in her manner that made the woman appear to see right through Georgiana and even to somehow sympathize with her.

"I have no family," Georgiana told her prospective employer. It seemed an unusual question, but she answered truthfully. "I never knew my father, and Mum died mere weeks after I went into service at the age of twelve." She could be mistaken, but it seemed her answer had somehow met with the shop owner's approval.

"Can you begin immediately?" the woman asked. When Georgiana nodded, she was steered toward the back of the shop. The light was dim, but she could see five women with their heads bent over piles of fabric, their fingers moving swiftly. Three of the women were middle-aged and appeared tired and worn. She recognized one of them as the woman who had been fitting the Roman style robe to a customer minutes earlier. The other two were closer to Georgiana's own age. One was plump with a sour expression on her face. She too had been out front when Georgiana arrived. The other young woman seemed to be little more than a nervous, flighty bird. Her fingers made rapid jerky stabs at the cloth she held on her lap. Georgiana could also see one vacant stool. The shop owner led her to it.

Georgiana was issued one needle and told that if it were broken or lost, she must buy her own replacement. Her new employer pointed to a half-completed gown and a sketch that lay atop a battered sewing bag. Without so much as a discussion of salary or an introduction to the other seamstresses, she was left to begin her new career.

Making the tiny, neat stitches women like Lady Burton would expect was harder than she'd anticipated. It was also much more difficult to match pieces together in the right order than she'd had any idea it would be. The other women worked doggedly and primarily ignored her. Almost a week passed before she learned all their names. It didn't take that long to learn her employer was none other than Madam DuPont, a clothier famous for her fashionable, elaborate designs who refused her gowns to the titled and wealthy society women. Her creations were reserved for the fashionably impure. Numbered among her clientele were the loveliest ladies of the night, the mistresses of titled gentlemen, and the more successful actresses.

Georgiana returned to her room with a headache from eyestrain that night and each night after. As summer turned to fall, the condition grew worse. The backroom where she worked was in dire need of light, but since the seamstresses had to pay for their own oil for the tiny lamp in the room, they struggled to work with the small amount of light that fought its way through the workroom's one small, grimy window. Making matters worse was the close work required to ornament the gowns with excessive lace, ribbons, braid, and glittering diamante. The shop was heavily patronized, and keeping up with the orders was more than could be expected of but six seamstresses.

Hoping to improve the light and rid herself of the headache that plagued her day and night, Georgiana carried water and a bit of soap to work early one morning to clean the window. Soap was an expensive luxury, but one she considered a necessity, so she took but a sliver of the cake she'd purchased shortly after arriving in London. As she scrubbed at the grime, the other seamstresses arrived. None spoke to her, but the harried older woman who was allowed to fit Madam's creations to the customers who had ordered them, did offer a weak smile. Madam DuPont arrived just as Georgiana gave the window one last swipe and immediately reprimanded her for wasting time she should be spending plying her needle.

The other women were all much faster than Georgiana and not inclined to friendliness, though the one who had briefly smiled at her suggested she stick her needle in the bit of soap she had left after washing the window. The seamstress assured her the soap would sharpen her needle, causing it to glide through the fabric more easily.

"It'll take more than a sharper needle to turn the strumpet into a seamstress," the stringy-haired blonde sneered. Georgiana bit back the sharp retort that came to her lips and chose to pretend she hadn't heard the offensive remark.

After thrusting her needle through the bit of soap, she was pleased with the remarkable difference the small hint made in her speed and the neatness of her stitches. Out of gratitude and a hunger for someone to talk with, she shared the sliver with the woman who had given her the tip. The seamstress took it, passed her needle through it several times, then passed it on to the others without first consulting Georgiana. The last seamstress, the rude blonde, tossed the bit of soap into her own bag when she finished sharpening her needle. She gave Georgiana a haughty glare as though challenging her to dispute her right to claim the scrap of soap. With difficulty, Georgiana resisted claiming her property. Finding the miserable seamstress position had taken weeks and had exhausted her resources; she couldn't risk losing it.

"Anne!" Madam DuPont entered the back room. "Your customer is waiting." The young woman rose languidly to her feet, bag in hand, making no effort to hide the smirk she sent Georgiana's way.

"As for the rest of you, you really must work faster," Madam DuPont chided. "If you were all as quick with your needles as Anne, you might actually earn your wages. If those gowns are not finished by the end of the day, I will find it necessary to dock your pay."

It took considerable effort to hide the resentment Madam's words brought to Georgiana's heart. Anne's habit of appropriating the other seamstress's supplies and the faulty measurements she gave them for projects they were assigned, along with her air of superiority over the other seamstresses did not endear her to any of them. None of them dared complain for fear she would retaliate by ruining the gowns they worked on.

Georgiana sensed something more in Anne's attitude toward her. It was apparent the young woman had taken a distinct aversion to Georgiana personally. She never missed an opportunity to make cutting remarks concerning Georgiana's work or appearance. Georgiana recognized the signs of jealousy, though why the other woman was jealous of her, she couldn't guess.

One afternoon, as she reached to place a finished gown on one of the hooks where completed work was placed pending the customer's final fitting and approval, the button at her left wrist slipped free. Her cuff gaped open, exposing the bracelet. Before she could pull the cuff back in place, a hand gripped her wrist.

"What's this?" Anne plucked at the bracelet. "A worthless bauble from your lover?"

"'Tis only a country fair token given to me by my papa when I was a child," Georgiana improvised. She knew that the best protection against theft was to trivialize the bracelet's value. She also knew it was dangerous to wear the bracelet to work, but leaving it in her room seemed far more risky. Not only was there a risk of losing the bracelet to thieves if she left it in her room, but there was also the constant dread that Sydney might happen upon her. He knew she could identify him as the thief who attacked the Wellington party. A mere woman couldn't testify against him in court, but he couldn't afford to have his name bandied about in speculation that he was the notorious footpad who shot Lord Haven, the Earl of Dorchester's heir. If Sydney discovered her, she would have to run. If forced to run, she wouldn't be able to take the chance of returning to her room for the jewels; therefore she kept them with her.

"I believe the stones are bits of colored glass that melted when a church burned." She repeated what Gwen had told her of the original lumps of glass in their shoddy setting.

"It's worse than worthless. Look how the cheap metal turns your arm green." Anne gave the bracelet a vicious twist before releasing it. "I wouldn't be caught dead wearing anything so gaudy as all those different colored pieces of glass." Anne laughed in smug satisfaction as she pointed to the mark on Georgiana's arm. Once, Georgiana had been sick to discover the chain was neither silver nor pewter, but now she was glad that the setting proclaimed the trinket as cheap.

Georgiana took advantage of the other woman's laughter to fasten her sleeve. When she reached her room that night, as tired as she was, she took the time to tighten the button which had come loose.

Georgiana rushed to work the day she was to receive her first wages. Seeing the other seamstresses weren't laughing and joking the way servants in the big houses generally greeted their quarterly pay, she began to worry. It wasn't until evening, when the seamstresses were preparing to depart, that Madam DuPont handed them each a small packet. Georgiana stuffed hers in her pocket and made her way to her room. Once there, she ripped open the packet and emptied its contents onto her bed. *There must be a mistake!* She was horrified by the pitifully small amount she'd received. Staring at it, she knew it would barely pay her rent and leave little for food. There would be nothing to save for passage to America.

6

The next month, her pay packet was similarly small, and she opened it before leaving the shop. Madam DuPont stood nearby as Georgiana counted the few coins.

"This can't be right," Georgiana protested.

"You're still learning. Surely you didn't expect full wages before learning to keep up with the others? Though you could soon be earning a great deal more," the older woman said. "My friend Celeste runs a fashionable club for gentlemen. She might be interested in a young woman with your face and form."

"Oh, no, ma'am," Georgiana stammered. "I'd not sell myself."

In spite of her refusal, Madam seemed serenely confident Georgiana would change her mind. Scarcely a day went by without a subtle invitation for Georgiana to meet Celeste. It didn't take long for the hints and suggestions to change to coercion. Her employer meant to force her to change her mind.

One day in mid-November, Georgiana arrived at her post to discover a long seam she had labored over for two hours the previous day was undone. Streaks of mud, a few drops of blood as though she'd pricked her finger while stitching, and a broken needle followed in the succeeding days and weeks. The other seamstresses professed to know nothing about the mishaps. After one emphatic refusal to work for Celeste, an expensive panel for the dress she'd been laboring over was slashed, and Madam informed her the cost of the fabric would be deducted from her wages. Georgiana seethed with rage. She knew what was happening.

Out of self-defense, she began sneaking her work home with her, hidden beneath the gray pelisse, in the shabby bag she'd inherited along with her seamstress's stool. How she wished she could simply leave and find other employment, but the days were growing short, and she worked long hours. She didn't dare take time from the employment she'd searched so long to find for more searching.

Leaving the shop late one evening with the heavy bag, she noticed Anne lingering near the nearby street corner. A closed carriage stopped. A gentleman poked his head through the curtains, spoke briefly with Anne, then after a quick glance around, the girl climbed inside the carriage.

"She'll be worthless tomorrow."

Georgiana turned to see the older woman who had once smiled at her, staring after the carriage with a dark look of disapproval.

"If Madam finds out, she'll dismiss her," the woman continued.

"But . . ." Georgiana stammered. She'd suspected for some time that Anne had another source of income, because her wardrobe was better than that of the other seamstresses and she kept a steady supply of sweets close at hand. *But surely what Anne is doing is no different from what Madam is attempting to force me into doing.* The expression on her face must have given away her dark thoughts, or perhaps the woman knew more than Georgiana had supposed.

She gave Georgiana a strange look, then seeming to take pity on her, explained, "I have worked for Madam DuPont for a long time. Once she and I were young and beautiful and she ran a very different kind of business. When she opened her dress shop, she turned her previous business over to Celeste Fontaine, who formerly was her favorite employee. I was too old to remain with Celeste, and Madam, out of pity for the past we shared, made room for me in her shop. Then too, I have an eye for fashion and fabrics.

"Celeste pays Madam a percentage of her profits, and Madam finds beautiful young girls who are willing to enter Celeste's employ. You are a beauty and without family, just the sort of young woman Celeste is looking for. Anne is not beautiful, though she fancies she is. She came to Madam DuPont because she had heard the rumor that Celeste hires only girls approved by Madam, and Anne wants to work for Celeste. Celeste's establishment, however, is very exclusive, and she has no desire to employ Anne, but she is in desperate need of a new girl, and Madam DuPont is greedy for the generous fee Celeste will pay her. Anne is convinced that if you were out of the way, Celeste would offer the position to her. I'm afraid she will soon resort to physical attacks to remove the threat she considers you to be. You will be safe from Anne if you go to Celeste. It is better anyway for you to go willingly, for soon Madam will tire of your stubborn resistance, and you will discover you have lost the opportunity to bargain."

Georgiana tossed and turned that night in her cold room. She couldn't afford fuel to heat the room. But it wasn't the cold keeping her awake. The seamstress had confirmed her concerns over Madam DuPont and her friend, Celeste Fontaine. She must leave Madam DuPont's shop. *But I can't leave before I receive my next pay packet. I'll starve if I leave without the coins I have coming. But to stay is to risk being forced to work for Celeste.* She ran her fingers across the bracelet and thought of the bits of glass she had replaced. They had once been part of a church window. She'd been inside a church a few times in her life and had enjoyed the peace and quiet there. She found herself wishing she'd learned how to pray.

The following day, Anne smirked and preened, showing off a new pair of earrings. The older seamstress said nothing to indicate what she and Georgiana had seen the previous evening and neither did Georgiana, yet there was something malicious in the way Anne seemed to taunt Georgiana with the jewelry and the way each time she passed by, Georgiana's scissors or threads were brushed to the floor. A few days later, Anne flung a pair of scissors across the room, narrowly missing Georgiana's face.

Georgiana's next pay packet paid her rent and nothing more, but she didn't dare complain. That night, she tossed and turned on her bed once more and worried about what would become of her. She expected the harassment would continue until she owed more than she earned, then she would be forced to choose between debtors' prison and working for Celeste. If Anne didn't manage to disfigure or maim her first. She couldn't let either happen. If she worked for Celeste, she would never attain the respectability she had yearned for all of her life. She touched the bracelet. Perhaps it was already too late. *Dear God,* she whispered. *Tell me what to do.* Silence met her plea. She'd been foolish to think she could make up a prayer or hope God would care about a thief.

It was dawn when she crept out of bed and donned her plain work gown with cold, shaking fingers. She would resign today. A sense of urgency told her she didn't have much time. She didn't know what would become of her, but she chose not to dwell on that fear lest she talk herself out of resigning her position. She was glad she hadn't signed a contract. Madam couldn't haul her before a magistrate for failing to abide by their agreement.

Perhaps Madam was right about one thing, she thought as she drew her cloak close about her shoulders for the walk to the shop. She was too picky. Taverns were plentiful along the waterfront, and she would look for work in one of them, serving grog or helping in the kitchen. At least she'd be warm.

When she arrived at the shop, Georgiana moved the gown she'd taken home with her from her basket to the rod where finished gowns and those awaiting a fitting were hung. Madam arrived shortly after and began flinging gowns about, searching for a gown promised to the beautiful songstress Olivia Samuels, who would arrive in minutes for a fitting.

Georgiana and the other seamstresses joined in the search for the missing gown. It soon became apparent more than one gown was missing, as was Anne, the seamstress who had worked on the dress for Miss Samuels. The faces of the searching women turned pale, revealing their fear they would be charged for the missing items. Georgiana was glad she'd taken the dress she was responsible for to her room the previous night.

"What is this?" Madam clutched the dress Georgiana had returned.

"The gown for Lord Brenthaven's new mistress," Georgiana stammered, fearful that in her rage, Madam would shred the dress and demand she start over.

"Madam DuPont?" an anxious voice called from the front of the shop. Georgiana welcomed the interruption, as she could see Madam was torn. She looked at the gown, then at Georgiana before flinging the dress toward her.

"It's from the same silk as Miss Samuel's gown, but much too plain. Try it on the customer, then make the alterations. Tell her you haven't finished the trim, but will add lace and braid at once. You can make a new gown for the Brenthaven mistress later. If you cost me a customer, you'll pay!" Her voice was harsh in speaking to Georgiana, but it softened and her accent became more pronounced as she called out, "Dear Miss Samuels, we were just tidying up a bit before your arrival. The gown is ready for fitting if you would please step into a fitting room."

Georgiana gathered up the yards of silk, tape measure, and pins before making her way to the fitting room. It wasn't what she'd meant to do that morning, but she could resign her position once Miss Samuels was on her way. She'd heard the lovely soprano sing more than a year ago at a private entertainment Lady Burton had hosted long before her hasty retreat to the country. She didn't care how much trouble Anne's departure might cause Madam, but she didn't wish the singer to be inconvenienced.

"I'm so sorry to keep you waiting," Madam spoke to Olivia in a charming voice as she ushered Georgiana into the fitting room. "The employee who took your order is no longer employed here, and this young lady has taken over her accounts. I hope she will suit. Please call for me if anything is amiss." She finished by apologizing again before leaving Georgiana and Miss Samuels alone in the fitting room.

It occurred to Georgiana that the situation might be a setup, but if not, then it might be the means of stopping Madam's determined push to force her into Celeste's employ. If she proved herself capable of fitting and measuring, perhaps her employer would need her badly enough to change her mind about forcing her to work for Celeste.

"Miss," Georgiana hesitantly held out the dress for Miss Samuels to step into. She then helped her smooth it into place. As she began to fasten the row of tiny buttons down the back of the gown, she was pleased to see it was a better fit than she had expected. The waist would need taking in, and the hem should be taken up. The songbird was known for her powerful voice, but her stature was almost diminutive. Georgiana was glad to see that little else would be required to make the garment a perfect fit.

"Perhaps a bit of white fur at the neckline?" The singer examined herself critically in the glass, tugging at the neckline, which showed only a single, narrow row of lace.

"Will you be wearing jewels?" Georgiana countered.

"Yes, I plan to wear a lovely set of sapphires and diamonds." She smiled, and Georgiana suspected the jewels were a gift from a favorite admirer.

"Fur could easily be added to the bodice if you desire, but it would distract attention from your jewelry and the lovely line of your throat. If your heart is set on fur, you might consider a wide strip added to the hemline to add drama to each step you take and a sprinkle of diamante across the overskirt." Georgiana suggested.

"Oh, yes!" Olivia Samuels clapped her slender hands. Then, turning to the tall glass, she brushed her fingers against her hair, pulling it back. "And should I wear my hair up or down?" she asked her reflection in the mirror.

"If I might suggest . . ." Georgiana reached for the other woman's hair and deftly twisted it into a puffy knot atop her head, allowing one long curl to cascade over her shoulder. "With your hair piled on top of your head, your ear bobs will draw attention to your face, and the one escaping curl will enhance your femininity."

"You're really very clever," Olivia said. "I think I'll take your suggestions—all of them."

Georgiana carefully helped Olivia out of the dress and back into the gown in which she'd arrived.

While Olivia stopped to talk with Madam, Georgiana gathered up the gown and carried it to her stool to begin the alterations.

"My dress will be ready by tomorrow night?" she heard the inquiry addressed to Madam and Madam's assurance that it would be, followed by the silvery tinkle of the bell above the door as the customer left.

Georgiana threaded her needle and began the stitches that would pull the waist tighter. While she stitched, she held her breath, rehearsing the words she'd planned for telling Madam that she was leaving, but the shop owner never ventured into the backroom. Attaching the fur was difficult since it was much heavier than the airy silk, and she had to be wary of pricking a finger as she forced the needle through the leather-like thickness. By the time the shop grew too dark to work any longer, the dress was finished. She considered taking it with her when she left to avoid the risk of malicious damage to her creation before she returned, but the finished garment was too bulky to hide in her bag. Besides she didn't plan to return. She would tell Madam she was leaving right now.

Gathering up her needle and untouched crust of bread she'd brought for her lunch, she made her way to the front of the shop. She didn't see her employer, so it seemed she must return one more time in order to resign. Her shoulders slumped. Before she could push open the door to the street, Madam DuPont's voice came from behind her. She too sounded tired and defeated.

"Take the gown with you. Miss Samuels has requested that you begin employment with her immediately. I trust that is satisfactory?" There was an even tone to the woman's voice, revealing neither anger nor satisfaction that their duel was at an end.

7

"You came!" Miss Samuels greeted Georgiana enthusiastically when she presented herself at the singer's townhouse the next morning. "I thought you would, and I'm seldom wrong about a person's character."

"You knew . . ." Georgiana blushed, unable to go on.

"Oh, yes. There's a great deal of gossip among singers and actresses. The arrangement between Madam DuPont and Madam Celeste is quite well known. The moment I saw you, I knew Celeste's establishment was the reason Madam DuPont hired you and has kept you hidden in the backroom. It is my good fortune that you are also an excellent seamstress and know something of arranging hair."

Olivia insisted Georgiana move into a room in her house. It wasn't one of the grand houses such as the ones she'd previously worked in, but her room was more comfortable than the one over the bakery had been, and with winter just beginning, it would certainly be much warmer. She was pleasantly surprised when the other members of the household treated her with courtesy and welcomed her into the household. The staff was small, consisting of a housekeeper, Mrs. Betz, who also served as the cook, a maid, Elsa, and the housekeeper's husband, who tended the small garden and drove Miss Samuels's carriage. He also acted as butler when needed. He walked with a strange lurching step Georgiana learned came from an accident at sea.

"Welcome, Miss," Mr. Betz greeted her. His wife followed suit.

"Your room is ready, and I put fresh sheets on the bed." Elsa ducked her head and smiled. Her shyness made the diminutive maid look much too young for her post.

Georgiana acknowledged their welcome and made a silent vow to not hold herself aloof from their friendly warmth. She had never cultivated friendships with the other servants at her previous places of employment, but she felt drawn to Elsa and the Betzes. She had been alone far too long.

Adjusting to the household was made easy by the other servants' willingness to befriend her and by her new mistress's sunny disposition. Georgiana's days were soon filled with caring for the songstress's wardrobe and dressing her for her performances. Olivia owned many beautiful gowns, and preparing her wardrobe and hairstyle was a pleasure.

It didn't take long to discover that Olivia was not only kind, but generous. Whenever she tired of a gown, she gave it to Georgiana to restyle for herself or Elsa. Georgiana had never worked for a mistress so generous and unfailingly polite, who treated her employees as dear friends. She never tired of listening to Olivia sing or talk about her career and the exciting people she met. Sometimes they giggled together like sisters, and Georgiana didn't mind when her mistress shortened her name to Georgie.

December faded into January, and Georgiana began to relax. She'd seen nothing of the Burtons or Wellingtons, nor any of her previous employers. In the back of her mind, she knew that when Parliament convened in a few weeks and Viscount Burton assumed his seat there, the London season would also begin. Then she would be at greater risk, but for the present, she was content to enjoy working for Olivia Samuels.

Olivia had sung at a number of simple entertainments through the early winter, and the demand for her services had grown through the holiday season. Georgiana was grateful her mistress didn't accept any invitations to attend holiday house parties a distance from the city, though her trepidation grew as the season approached. Servants were generally a faceless lot as far as the wealthy were concerned, but still she dreaded the possibility of recognition. The increased pace of the social season would mean Georgiana would have to be more vigilant about staying out of sight.

Almost as if she knew of Georgiana's reluctance to appear in public, Olivia didn't require her to accompany her when she sang at private entertainments hosted by dowagers eager to announce their arrival in London. And by taking care to remain in Olivia's dressing room when she accompanied her to the theatre, Georgiana was able to avoid contact with anyone who might recognize her.

She had worried at first about accompanying Olivia to the theatre, as she was well aware that some actresses and performers entertained gentlemen following their performances, and she had no desire to stumble onto anyone backstage or in the hallway who might recognize her. She was relieved and thankful to discover Olivia met her male admirers—and she had plenty of them—in the green room but never brought them back to her dressing room. A certain merchant marine officer, a Robert, called occasionally at the house and stayed the night, but Olivia did not hold open house each afternoon or invite any of her other admirers to her home. Instead, she devoted her afternoons to practicing her music.

Through the winter months, Georgiana began to relax and take pleasure in her new situation, but as landowners flocked to London for the peak of the parliamentary session following Easter and their families arrived to see and be seen at the more important social extravaganzas, her fears returned. She hadn't known Sydney as well as she'd thought, but she did know he was tenacious, stubborn, and unforgiving. She'd thwarted his plans for her, shot him, and knew his criminal identity. Though months had passed since she'd last seen him, she knew she was not safe from his retribution. She wouldn't be truly safe until she reached America.

Georgiana was well acquainted with the social mores of the gentry and took extra pains to avoid places where she might be noticed. She stayed indoors more and took care to change her hairstyle. She even acquired an unstylish poke bonnet to wear while running errands for Olivia, and she avoided the more fashionable shops. Catching sight of a familiar coat of arms on a carriage door would have her ducking into side streets, and occasionally she bribed Elsa to purchase ribbons or thread in her stead.

After the Easter break, Georgiana was kept busy almost every night as the hectic pace accelerated, taking on almost a frenzy of activity. On the fourth consecutive night of Olivia's performance in the new opera house, Georgiana found her eyes growing heavy while she waited for the thunderous applause that would signal the end of Olivia's segment of the show.

Working for the singer was the best position Georgiana had ever had, and the hoard of coins she was accumulating in the small bag she kept at the bottom of her sewing bag was growing steadily. It would take most of another year to accumulate enough to pay for her passage to America, but the coins were multiplying much faster than Georgiana had hoped, certainly far faster than would have been possible if she'd continued working as a seamstress. She wouldn't feel completely safe until she reached America, but already she dreaded saying good-bye to Olivia and the other residents of Olivia's house.

"Georgie, we must hurry," Olivia swept into the dressing room, surprising Georgiana, who had been dreaming of the life she would trade her jewels for when she reached America. Surely Olivia's performance hadn't ended already.

"The show . . .?"

"I will not sing again tonight! The rabble are unusually drunk and are throwing vegetables at the stage. My dress is

ruined, and I shall have a bruise on my cheek for a week."
She rubbed the aggrieved spot with her fingers. "A couple
of young dandies are egging the peasants on, and I will not
stay to be injured. But we must leave quickly before the
manager finds me and insists I return to the stage for my
next number." She made no attempt to hide her anger as
she began snatching up her cape and the small casket that
held her jewelry. Georgiana gathered up Olivia's cosmetics
case and her own few belongings from the dressing room.
With her arms full, she followed Olivia to the door.

Olivia opened the door a crack. Such caution on
Olivia's part was unusual and caused Georgiana to
become fearful. A loud burst of laughter had Olivia
hastily closing the door again.

"Where did she go?" A drunken voice called. "I mean
to have her afore I get leg-shackled." The shout was
followed by raucous laughter. Georgiana felt the blood
drain from her face. The voice came from none other
than Sydney Burton. She couldn't go out there.

"They've come backstage!" Olivia fumed. "That devil
Sydney Burton will wed the Wellington miss tomorrow.
Sydney's father discovered last spring that the dolt was
pestering me to become his mistress and sent him to the
country before his future father-in-law caught wind of his
intentions. Tonight he and his drunken cronies were
turned away at both Whites and Madam Celeste's for
creating disturbances, so they came here looking for
substitutes. They must have bribed the stage manager to
look the other way in order to gain entrance to the
dressing rooms."

Laughter and the not-so-outraged squeals coming down the hall were drawing closer. Georgiana peered around the room in panic. *I have to get out of here. I can't let him find me.*

"I am a singer, not a . . ." Olivia's outraged voice was approaching hysteria and it registered in Georgiana's mind that her mistress was as frightened as she. "I won't be forced into becoming any man's mistress. Last time he caught me, he beat me until I almost lost consciousness. I barely managed to stop him with the dagger Robert insists I carry beneath my skirt. It took months for the bruises to heal, and I missed several months of the engagements I depend on for my income. Save for Robert's intervention, I would have been sent to prison for attacking a peer."

Olivia's voice rose to a shrill cry. Fearing Sydney would hear and come to investigate, Georgiana grasped her employer's shoulders, shaking her until her shrieks ended in sobs. Her own emotions were approaching hysteria too, but she couldn't let Sydney find them. Olivia's revelation that she was the one who had wounded Sydney was startling, but it only intensified Georgiana's concern that they might be discovered. She looked around the room, desperate for a way out. She thought of the tiny pistol in her sewing bag, then discarded any thought of using it. It only held one piece of lead. Regardless, she would hang if she shot a member of the gentry.

"Come. This way." She grasped Olivia's arm. Olivia appeared to have sunk into some kind of hysterical shock, and Georgiana wasn't certain the other woman would follow her—or if she could even hear her. To her relief, Olivia followed her lead as docilely as a frightened child.

Georgiana led her to the small maid's room attached to the star's dressing room. Once inside the tiny space, she whispered, "Beneath the cot, there is a panel that opens to hide the night soil bucket. The space is just large enough for us to crawl inside."

She knelt, removed the bucket, and set it in a corner. Returning to Olivia's side, she took her mistress's jewel casket and cloak, along with her own sewing bag and pelisse, and stuffed them into the space under the cot. She then urged Olivia to crawl inside the opening. Olivia hesitated, wrinkling her nose.

Pounding on the dressing room door provided the impetus to overcome Olivia's squeamishness, and both young women lost no time crawling inside the narrow, dark space. Georgiana slid the panel closed behind them. Then, gripping each other's hands, they lay still, scarcely daring to breathe.

The splintering of wood heralded the invasion of Olivia's dressing room. Running footsteps could be heard followed by disappointed male voices. The door to the maid's room was flung open so hard it reverberated against the wall, but as near as Georgiana could tell, none of the men actually entered the room. She couldn't be certain how many there were, but she thought she detected at least three separate voices. Sydney's was the only voice she recognized.

Crude jokes and laughter continued for several minutes as Syndey and his friends searched the dressing room.

Several objects fell, crashing to the floor to the amusement of the drunken invaders, but soon they moved back to the hallway where their voices continued to elicit screams and the sound of scurrying footsteps. After a few minutes, the stage manager's deep voice bellowed a demand that the troublemakers leave. He was backed up by several other deep voices and the titter of female voices. Pandemonium continued for several more minutes, then was gradually replaced by silence.

Neither woman made a move to leave their hiding place until Georgiana's foot began to cramp, then her shoulder. Cautiously, she opened the panel a crack and peered out. The room was black. Turning her head, she listened for any sound coming from the hall. Hearing nothing, she crawled out and turned to help Olivia, then knelt to retrieve the items she'd thrust far to the back of their hiding place. She had to crawl halfway back inside to reach them.

"Georgie," Olivia's voice came to her, sounding fearful. "I think the theatre is on fire."

"What?" Georgiana bumped her head as she withdrew it too quickly. Regaining her feet, she sniffed. A faint whiff of smoke floated in the air. Grasping the jewel case under one arm and holding her bag and Olivia's cape in the other, she attempted to feel her way in the darkened room toward the door.

"We've got to get out of here." Olivia found the door first. Once inside the dressing room, she rushed toward the door that led from it to the hall. She flung it open, then reeled backward. Smoke boiled into the dressing room, and a flickering pattern of flames leaped toward the open door. Georgiana rushed forward to shove the door closed again.

"The window," Olivia screamed as she ran toward the small window that opened two stories above a stone court.

"Wait!" Georgiana caught her arm. "We'll be killed if we jump, and if we open the window before we're ready to leave, the fire will burn faster."

"I'm not waiting to burn to death." Olivia struggled to free herself.

"If we fashion a rope out of your dress sashes, we won't have so far to fall." Georgiana waited only long enough for her words to register with Olivia before releasing her to run toward the wardrobe.

"We can use the curtain ties, too." Olivia jerked one long curtain panel free. She reached for the rope tie that was used to hold the drapes back. Discovering it was sturdy, she found the other one and tied them together.

"I'm not certain I can knot them well enough," Georgiana expressed her doubts as she carried Olivia's sashes closer to the window where a small amount of light filtered into the room.

"Leave that to me." Olivia reached for the long sashes. "Robert is a sailor, and he taught me to tie knots." Her words ended in a cough, but her fingers moved quickly, fashioning a rope. Olivia coughed again, and Georgiana found she too was struggling for breath. She straightened the sashes and handed them to Olivia, who joined them into a brightly colored rope and linked them to the curtain ties.

"Do you suppose it's long enough?" Olivia's voice was now a harsh whisper as she finished tying the last sash.

"No, but it's all we have, and we must go." Georgiana carried one end of the rope to the window while Olivia tied the other end to one leg of the heavy armoire. The exertion left them both gasping for breath.

"Now," Georgiana croaked. "We can open the window."

Georgiana released the catch and shoved at the window. It didn't move. Olivia joined her, and together they pushed, trying to lift it. Whether it was paint or winter's grime that held the window closed, Georgiana couldn't guess. Their only other option was to shatter the glass and risk injury from broken shards as they climbed through it. Olivia turned to gain a better hold and screamed.

Georgiana glanced over her shoulder to see flames reaching through the door. Desperation lent both girls strength, and the window flew open. Olivia threw out the free end of their rope and without waiting to see how far it fell, Georgiana urged Olivia over the sill.

Not wishing to add her weight to Olivia's, Georgiana waited, listening for a signal that the other woman had made it to the ground. Her back was growing hot, and from the corner of her eye, she saw flames creeping along the wall toward her. She couldn't wait any longer.

"Hurry," she screamed to Olivia.

Crackles and hisses added to the heat behind her, warning that the fire was moving closer. She glanced down to see flames licking at the sewing bag which lay beside Olivia's jewelry casket where both women had dropped them beneath the window. She paused long enough to drop the casket inside the sewing bag, wrap both in Olivia's cape, and fling the bundle out the window before climbing over the window ledge. She grasped the makeshift rope and began to slide toward the ground, only slowed in her descent by the series of knots.

Suddenly she was falling.

There was no time to wonder if the fire had burned through the rope or if a knot had come untied. Her landing was almost immediate. It was also softer than she'd expected, and it took a moment to realize she was lying on top of Olivia.

"Are you all right?" She moaned between paroxysms of strangled coughs while endeavoring to move off of Olivia.

"Let's go home," Olivia gasped, clearly winded.

Stumbling and coughing, they helped each other to their feet, then stood, holding onto each other and swaying precariously. Two things registered after a few moments. Sounds were coming from the front of the building, and a deluge of rain was pouring from the sky upon them.

"Shall we alert the firefighters?" Georgiana asked, assuming the sounds coming from the front of the theatre were coming from the fire brigade.

"No," Olivia shuddered. "Sydney and his friends might still be around here, and even if they aren't, we wouldn't be safe from the thieves who rush to fires to pick over the rubble for coins or jewels abandoned by their owners."

"But without a coach . . ."

"We'll have to risk it." Olivia turned toward the alley, and Georgiana rushed to catch up to her. She stumbled over a small, soft obstruction. Her despair lessened when she recognized the bundle she'd tossed from the window. She lost no time gathering it up.

"We'll be perfectly safe," Olivia turned to add. "We look like hags and have nothing of value that might attract thieves."

"At least cover your head," Georgiana admonished, pulling Olivia's cloak over the other woman's hair. "And we aren't without valuables as much as you think," she went on. "I tossed my small savings and your jewels out the window in this bag." She held up the sewing bag to show Olivia, then tucked it inside the front of her dress where it would be out of sight. It also served to make her appear older and more shapeless.

"My jewels?" Olivia croaked, then dissolved in a fit of coughing. She flung her arms around Georgiana and leaned against her weakly, unable to speak. Georgiana put her arm around Olivia, and Olivia drew her cloak around them both. They had a long walk ahead of them.

Keeping to the shadows and huddling together against the rain, they moved past a nearby park, which was notorious for footpads, and kept walking steadily toward Olivia's house, passing through narrow, cluttered streets, shrouded in darkness and notorious for their crime and squalor. They jumped at each shadow that slid threateningly from a gaping alley, ripe with the stench of rotting filth. Rats scurried between buildings, and the pathetic shapes of women and children filled doorways that reeked of gin. Olivia spoke only once.

"The rain will help put out the fire and draw looters to the opera house with the hope of salvaging valuables that might have survived the flames." She finished with a cough.

"Won't the Watch help?" Georgiana asked.

"Perhaps, but the best protection will come from Mr. Russell, the stage manager. By now he should be marshaling the gang of cutthroats he employs as guards."

A carriage drew close and seemed to slow. The two young women shrank back into a narrow alleyway. After a slight hesitation, the carriage went on. Minutes later, the sound of footsteps had them once more seeking the shadows. The thud of hurrying steps passed them by.

Olivia's cough grew worse the farther they traveled, and when her steps began to slow, Georgiana put an arm around her waist to hurry her lagging steps. The sodden cloak no longer offered any protection from the cold, but Georgiana positioned it to protect Olivia from the driving rain as much as possible. It also served to hide the singer's face and golden mane. Georgiana was cold and thoroughly soaked, but Olivia seemed to be in worse shape. Both Olivia's shoes and her own had disintegrated, leaving them to splash through puddles with only the meager protection of their stockings, which soon were nothing but tattered shreds. Each step seemed to drain a little more of the slight energy Georgiana had left, but she felt a compelling need to protect Olivia, the only mistress she'd ever had who had treated her kindly. She'd known few friends in her life and valued Olivia the more because of it.

At last they entered a familiar narrow street and saw lights on the lower floor of Olivia's house. Georgiana felt tears slide down her face on seeing it. She'd almost despaired of reaching that haven.

"We're almost home," she told Olivia, who made no response, though her body seemed to sag more heavily against Georgiana. A carriage splashed past them, then drew to a halt. Georgiana stiffened, then she recognized Olivia's coachman. Mr. Betz leaped to the road and dashed toward them.

"Miss Samuels, I searched everywhere for you," he called out. "I was afraid you had perished in the flames."

Olivia collapsed, dragging Georgiana with her to the muddy ground. The coachman reached for Olivia, lifting her into his sturdy arms. He looked around as though uncertain whether to carry her the short distance to the house or place her in the carriage. He chose the carriage and quickly thrust her inside, leaving Georgiana to scramble on her own to Olivia's side.

The housekeeper and maid took over Olivia's care the moment the coachman burst through the door carrying their mistress, though the housekeeper, with thoughtful thoroughness, instructed the maid to fill a tub with hot water for Georgiana along with one for Olivia in their respective sleeping chambers.

Alone in her small room, Georgiana clumsily removed her clothing and struggled with the clasp on her bracelet. Her numb fingers refused to cooperate. At length, she had to use her teeth to release the clasp. She set the bracelet on a stool beside her bed, then gratefully sank into the warm depths of the tin tub. Only when the young maid, Elsa, timidly handed her a warmed towel and suggested she go to bed, did she gather enough strength to climb out of the comforting water. She made a mental note to thank Elsa for her warmed bed just before slipping into oblivion.

It was well past noon the following day when Georgiana awoke. The house was still, but in the distance she could hear the clamoring of church bells. For just a moment, she thought about Sydney. She no longer loved him, but she felt an ache of regret for the bright dream she'd lost. A tinge of pity for his innocent bride surfaced for just a moment, then she leaped out of bed. From habit, her right hand brushed her left wrist. The bracelet was gone. Her eyes went to the spot where she had undressed. There was nothing there.

She took a step toward the spot, and her toe struck the small stool beside her bed, tipping it over. The bracelet clattered to the floor. She grasped it and fastened it to its customary place on her wrist before starting to search for her sewing bag.

She found the bag hanging on a peg beside her freshly laundered dress. She tore the bag open and was assailed with a mixture of emotions. Olivia's jewel casket sat on top of a damp bit of cloth Georgiana had been working on while she waited in the dressing room for Olivia to finish her performance. Beneath it was the leather bag with a drawstring and the silver derringer. Opening the bag, she found every coin accounted for. Olivia's staff were honest, caring people. *Only I,* Georgiana thought with the first faint stirrings of regret, *am a thief.* She touched the bracelet, and for the first time experienced a deep pang of remorse.

A knock on the door interrupted her thoughts, and she tucked the bag of coins back inside the sewing bag before opening the door a crack.

"Would you like some breakfast?" Elsa stood smiling outside her door with a heavy tray balanced on one hand.

"Oh my!" Georgiana opened the door wider. "It isn't your job to wait on me."

"I chose to bring you a tray." Elsa entered the room and set the tray on the stool. "Miss Samuels is awake, and she said you saved her life. She has been good to me, took me in when I was to be sent to a prison colony because I couldn't pay my father's debts after he was run over by a carriage. If anything happened to Miss Samuels, I don't know what would become of me." It was becoming apparent to Georgiana that Olivia had acquired her staff largely through her compassionate nature.

"You're both kind and efficient and would easily find another place," Georgiana assured the girl. "But I don't believe any other mistress would protect you so well from unscrupulous sons or husbands." She seated herself on the edge of the bed and began to eat, relishing the cook's flaky croissants slathered with rich, fresh butter.

"Miss Samuels asked to see you as soon as you are awake and have had a chance to eat," Elsa informed her. "I'll leave you now to your breakfast. As soon as you finish, please join her in her bedchamber."

Georgiana set her cup down and reached for the draw-string holding her bed gown. She interspersed bites of her breakfast with donning a day dress and combing out her hair before coiling it artfully atop her head. When she finished, she picked up the tray. Elsa had been kind to bring the tray to her, but she would return it to the kitchen herself on the way to see Olivia. She gathered up Olivia's jewel casket and balanced it on the tray. Olivia would be anxious for its return, and it was of extreme importance to Georgiana that her mistress receive the casket without a single jewel missing.

* * *

Georgiana was sitting beside Olivia's bed urging her to drink the concoction Cook sent up to ease her cough when a tap sounded at the door. Before being invited to enter, Miss Samuels's seafaring man strode into the room. He was a fine figure of a man with his broad shoulders and narrow waist. His features were regular, and his eyes amazingly blue. It was easy to see why Olivia paid scant attention to her other admirers.

"Olivia, luv, what have you done to yourself?" The large man knelt beside the bed, and Georgiana saw he was not only a handsome man, but more youthful than she had supposed, having only seen him previously from across a room. He took Olivia's hand in his and looked at her appraisingly, almost in a fatherly manner. He didn't act at all as Georgiana might expect a man in love to act. Nevertheless, she stood, prepared to make a careful exit.

A scratchy sound came from Olivia's throat that sounded like she was trying to say, "Georgie," then "Robert," as though she were attempting to introduce the two to each other. She grasped Georgiana's hand tighter as she struggled to speak. The captain turned to Georgiana. "What the blazes happened? I got a glimpse of a paper this morning just as I arrived in London that claimed my Olivia and her maid, one Georgiana Fenwick, had died in the opera house fire last night. I assume you are Georgiana Fenwick?"

Georgiana was speechless as his words sank in. Neither she nor Olivia had considered that it would be assumed that they had died in the fire. Worse yet, she had been identified by name in the morning paper as a connection of Olivia's. When it was discovered that Olivia had survived the fire, might Sydney guess she had survived as well? If so, he would come looking not only for Olivia, but for her as well.

"Well?" The captain rose to his full height and looked down at Georgiana. She had never been so close to such a large man before. Her head came just to his shoulder. He smelled of something spicy, and there was nothing cruel or intimidating in the look he gave her. Quite the opposite, in fact. The deep blue of his eyes seemed to pull her toward him, and she sensed his concern included her as well as Olivia. She could see why Olivia cared for him. There was something about him that made her feel safe. She found herself relating the facts of their ordeal. At several points, Olivia croaked a word or nodded her head. When Georgiana finished her story, Captain Carver stroked his chin as though deep in thought for several minutes.

"Lord Burton's spawn, hmm." He smiled, and Georgiana barely averted a gasp. The gentle giant was gone. There was something terrifying rather than jovial behind that smile. She could almost feel pity for Sydney. This man wasn't one she would ever want to anger, but there was something reassuring in knowing he was no friend of Sydney's.

9

"Mind if I join you?" Georgiana looked up, surprised to see Captain Carver standing in the doorway to the morning room where she'd made her way for afternoon tea. It was a compromise she had reached with Elsa, since the maid was adamant concerning taking Georgiana a tray and Georgiana hadn't wished the girl to carry any more heavy trays up the stairs. Olivia had often taken tea or eaten her breakfast in the sunny room and on frequent occasions had invited Georgiana to join her and had given her leave to make use of the room. Georgiana knew a place had been set for the captain in the dining room, but now he stood, plate in hand, before her.

"No. That is, I have no objection to your sitting here. I can go—"

"Don't leave." He was beside her, his hand extended as if to prevent her departure. "I would like you to stay."

"If you wish." She settled back on the chair she'd been about to vacate, feeling a bit perplexed. Perhaps the captain merely wished to further discuss the events of the previous night. "There is little more I can tell you about what transpired at the theatre. I was unaware of Miss Samuels's previous difficulties with Sydney Burton."

"It is neither Olivia nor that young rapscallion I wish to discuss." Captain Carver settled himself across from her on a chair Georgiana would have thought much too dainty for such a large man. He placed his heavily laden plate on the graceful table separating them, where Olivia was accustomed to managing her accounts and scribbling her correspondence. Instead of appearing foolishly out of place, the captain looked right at home and much too handsome for Georgiana's peace of mind.

"I wish to learn more about you," he said in an offhand voice while reaching for a jam-filled tart on his plate. Georgiana felt a flare of dismay. Surely he wasn't attempting to flirt with her. There was no way she would entertain such disloyalty to Olivia. A second thought was even more ominous. Had he perhaps found dissatisfaction with her conduct? For a servant to eat anywhere other than in the kitchen or to address her employer by her first name was cause for dismissal in most houses. Did he blame her for not protecting Olivia better? Surely he hadn't discovered she had stolen valuable gems from her previous employer.

"What do you wish to know, sir?" she asked, hesitant to volunteer information but reluctant to appear less than forthright.

"Oh, where were you born? Where were you employed before meeting Olivia? Is your family nearby? Do you prefer blackberry or red currant tarts?" He smiled, and Georgiana felt like the sun had emerged on a cloudy day.

"I know little of my father. He died before my birth," Georgiana struggled to place her story in the best light possible and ignore the pounding in her chest. "My mother met him while they were employed in the same household, he as tutor to the heir and she as governess to the young ladies of the family. My mother, who has been dead these ten years, took work as a lady's maid in another household following his death and her charges' marriages. I followed her into domestic service at the age of twelve." She paused, but he indicated she should continue, which she did, haltingly at first, since she found it unfathomable that a sea captain could truly be interested in a lady's maidservant.

"Because of a flair for dressing hair, my responsibilities changed to that of hairdresser. I left my last post due to the inappropriate attentions of my employer's son. I tried my hand as a seamstress, but was not happy with the work until Miss Samuels came to the shop for a fitting. She offered me employment as her personal wardrobe mistress and hairdresser." She told the truth, omitting names or identifying places, well aware an incomplete truth is easier to remember than a lie.

"And are you happy in Olivia's employ?" Captain Carver smiled invitingly, encouraging her confidence, but she feared a trap. She nodded her head to the captain's question while trying to remain calm. *What if Olivia's Robert meant to see her dismissed? Or might he make an improper proposition?* As if sensing her reluctance to confide in him, he emptied his plate with almost methodical deliberation while launching into a tale of his own boyhood yearning to go to sea and how his father had taken pity on him, making him his cabin boy when he was but ten years of age.

"It was a difficult voyage. Many lives were lost, including that of my father," he confided. Georgiana felt a surge of sympathy for the lad orphaned so early by the sea. Before she could offer condolences, the captain continued. "My mother kept me by her side until she rewed. I tried my best to be a dutiful son, keeping the wood box filled, hiring out to returning fishermen for a few coins, and studying the lessons she set for me, but I missed the sea and longed to feel a deck beneath my feet once more. Mother's new husband was another seafaring man, and knowing my heart's desire, she consented to my becoming his cabin boy as I had been my father's. I was overjoyed to set sail once more. From cabin boy, I worked my way up to becoming an officer by seizing every opportunity given me.

"Not long after I made first mate, I was invited to dinner at the home of a man with two sons. The older had plans to eventually take over his father's small ship-building business near Liverpool, but the younger son wished to build his own business in America and was looking for partners. His proposition appealed to me, and two years later I set sail as the captain of the first ship to leave his Boston yard. He gave me the honor of christening her, which is why she is called the *Nightingale*, named for my own sweet Olivia."

Conversation which began so stiffly came more easily, and Georgiana was surprised when Mrs. Betz poked her head around the door. "There's a bloke at the door asking for you, Captain," she said.

"Thank you, Mrs. Betz." He rose to his feet, then holding out a hand to Georgiana, assisted her to rise.

"Olivia is sleeping, with young Elsa in the chair beside her bed. You must retire to your room and rest as well, while you can. Though you seem quite recovered from your ordeal, we must not take chances with your health. Thank you for sharing your tea with me." He bowed slightly before taking his leave.

Georgiana watched him leave the room with a sense of bemusement. For such a large man, he was amazingly quick and light on his feet. She didn't know what to think of the conversation that had just transpired. The captain had seemed solicitous of her rather than threatening. There had been nothing improper in his behavior toward her, unless it was improper for him to share tea with a servant.

Spending so much time at sea, and with Olivia asleep, it was likely he was lonely and merely wished company. She was making too much of it, she decided. She gathered up the plates and cups. She'd carry them to the kitchen to spare Elsa the extra task.

* * *

The light was wrong when Georgiana awoke. It should have been late afternoon, but it was the bright rays of morning shining through windows where curtains had not been drawn that woke her. Appalled that she had slept through dinner and hadn't yet seen to her mistress, she rushed to dress. Olivia had enough to worry about without wondering if her maid was going to arrive to help her with her toilette.

She quickly selected a dark green gown, which happened to suit her coloring particularly well. Next she brushed her long locks into a simple knot at the nape of her neck, allowing slender ringlets to frame either side of her face. She had barely pushed the last pin into place when there was a knock on her bedroom door. She hurried to answer it.

"Elsa!" Spying the heavy tray the girl carried, Georgiana took it from the smaller girl and set it on a small table near her bed, then turned to her. "I am quite recovered. There is no need to wait on me."

"Captain Carver said I should bring you a tray and tell you there is no need to hurry this morning, then I am to take a nap. Miss Olivia has no intention of leaving her bed this day. And he insists on feeding her himself."

"Captain Carver has quite taken over the household it seems," Georgiana observed.

"Oh, no. Mrs. Betz is still in charge. She keeps a heavy skillet to hand and has provided Mr. Betz with a rolling pin should the Honorable Sydney Burton make an attempt to call on Miss Olivia." She ended on a giggle, and Georgiana found herself smiling at the picture painted by the young maid.

Georgiana ate her breakfast quickly, nagged by guilt over leaving the other servants to shoulder alone the extra load brought on by Olivia's illness and a guest in the house. Admittedly, Captain Carver wasn't behaving much like a guest.

When she reached Olivia's sitting room, she found the bedroom door standing open and the captain seated in a chair he'd pulled close to Olivia's bedside. She was propped on a pile of pillows with her hair down and a lacy bed jacket fastened at her throat, looking wan, but pleased at the attention from her admirer. He looked up from the newspaper he'd been reading to her, and a smile brought crinkles to the corners of his eyes.

"Good morning, miss." Captain Carver seemed to be appraising her appearance and approving of what he saw. Georgiana was suddenly glad that her coloring hid the blush she felt creeping up her neck better than she might have fared had she been as pale as Olivia.

"Good morning, sir," she returned his greeting with a quick bob of her head, then turned to Olivia. "I apologize for my tardiness. Is your cough improved?"

"Dear Georgie," Olivia reached for her hands. "I owe you my life. My panic would surely have led to my death without your level-headed response to all that happened at the theatre two nights ago," she spoke in a whisper.

"Don't tire your voice. You saved my life every bit as much as I saved yours." She smiled at her friend and gently squeezed her hands. "Who broke my fall when I tumbled toward the ground? Now let's speak no more of it. If you would like me to plait your hair, merely nod your head." A nod of the flaxen head sent Georgiana scurrying to find a brush and ribbons to match Olivia's bed gown.

While weaving two long plaits, Georgiana was aware that Robert Carver had removed himself to stand before the tall windows overlooking Olivia's small garden. He stood with his back to the two women and appeared deep in thought.

"There! You look lovely," she pronounced upon completing her task.

"You do indeed look lovely," the captain said, echoing her words as he turned toward the two women. Georgiana had the uncomfortable feeling the gentleman was including her in the compliment.

"Sir," she began, thinking to excuse herself if he and Olivia wished to be alone.

"My name is Robert." He smiled the friendly smile that made her heart seem to skip a beat. "Neither 'sir' nor 'captain' are at all necessary. I've noticed you are on a first-name basis with Olivia, and so it shall be with me."

"But—"

"No, I shall not hear any argument." He turned his attention back to Olivia, much to Georgiana's relief. It seemed quite scandalous to address a man of such dignity by his given name. She returned her thoughts to Olivia just as she whispered to her admirer, "I shall nap while you are away."

"If your guest has business to attend to," Georgiana told Olivia, "I'll fetch the cream silk you selected for the Cardiff extravaganza and begin setting the stitches right here, where if you should need anything, I will be close at hand."

"I do have a matter to attend to," the captain said. "And it will relieve my mind to know you are sitting with Olivia." Taking Olivia's hand, he pressed his lips to the back of it and assured her he wouldn't be long.

"Mrs. Betz will be put out if you don't take time to eat breakfast." Olivia's whispering voice ruined her attempt to be severe in admonishing the man to take breakfast before leaving to conduct his business.

"Aye, aye, Captain." Robert sent Olivia a mocking salute, then had the audacity to wink at Georgiana. Lowering her eyes, she made a hurried departure in search of the fabric she'd already cut for her mistress's new gown.

Tears came to Georgiana's eyes as she drew the unfinished gown from the trunk where she had placed it before leaving for the theatre two nights ago. With her hands, she smoothed the delicate fabric, imagining how lovely Olivia would be in the finished gown. *Oh, why did he come here? It would have been better had he been far at sea just now.* Immediately she regretted her thoughts. Olivia gained a great deal of pleasure from Robert's presence, and she didn't begrudge her mistress any joy. *It's just that I don't want to lose another job over a man.* Gathering up her sewing bag and selecting the proper threads took just a moment more. If luck were with her, he would soon put to sea.

Olivia was alone and seemed to be sleeping when Georgiana slipped back into the room. She settled herself in the roomy chair Robert had occupied earlier. Her fingers moved swiftly as she drew her needle in and out of the delicate fabric, and she had almost completed an entire seam when Olivia opened her eyes.

"You do like him, don't you?" she asked in a sleepy voice. There was no need to explain whom she meant.

"I can see that he loves you very much," Georgiana attempted to sidestep the question, worried where this was leading.

"Of course he loves me." Olivia sounded impatient. "But I was speaking of you. Robert seldom shows his feelings, but he has made no attempt to conceal his admiration for you."

"I've done nothing to encourage him or invite his attention." She spoke calmly, but her cheeks were flaming. It took all of the self-control she could muster to continue setting the tiny stitches. But after only a moment, she stopped. It was useless to continue. The delicate fabric would show every wrong stitch. The gown would be ruined if she had to pull out the thread and begin again.

"Georgie, look at me." Olivia's voice sounded stronger.

Georgiana raised her face, fearful of what she would see. At that moment, she hated Robert. Why couldn't he have stayed away? She couldn't bear for Olivia to hold her in contempt.

"Georgie, it doesn't matter to Robert that you are in my employ. He's almost more American than English in his views, and he's never set any store by the pretensions of those who have titles or wealth."

"Please." Tears spilled from Georgiana's eyes, and she hurriedly thrust the creamy silk aside to protect it from becoming stained. "I have not and never will betray you."

"Betray me?" Olivia looked puzzled, then a gentle smile curved her lips. "Forgive me, dear Georgie. I forgot I had never explained this. When I began my singing career, I discovered that any woman who sets foot on a public stage is thought to be a prostitute, and at first, I was continually harassed by gentlemen who took offense at my refusal to become their mistress. One night, Robert accompanied me to the theatre and after my performance escorted me home. A rumor quickly spread concerning my captain and I never refuted it because it brought me a measure of peace from presumptuous boors. Robert is my brother."

"Brother?" Georgiana heard her own voice squeak to a higher level.

"Not a brother in the usual sense." Olivia began a chuckle that ended in a paroxysm of coughing. Georgiana lifted a glass to her friend's lips, and when Olivia could speak again, she continued. "Robert's father died when Robert was but a lad. In just under two years, his mother wed my father who was also alone but for a wee daughter whose mother had died in childbirth. Thus we have different surnames. Robert took his role as elder brother seriously and made my childhood sweet. When both our parents succumbed to cholera while I was little more than a child, he took over my guardianship, saw to my education, and supported my passion for music. I love him dearly, but he is my brother in every way that counts."

Georgiana was embarrassed she hadn't seen the relationship for what it was. At the same time, she was surprised to feel her heart soar, knowing Robert was not involved with dear Olivia in the way she had presumed.

"Now tell me," Olivia renewed her earlier question. "What do you think of my dashing brother?"

A crash from the first floor echoed through the house, followed by shouting and a woman's scream, saving Georgiana from answering. Instinctively, the two women grasped for each other's hands, and their hearts pounded. They listened for footsteps ascending the stairs, but the sound did not come. At last, Georgiana whispered, "I'll tiptoe to the top of the stairs to see what is happening. If Sydney has broken in, I'll fly right back and barricade the door."

"Sydney married the day after the fire. Robert said he and his bride set sail for the continent yesterday, so I think we're safe from him for now. They're expected to be gone a year." Olivia straightened her shoulders and released Georgiana's hand in an attempt to be brave. Her words managed to lend Georgiana more confidence, and she stepped toward the door, peered cautiously down the hall, then on seeing nothing unusual, sped quietly down its length to the top of the stairs. Leaning as far out as she dared, she searched the entryway from where the noise had seemed to originate.

At first, she saw only two legs, ending in heavy, leather brogues, stretched across the marble entryway floor. Leaning further, she spied Elsa, with an umbrella stand in her hands, standing over a sturdy young man who lay sprawled on the floor. Shouting at each other across the unfortunate lad's prostate form were the Betzes, weapons in hand. Each time the young man tried to sit up, he was threatened with Mrs. Betz's skillet, Mr. Betz's rolling pin, and the unwieldy umbrella stand clutched by Elsa.

"What is this?" Georgiana hurried down the flight of stairs.

"I saw him from my window in the rear garden, peeking behind bushes and staring up at windows," Elsa reported.

"She reported to me, as was her duty," Mr. Betz added.

"He attempted to enter by my kitchen, but I sent him on his way," Mrs. Betz contributed to the explanation. She glared in a warning fashion at the unfortunate youth.

"He lifted the knocker as though he had a right to expect entrance. The moment he stepped inside, I knew he was no gentleman and should make his business known at the back door. When he refused to leave, I had no choice but to take action." Mr. Betz puffed out his chest as he took credit for the lump on the young man's head.

"What do you have to say for yourself?" Georgiana gazed sternly at the man on the floor. His sturdy form and ruffled hair gave him the look of an innocent cherub. He flashed her a roguish grin before replying.

"My name's James O'Connell, miss. Captain Carver engaged my services just this morning to guard his sister. Being the thorough sort, I examined the premises for weaknesses before presenting myself at the door. I think I can inform the captain that any miscreant who gets past me will surely be felled by Miss Samuels's vigilant staff."

"How do we know you're who you claim to be?" Mr. Betz asked, still brandishing Mrs. Betz's rolling pin.

"Do you mind if I stand? The captain's letter is in my pocket and it is quite impossible to retrieve while I am lying upon it."

Georgiana indicated he should rise. The trio of onlookers brandished their weapons as a warning. On gaining his feet, he reached with exaggerated care into his breeches pocket and withdrew a page that appeared to have been ripped from a journal or logbook. He handed the sheet to Mr. Betz, who squinted at it, then passed it to Georgiana. Georgiana stumbled through it, reading aloud and sounding out slowly the longer words.

"The bearer of this missive has con-trac-ted for 50 pounds per annum to provide pro-tec-tion for Olivia Samuels and her household beginning im-me-di-ate-ly. He has been in-struc-ted in the duties of butler to keep private his true purpose. On pre-sent-ing this letter to Virgil Betz, he will com-mence his duties at once." It held two signatures. That of Captain Robert Carver and a scribbled scrawl that read James O'Connell.

10 ᷒

"Oh, you poor man!" Elsa was the first to react. The umbrella stand in her arms landed on the floor with a thud. "If I'd known . . . but the captain didn't say."

"Come right this way," Mrs. Betz took charge. "A cool cloth will help that lump, and you might wish to sample the peach scones I've prepared for tea." She reached for the stranger's arm. Elsa fluttered about, opening doors and offering apologies.

"Go along now," Mr. Betz advised. "I'll keep my eye on the door until you return, and young Elsa will have your room ready when you finish." He cast Elsa a meaningful look, sending her scurrying to prepare the room. Georgiana noticed that James's eyes followed the young maid as she disappeared in the direction of the back stairs.

"Now, don't be harsh with the lass," James cautioned the Betzes. "She did right to question my right to be examining the house and gardens."

"She's a good lass," Mr. Betz concurred.

"Welcome to our ranks." Georgiana stepped forward and offered her hand. "I am Georgiana Fenwick, Miss Olivia's personal maid. Our mistress would welcome you herself, but as I'm sure Captain Carver explained, she has been the victim of an unfortunate incident. We shall all rest better knowing you are here."

"Thank you, miss. Captain Carver spoke highly of your good sense." His words brought a tingle of pleasure to Georgiana. She was smiling when she returned to Olivia, who was sitting up in bed looking concerned. Georgiana related all that had happened, and Olivia lay back, reassured.

"Dear Robert! I should have expected he would take such a measure to ensure my safety." The excitement seemed to exhaust her, and she soon closed her eyes. When Georgiana judged that her mistress was asleep, she once more picked up the silk fabric, and her fingers flew as she resumed work on the gown.

It was teatime when the door leading from Olivia's sitting room opened and Robert, balancing a tea tray, strode to Olivia's bedside. Seeing his burden, Georgiana set aside her sewing and cleared a space on a low table beside the bed for the tray. When Robert had freed himself of the tray, he looked to Olivia just as she opened her eyes.

"Robert," she whispered, "it was kind of you to hire James to look after us. Georgiana, you must tell Robert all about the lad's momentous arrival."

Robert laughed. "I've already heard the tale thrice over. First from the young man himself, then from the Betzes. Elsa added her version from the upstairs hall where she seems to have found a prodigious amount of dust in need of removal, just where she has a bird's-eye view of your new butler's post." Both Georgiana and Olivia joined his booming laughter.

"If you'll excuse me," Georgiana said, "I'll leave you to your tea now."

"No, no," Robert protested. "I brought more than enough for three. You must stay and keep us company."

"Yes, do," Olivia echoed.

So began days of sitting quietly beside Olivia with her sewing and evenings spent with Olivia and Robert sharing tea, then playing games and listening to Robert's tales of the sea. Much to Georgiana's pleasure, Robert continued, on a regular basis, finding his way to the morning room for a pleasant chat over breakfast. He was an early riser, as was she, and when the meal was concluded, he invariably bowed low over her hand and wished her good day before seeking out James for a brief consultation. Then he was off to check on the *Nightingale* while Georgiana cleared away their dishes and fetched a breakfast tray for Olivia.

"I think I should like to try my hand at embroidery," Olivia announced one morning. None of Georgiana's silks would do for the tapestry her mistress wished to undertake, and since Elsa was busy turning out the front parlor and making sheep's eyes at James, Georgiana promised to search for the necessary silks herself at a shop two streets over.

Donning a sedate green cloak and bonnet Olivia had given her, Georgiana let herself out the kitchen door and walked with rapid steps to the end of the street. It was her first outing since the fire, and at first she was nervous. She found herself casting glances over her shoulder at frequent intervals, but the sun was shining, and it was quite pleasant to escape the house for a short time. When she spied the thread shop on the opposite side of the street, she checked for traffic, then lifted her skirt and scurried across.

Reaching the shop, she took her time selecting the colors. It was important to find the exact hues Olivia desired. When she was satisfied that she had found the correct silks, she handed the coin Olivia had given her to the shop mistress and tucked her small parcel in the pocket of her cloak.

Stepping outside the shop, she looked about, enjoying the sounds of carriages, people's voices, and a small boy chasing a hoop down the street. A team of carriage horses slumbered in the sun nearby, still attached to a heavy wagon, their driver drowsing on the seat. A gentleman, perched high on the seat of a bright red and yellow phaeton, snapped the reins, urging his horse to a faster trot. When it had passed, she stepped onto the street. Two thirds of the way across the street, the thunder of heavy hooves made her aware of a conveyance bearing down upon her. From the corner of her eye, she saw the team of draft horses that had been idling at the side of the street, charging at full speed toward her.

Making a lunge to escape their pounding hoofs, her slipper came down on the front of her petticoat, pitching her forward. A scream escaped her throat as she felt herself falling. The horses were so close she could almost feel their snorting breath. Between their great, shaggy heads, she caught a glimpse of the driver, urging his animals on, his dark, maniacal features twisted with unholy mirth. There was no way to stop her fall. Even if she rolled as she fell, she would be trampled beneath the horses' hooves.

She felt herself flying. She would have supposed herself dead, but the jolt of her body striking a solid object and the whoosh of air leaving her lungs was too painful for allowing her to contemplate that state. Then she felt arms cradling her close to a broad chest. Lifting her face, her eyes met Robert's.

"Are you all right?" he asked.

She was barely aware enough to be comforted by the concern in his voice. When she was calm enough to speak, her voice escaped as a whisper. "I tripped."

Robert scowled and cast his eyes in the direction the team and wagon had disappeared. She could tell he was torn between seeing if she were injured and following the disappearing wagon.

"I'll see you home," he said at length. With all that had happened and her heart still pounding, she still took comfort in knowing he placed her needs first. After Robert had remounted his horse and it clopped sedately down the street, she grew calmer. She remembered the face she'd seen and questioned whether she'd really seen Raul or if her imagination, stoked by the horror of the situation, had conjured the face she dreaded before her. She also became aware of how soothing it was to lean her face against Robert's broad chest, feel the coarse weave of his jacket against her cheek, and hear the even rhythm of his breath above her ear.

They reached Olivia's house too soon, and Robert brought his mount to a halt. Reluctantly, Olivia straightened.

"Thank you," she remembered her manners before sliding to the ground.

"I'll not be long, then we shall talk," Robert said, his manner alarmingly stiff. "I must return my mount to the stable." Seeing her puzzled expression, he went on. "I'm away so much, I don't keep a mount of my own. There's a livery not far from here where I obtain an animal while I am ashore. Olivia's team and carriage are cared for there as well."

She hurried inside the house, never doubting Robert would demand every detail of her near-disaster when they met again. She contemplated how much to tell him. At length she decided she would tell him everything, save that she knew the identity of the driver. Withholding that small detail wasn't truly a lie. The escapade had happened so quickly, she really couldn't be certain whether she had really seen the gypsy.

Once she'd calmed herself and changed her gown, she carried the silks to Olivia. They sat in companionable silence sewing for some time. When Robert arrived, they were both busily engaged in needlework. He pulled a chair closer, watching for several minutes. His close observation caused Georgiana's hands to tremble the slightest bit, just enough that she missed a stitch and would have the bothersome task of correcting the error when she returned to her room.

"I'm surprised you find our stitches so fascinating," Olivia teased her brother.

"It isn't the stitches I find fascinating." He looked closer at Georgiana, who took care not to lift her eyes. "I'm waiting for an explanation."

Olivia looked from him to Georgiana and back. "This concerns Georgiana, I assume. Dear Georgie, what have you done to have poor Robert in such a pother?"

"'Tis a serious matter." Robert continued to look at Georgiana, though he addressed Olivia. "I met your Georgie quite by accident crossing a busy street. She tripped and was about to fall beneath the hooves of a team that was racing much too fast for an area frequented by women and children. If I hadn't happened along, she would have been crushed."

"Georgie!" Olivia squealed. "It's not like you to be so careless."

"I wasn't careless." She lifted her head, stung by the accusation. "I checked carefully for vehicles using the street. A wagon was parked a short distance up the street. The horses were dozing as was the driver. I waited for a phaeton to pass before stepping into the street. Suddenly the wagon and team were charging toward me. I tried to get out of the way, but I stepped on the hem of my petticoat. As I began to fall, I saw the driver urging the team to run faster toward me."

"It was deliberate then?" Robert's visage turned stern. "Describe the man you saw." It was more command than request.

"He was young, dark, with black curls." She couldn't quite suppress the shudder that came over her as she described Raul.

"I'm glad you were not careless," Robert said by way of apology.

"And I shall be grateful forever that you were nearby to rescue me." Their eyes met, and Georgiana felt a familiar flutter in her chest.

Robert promised to make inquiries, then seeing that the story had upset Olivia, he set about trying to restore her to good cheer. When the tea tray arrived, she picked at her dinner and declared herself tired and ready to sleep earlier than had become her custom.

Olivia grew quieter each day and her appetite disappeared. She had been nearly recovered, and now her cough returned. Each morning, Mrs. Betz prepared a tempting treat to coax their mistress's appetite, but Georgiana had little success in persuading Olivia to sample the delicacies.

"Olivia, you must eat," Georgiana urged when, after two weeks, the singer had not regained her appetite. "You are not getting better, and I fear it is because you do not eat."

"Eating makes me cough," Olivia complained. She lifted her cup and sipped slowly at her tea. "Besides, I don't feel well enough to eat."

"You can't live on tea alone. If you don't eat, you'll not become strong enough to walk across a stage, and you'll be so thin, I'll have to take the cream silk in again."

"I'm sorry I'm such a bother." Tears glittered in Olivia's eyes, and Georgiana hastened to reassure her.

"You're not a bother. I just want you to be well again. I fear you'll not get well if you don't eat the food Mrs. Betz prepares for you. And if you aren't strong enough to stroll about your room, how will you stand on a stage? Here, let me prop the pillows behind you. You seem to breathe better when you sit." She fussed with piling pillows behind Olivia's back. When she finished, Olivia clasped her hands, holding Georgiana beside her bed.

"I'm quite afraid, you know. Sydney Burton is not like other men. I've heard that he was sent down from Eton because he took revenge on a lad who beat him at some match the boys engaged in. He pushed the lad beneath the water of a nearby pond and held him down by his hair until a passing teacher pried his fingers loose. And there was an actress who caught his fancy one night, then the next, she showed bruises and complained to the other girls that he was rough and mean. That night she disappeared and was never heard from again. I feel certain Sydney was responsible for her disappearance. He won't forget I refused him, and he'll be back."

"You're safe for now. Robert said so," Georgiana attempted to soothe her mistress. But there was no one to soothe her own fears. Sydney would return one day. What then? She suspected he had hired Raul to kill her before he returned from his wedding trip. It was quite possible that Olivia, too, had connected the attack on Georgiana to a hired assassin, and it was this suspicion that aggravated her illness.

Olivia took a turn for the worse that night, and Robert sent for a doctor. When the doctor arrived, James escorted him to Olivia's bedchamber. He was a small man who swaggered with his own importance. James showed him to the sick room, and he went directly to Robert to introduce himself and make clear to Robert that there would be an extra charge for being summoned during the night.

"I expected as much," Robert nodded. "Now if you will, my sister is in need of your services." The doctor didn't appear pleased to be reminded of his patient. He turned toward Olivia with a resigned expression on his face until he saw Elsa and Georgiana, who were taking turns bathing Olivia's fevered face with rags soaked in a basin of perfumed water.

"Stop that at once," he demanded. "Washing a sick person, especially at night, will worsen her condition by encouraging the miasma that afflicts her. If she dies, you foolish women will be to blame. Get out of here. Leave at once."

Georgiana looked to Robert for an indication of whether or not she should leave. He appeared confused for just a moment, then suggested she and Elsa retire to the kitchen for the supper they'd missed earlier and requested they send up Mrs. Betz, who could assist Olivia should it be necessary to remove her robe.

Elsa left at once, but leaving Olivia in the doctor's hands wasn't easy for Georgiana. She'd taken a dislike to the pompous man at once, even before he'd shouted his disapproval of the method she and Elsa were using to reduce Olivia's fever. Since childhood, she'd observed that fevers were often reduced by the simple application of cool, wet cloths. She soon discovered she wasn't alone in her disdain for the doctor.

Georgiana found Elsa in the kitchen vigorously scrubbing pots. "I'd like to take one of these pots to the doctor's head. He'll do the mistress no good," Elsa proclaimed. "I know the popular opinion is that washing or submerging oneself in water is dangerous, but I cannot accept that view. My mum was of the opinion that dishes and babes were both better for a good scrub, and I quite agree. The doctor has grime beneath his nails and a stench about him that cannot be good for dear Olivia."

"On one occasion I was present when a man was being doctored by a former soldier who had dealt with a number of wounds and illnesses." Georgiana thought of the Earl of Wellington's man treating the bullet hole in the earl's shoulder. "He was at great pains to make certain no dirt lodged in the wound. He went so far as to wash the wound with brandy. And my mother was often called to nurse other servants through their illnesses. She claimed cooling with dampened cloths served far better than the piling on of quilts to break a fever."

Hearing a sound in the hall a few minutes later, the women rushed to the door in time to see James hand the doctor his hat and stick. He appeared to be highly offended and much put upon. The women, however, were glad to see him go.

"That was quick," Georgiana said.

"I hope he hasn't made Miss Olivia more ill," Elsa muttered.

Together they raced toward the back stairs and dashed up them to the hall that led to Olivia's suite. A sickening odor greeted them when they poked their heads inside.

"Come in." Robert's voice was sharp, and Georgiana wondered if he was angry with them. She entered to see

Olivia, held fast by Robert, retching into a basin held by Mrs. Betz.

"Now, now, dearie," Mrs. Betz uttered over and over.

"Did that doctor do this?" Elsa demanded to know. She picked up a glass on the bedside table and sniffed. She wrinkled her nose and set it back down.

"Surely this can't help her?" Georgiana turned to Robert. "She has eaten almost nothing for days. She needs to put something in her stomach, not lose the little she has there."

"I have my doubts," Robert conceded. "Sometimes I think a ship's cook knows more about doctoring than all the medical men in London."

"The stench alone will make her more ill." Georgiana unclasped the window.

"No," Mrs. Betz protested. "The doctor said her illness is caused by foul air coming up from the ground. Night air will make it worse." Reluctantly, Georgiana closed the window, but not before a rush of air dissipated the worst of the odor.

When Olivia hung exhausted on Robert's arm and there were no more gastric spasms, he tucked her back in bed. Mrs. Betz scurried to pile additional quilts over her. "The doctor said she must sweat out the miasma."

"One of your mustard plasters would serve her far better," Georgiana muttered. She strongly suspected the doctor knew no more about illnesses and their causes than did she. She couldn't prove it, but it seemed to her Olivia was returning to good health until Georgiana's near-accident. Suddenly, Georgiana saw the incident as

Olivia must have viewed it. Georgiana had left Olivia's house wearing clothing that had once belonged to Olivia. If the incident had been deliberate as Georgiana had stated she believed it to be, then it was possible someone had attempted to kill Olivia. Olivia's decline was due to her belief that Sydney had hired someone to kill her! Georgiana's suspicions were the same, but she didn't believe it was a matter of mistaken identity. She had no doubt Raul had recognized her and meant for Georgiana to be trampled. She'd taken great care since that day to never leave the house or show herself at her window, but now she wondered if that were enough.

All night, Robert and Georgiana sat by Olivia's side, and Georgiana wrestled with her conscience. Around and around she twisted the bracelet on her arm and wondered if she should tell Olivia of her own connection to Sydney. If Olivia knew Sydney had more reason to attack Georgiana than Olivia, her mistress might worry less and begin to get well. Perhaps she could ease Olivia's mind by revealing her former relationship with Sydney. Olivia would not want her to remain in her home once she knew Georgiana was Sydney's target. Contemplating leaving Olivia brought tears to Georgiana's eyes. Once she confessed, she would have to take her few coins and see if they would purchase a seat on the Liverpool train.

11

As time for Robert's departure drew closer, Olivia rallied again. She seemed to be on the mend, but Georgiana feared she was merely being brave to keep Robert from worrying while he was at sea. The last night before the *Nightingale* was to sail, Mrs. Betz prepared a special meal for Robert and Olivia. They invited Georgiana to join them.

Olivia laughed and seemed much more herself. Georgiana enjoyed her time with them a great deal. Both Olivia and Robert seemed bent on amusing her. They regaled her with tales of their childhood, and it was with sadness that Robert spoke seriously as they finished their dinner.

"I'll be leaving ere dawn," he said. "The *Nightingale* will set sail for Boston with the morning tide. I wish I could delay, little sister, until you are well, but much rides on the timely delivery of my passengers and cargo."

Tears came to Olivia's eyes, and Georgiana was surprised at how dark the room seemed to turn, as if a light she'd grown accustomed to had been extinguished. She would miss Robert too.

"You need not be concerned for your safety," Robert went on to say. "Sydney is expected to spend a year on the continent with his bride. I shall return before he does, and James will keep watch. He's dependable and knows others who will lend a hand should trouble arise."

"You've eased my mind greatly," Olivia whispered. "I have just one other concern . . ." She dropped her eyes and looked uncomfortable.

"Don't worry about household funds." Robert guessed the direction of her thoughts. "I met with my solicitor this morning and left sufficient funds to pay quarterly wages and all your expenses until you are able to resume singing. I knew you would hesitate to ask, but with young Burton cutting short two seasons in a row for you, I feared you might be somewhat short of funds."

"Thank you, Robert. I'll never be able to repay all your kindnesses."

"Just get well. That's all I ask." He pressed his lips to the back of her hand.

* * *

Following dinner, Robert excused himself to discuss a few matters with James and Mr. Betz. Georgiana prepared Olivia for the night and gave her a concoction Mrs. Betz sent up from the kitchen for her to drink. The housekeeper swore it would soothe Olivia's throat and help her sleep. It apparently worked, because Olivia was soon deep in sleep. Georgiana stitched for a time, then Elsa arrived, urging Georgiana to seek her own bed.

"I sleep quite comfortably here in the chair," Elsa insisted when Georgiana expressed concern for the many nights the young maid spent in the chair beside their mistress. "I'm smaller than you and am able to curl up quite like a bird in its nest."

Reluctantly, Georgiana left Olivia. The hour was late, but she was more cramped from her long hours in the sick room than sleepy. What she needed, she decided, was a turn about the garden. She returned to her room only long enough to fetch a light wrapper, then made her way down the back stairs and out the kitchen door.

The garden was small and filled with the scent of early summer roses. A wall encircled the patch of grass and flowers, and a half dozen trees stretched their branches in a thick, green canopy over the inviting space. A small structure that had once been a carriage house, but was now used by Mr. Betz to store his gardening tools, was almost hidden by thick shrubbery at the foot of the garden. A haze of smoke and fog hung over the city and, in the distance, Georgiana heard the shriek of a steam whistle from the ever-expanding railway system. It was too dark to see the blossoms in Mr. Betz's carefully tended flowerbeds, but she knew they were there by their rich aroma.

She wandered aimlessly down a faint path, unconsciously fingering her bracelet beneath the long sleeve of her dress, until she heard steps behind her. She turned, expecting to see James, who made a habit of a nightly turn about the garden. She was not disappointed to recognize Robert's broad shoulders and ambling gait instead of James's shorter, stocky form.

"Good evening," Robert greeted her formally as though they hadn't just parted a few hours earlier. "I peeked in to see Olivia asleep and Elsa curled in the big chair beside her nearly asleep as well. I was hoping you hadn't already retired for the night."

"I thought a turn about the garden might help me sleep better."

Robert chuckled. "I'm not accustomed to inactivity either and felt inclined to stretch a bit. I feel fortunate to have stumbled upon you taking a similar evening stroll and wish to say a private good-bye. I'll be leaving before the household is awake in the morning, and I'll travel easier knowing you are with Olivia. Do not hesitate to call in another doctor should her cough worsen, and try to keep her from keeping any engagements which might strain her voice before she is completely well. Please look after yourself as well."

"I'll do my best."

"I know you will." He touched her hand, then briefly carried it to his lips. "I'll be gone four months, six at most. I'll think of you often." He seemed about to say more. Instead, he released her hand and turned abruptly toward the house. In seconds, he was gone.

She stood as if rooted to the ground for a time, then slowly made her own way to the house and up to her room. She undressed and retired to her bed, where she tossed and turned, finding sleep difficult. Far into the night, her hand seemed to burn where Robert had touched his lips to the back of it.

She awoke bleary-eyed and feeling a bit down, knowing the captain had already departed. Olivia seemed somewhat depressed too, and they spent the morning quietly, each wrapped in her own thoughts. Everywhere

Georgiana turned, she seemed to remember something Robert had done or said at that spot.

It was several days before it occurred to her that she wasn't the only one struggling with feelings for a man who had appeared somewhat abruptly in her life. The new butler had managed to win the undying devotion of young Elsa. It seems she took one look at his stalwart shoulders and angelic smile and promptly fell in love. Georgiana couldn't help sympathizing. Her reaction to Robert left her wondering how she could have ever been enamored by Sydney.

Olivia didn't ask more questions concerning Georgiana's interest in Robert, but she spoke about him frequently enough that Georgiana learned that after their parents' deaths, he'd taken Olivia to sea with him for a year, then arranged voice lessons for her in Paris. He'd set her up in her own household in London following her training so that she could pursue her dream of a singing career. The more Georgiana learned of the captain, the greater her admiration for him grew.

Olivia seemed to be recovering nicely at first, then her cough began to grow worse again. She picked at her food and lost interest in her books or the newspaper that Mr. Betz carried to her room each morning. Worried, Georgiana followed Robert's instructions and sent Mr. Betz for a doctor, a different one than had come before. He left a bottle of laudanum, but after the first night, Olivia refused to swallow the vile medicine.

"Robert said it is dangerous and that it takes control of your mind," she explained in whispers to Georgiana. "He said he has seen men become so enslaved by it they committed murder to get it and didn't even remember afterward."

Georgiana didn't argue. She too had reservations about the use of the potion for more than the occasional emergency.

Georgiana entered Olivia's room one morning several weeks after the captain's departure to find Olivia in tears.

"It's gone," the young woman sobbed.

"Gone? Has something been stolen?" Alarmed, Georgiana rushed to Olivia's bedside.

"Not stolen, exactly," Olivia complained. "But it's gone nonetheless."

"What? Have you informed James?"

"No, it's not that sort of thing. It's my voice. I can no longer sing." She looked the picture of absolute misery with unchecked tears running down her cheeks.

"It's too soon to know." Georgiana tucked the quilt to Olivia's chin. "You've been ill."

"But I'm not getting better. I fear I've contracted some terrible disease and will never be able to sing again. I shall die without my music."

"You're much better today than you were a few weeks ago." Georgiana wouldn't allow herself to consider that Olivia might not get well. It wasn't just her fear of being without support or protection again that concerned her. She'd come to truly care for Olivia. "In a few weeks, you shall be your old self."

"The doctor called on me this morning," Olivia went on in a tired voice. "He said the only hope I have of recovery is to leave the city. He recommended six months on the coast, breathing the clean salt air."

"Should I begin packing?"

"No, I think I won't be going. I'm much too tired to travel so far." She lay her head back against her pillows and closed her eyes. Georgiana watched her for several minutes, then rose to tidy the room. As she put away bottles and brushes, she frequently glanced back toward Olivia, who appeared to be deeply asleep. Whatever would happen to Georgiana if Olivia did not recover? The question haunted her in the coming days as Olivia seemed to shrink against her pillows and spoke less and less often.

The season drifted to a conclusion, and the long sultry days of summer arrived with Olivia seldom leaving her bed. Georgiana began reading the newspapers in her stumbling fashion to Olivia each morning, hoping to encourage some interest from her mistress. Occasionally, a quote brought a slight smile, but mostly, Olivia never opened her eyes, until the morning Georgiana read that Sydney and his bride had returned early from the continent, where they had honeymooned in a villa on the Italian border.

Olivia's cheeks took on bright spots of color, and she sat up for the first time in weeks. "It's his fault, you know. He burned the theatre because I would not be his mistress." She looked sad for a moment, then went on. "I met him almost two years ago. He seemed so bright and charming, and I often found myself laughing in his presence. I didn't realize his low opinion of me until I allowed him to escort me to my dressing room one night after my performance. When I attempted to bid him good night, he shoved his way inside the room. He struck me several times and tried to force me to yield to him. I didn't know what to do, then I remembered the small knife Robert had given me. I stabbed wildly with it until it lodged in Sydney's throat and he fell to the floor. There was blood everywhere, and I feared I had killed him. Dear Robert appeared in my dressing room just in time to save Sydney and spirit me away before I could be arrested."

Olivia lay back down and the color faded from her cheeks. Georgiana was about to tiptoe from the room when Olivia spoke again. "I thought he loved me."

"Sydney loves no one but himself!"

Olivia opened her eyes and looked at Georgiana oddly. "You know him?" she asked.

Realizing she'd said more than she should have, Georgiana sighed deeply, then sank to her knees beside Olivia's bed. Though she had thought often of telling Olivia of her experience with Sydney, the time had never seemed right. Now, she knew, she had to speak.

"Yes," she admitted. "I know him well. I worked for his mother when she retired to the country, taking Sydney with her. My story is much like yours. I too thought he loved me. He pursued me, promising me marriage, then the night of his betrothal to Daphne Wellington, I narrowly escaped a plan he'd set into motion to take my virtue then leave me in the hands of a rogue from a nearby gypsy camp. I had to flee without a reference, leaving behind my few belongings." She felt the comforting pressure of Olivia's fingers squeezing her hand.

Struggling to see through a mist of tears, Georgiana took up reading the paper to Olivia again, hoping to restore her own emotional equilibrium. After a few minutes, a small paragraph caught her attention.

"Olivia, it is known that we survived the fire," she whispered. Olivia's lashes struggled to lift, then fell back to their usual repose. "There's a story on the back page of the paper that says rumors are rife that you and your maid survived the fire and are in seclusion while you recover. What will we do if Sydney sees this notice?"

Olivia's only response was a deep shudder. After that, she failed to respond at all to Georgiana's attempts to discuss the danger they faced. Instead, she seemed to slip further away. In the days to come, the household staff moved silently about the house, and the butler sent once more for the doctor. After only a short visit, the doctor left the house, shaking his head and promising to write to Captain Carver.

One evening as Georgiana joined the other servants around the kitchen table, she learned she wasn't the only one wondering and worrying. Captain Carver had promised the older servants pensions, but Elsa, James, and Georgiana had no such promise to rely on.

"I'm not worrying about us," Mrs. Betz avowed. "We've a son who will make room in his home for us, and the coins the captain promised will make life easier for our son's family. We'll be fine. We've managed to put a small amount by, and with two pensions, we'll scrape by better than most."

"We'll not look for another post. It's difficult when young and strong for a married couple to find employment together. At our age, it would be impossible." The house-keeper shook her head. "We're getting on in years and there's no one else quite like our Miss Olivia."

Elsa and James looked at each other, and Georgiana read the misery in their eyes. They were neither one confident of receiving a recommendation after working much shorter periods of time than the older servants. Not only was a pension unthought of for young employees with many good years ahead of them, but the chances of the pair hiring on in the same household were pretty dim, as the Betzes had pointed out.

Georgiana listened without adding to the conversation. She knew what occasioned it. The servants didn't expect their mistress to recover. She couldn't bear to put her own fear into words. Miss Olivia was more than her employer. She was the only real friend Georgiana had ever known. Without Olivia and her music and laughter, life would become dull and colorless. There was no telling what awful things she might be forced to resort to in order to survive. She remembered her plan to go to America, but even that dream had dimmed. In an unconscious motion, she touched her bracelet. Would it fetch enough to pay her passage to America? But where could she turn to find an honest assessment for stolen gems? She wished she could ask Olivia.

Later that night, she crept into her bed and lay staring for a long time at the shadows dancing on the ceiling. She was just drifting toward sleep when a sound caught her attention. It had seemed to come from the back of the house. Feeling confident it wasn't a loose shutter, she wondered if it might be the garden gate. She'd meant to tell Mr. Betz that she'd noticed it tended to be quite stiff and made a scraping sound when pushed. The sound could have been a stray dog, or even the shriek of a distant train, but the sound might have come from something more sinister. Now wide-awake, she couldn't rest until she checked. Climbing out of bed, she moved on silent feet toward the small window overlooking the back garden.

A bright moon illuminated the garden, leaving black shadows beneath the trees. A dark shape flitted between the hedge bordering Olivia's property and the carriage house. She rubbed her eyes, then staring intently, she spotted a second figure, then a third. Thieves! She had to warn James. Together, he and Mr. Betz might be able to protect the household.

Taking care not to touch the curtain, she backed toward her bed, snatching up her wrapper as she passed it on her way to the door. The door opened soundlessly on well-oiled hinges and she thrust her arms into her wrapper as she fled down the hall to the room where James slept. Fearful of alerting the thieves that they'd been seen, she rapped softly on the butler's door. Before she could raise her fist to knock again, he thrust it open.

"What is it, Miss Fenwick?"

"Thieves! I saw them in the back garden."

He shoved past her and she saw he was already dressed in britches with a pistol in his hand. She trailed behind him as far as the top of the stairs, then paused, feeling uncertain about following him farther. Perhaps she should go to Olivia to provide her comfort should James fire a shot.

She turned on her heel and fled down the hall to Miss Olivia's private wing, which overlooked the garden. She knocked softly, then entered. Elsa was sitting beside Olivia with her head bent forward against the bed's coverlet. A candle on the low table sputtered in a pool of wax providing the weakest of lights. The poor girl had fallen asleep while watching over her failing mistress.

"Elsa," Georgiana whispered, touching the maid's shoulder. She was reluctant to wake the girl, but she felt she must.

Startled awake, Elsa blinked owlishly, then focused on Georgiana. "What . . . Has Miss Olivia taken a turn for the worse?" She was shushed by a finger against Georgiana's lips.

"Prowlers are outside," she whispered. Elsa's eyes widened further. "James has gone to check."

"Should we wake Miss Olivia?" the maid whispered back.

"No, but I came to be with the both of you should she be awakened and become frightened."

Scratching came from across the room, and both young women turned toward the long window that separated Olivia's bedroom from a balcony overlooking the garden. A shadowy form was visible behind the curtains. Georgiana looked around for a weapon and, spying the fireplace poker, rushed to grasp it in her hand. She wished she'd brought Sydney's silver derringer with her.

She and Elsa would be no match for three men if the footpads gained entry to the room. Their only chance would be to take the housebreakers by surprise and thus prevent their entry. Gripping the poker, she determined to whack each one as he attempted to enter the window.

Hearing a whimper behind her, she turned to see Elsa cowering behind a bedpost.

"You'll have to help me." She motioned the maid toward the curtain. "When I give a signal, pull the curtains open quickly." Elsa swallowed her fear enough to creep across the room to the rope pull, while Georgiana settled across from her with the raised poker. Several quick raps against the window from the outside were followed by the tinkle of falling glass. The intruder had broken the window, and there was no time to lose.

"Now!" Georgiana whispered.

The curtain flew open, and Georgiana brought the poker down with all her might on a black-gloved hand that was reaching for the window lock through the broken pane. A howl of pain turned to curses. A scream erupted from behind Georgiana as she prepared to strike again, and a shot rang out from the garden, followed by the sound of something heavy crashing to the ground. More curses and the sound of scuffling followed. She turned toward the scream and saw Olivia pointing toward the window. Turning back, she caught just a glimpse of a second man disappearing over the edge of the balcony.

"Miss Olivia! He's gone now." Elsa ran toward her mistress. She put an arm around Olivia to lower her head back onto her pillow. Olivia shook off the arm and slid from the bed. On shaking limbs, she stumbled toward Georgiana.

"It was him! He has discovered where I live." She crumpled in a heap at Georgiana's feet. Georgiana didn't have to ask who Olivia thought their intruder was. She hadn't seen him well enough to make an identification, but breaking into Olivia's house was just the sort of thing Sydney would do.

"Mercy! What is happening?" Mrs. Betz exploded into the room. Seeing Olivia on the floor and Georgiana stooping to comfort her, she asked, "Is she hurt?"

"No, I believe she will be fine." Georgiana put her arms around Olivia and urged her toward her bed. "Has Mr. Betz gone to check on James?" she inquired over her shoulder.

"Yes," Mrs. Betz exclaimed.

"No, I will not return to bed." Olivia straightened. "I will dress, and we shall all meet in the drawing room to plan what we shall do. Elsa?" She held out a hand toward the maid who scurried to find a gown and slippers for her.

Mrs. Betz answered a tap on the door, and Georgiana was relieved to see Mr. Betz. At least one of their protectors was safe.

"They're gone," the older man boomed in a voice meant to be a whisper. "James shot one of them in the leg, but the other two carried him off. We couldn't get close enough to hold him, seeing as we weren't certain if they were armed. A neighbor sent for a constable, and he's wanting to speak to everyone in the household."

"You tell him we'll all be down as soon as we've dressed." Mrs. Betz sailed from the room in a voluminous night rail as though it were the grandest ball gown. Georgiana noticed as her husband followed Mrs. Betz down the hall that the tail of his nightshirt had come untucked from his hastily buttoned britches. Turning her attention back to Olivia and Elsa, she noticed the maid was the only fully dressed member of the household.

"Go ahead," Elsa spoke to her. "I'll see to Olivia's toilet."

Georgiana dressed quickly and, as a precaution, hid her bracelet and small bag of coins back in the sewing bag before descending the stairs. She felt naked without the bracelet, but thought it best she not be seen by a policeman with a valuable piece of jewelry.

When all of the servants were gathered in the drawing room, James, sporting a cut lip, numerous bruises, and an eye swollen almost shut, carried Miss Olivia down the stairs and placed her gently in a wingback chair near the constable. The constable inquired politely after Miss Samuels's health, then proceeded to question the household concerning the night's activities. First Georgiana was called on to recount all she had seen. She finished with a description of her actions, which resulted in smashing the intruder's hand.

Then James told of exiting the house via the library window and circling the house to the rear garden, where he knocked one man's head with the butt of his pistol. Leaving him lying in the grass, the butler had approached a man who was nursing an injured hand while attempting to hold a ladder against Miss Samuels's balcony. A third man crouched beside Miss Samuels's window.

"I called out for 'im to come down," James said. "My voice alerted the fellow holding the ladder and he ran toward me. I fired a shot at the thief attempting to enter the house just before I was knocked to the ground. I got in a few punches before the one I hit earlier joined in the fray. I was holding me own when the third man descended the ladder and began to shout, distracting me a bit, and I received a blow to my eye. It sent me tumbling, and when I regained my feet, I saw the two what had been laying into me helping the other one through the hedge. I ran after them, but by the time I reached the street, they'd already gained their carriage what was waitin' for 'em." Georgiana noticed that James's grammar slid toward his native Irish in his excitement.

"I don't believe I ever heard of housebreakers arriving in a carriage," the constable observed. Georgiana suspected the man had noted James's hint of Irish brogue and dismissed him as being without consequence because of it.

"Nor have I," James agreed. "Neither have I heard of common villains setting out to rob and kill dressed as gentlemen."

"Dressed as gentlemen?"

"Aye, their attire was as fine as any seen at Knightsbridge or Kensington Square."

"And did your ball go wild?"

"I don't believe so, sir. The one who had been on the roof was limping quite sorely when his friends helped him away. Another one's hand appeared quite useless."

"That would account for the blood I found on the ladder and followed to the alley." The constable frowned. "I found this small silver gun on the balcony too. It is not the sort of weapon one would expect a housebreaker to carry. If your housebreakers were indeed gentlemen— perhaps they weren't housebreakers at all." He cast a knowing look toward Olivia.

"They were not friends of mine." Olivia glared at the constable but did not offer any information concerning Sydney and his friends.

Georgiana wasn't the type of woman to swoon, but seeing the silver derringer resting in the constable's hand brought a buzz to her ears, and she was glad she was seated. The tiny gun perfectly matched the one she kept hidden at the bottom of her reticule. Seeing it now confirmed beyond the slightest doubt that Sydney's face had indeed been the face Olivia recognized at her window.

Minutes later, the constable excused himself, and James saw him to the door. He looked back once to say, "I'll keep a watch out for any gentlemen with a fresh limp or smashed fingers."

Georgiana suspected he had no such intention. In his mind, he'd already dismissed the case. Learning the perpetrators were possibly gentlemen reduced the break-in to the status of a prank instigated by tipsy young bucks. And he obviously didn't consider an opera singer to possess moral character. No doubt he assigned the whole disturbance to Olivia's profession. An opera singer with an Irish butler didn't merit an investigation

When James returned to the room, Olivia invited him to sit. She twisted her hands in her lap for several minutes while she worried something over in her mind. At last she spoke.

"I will have to go. Sydney will return, and I must be gone before he arrives."

"Where will you go?"

"How will you get there?"

"You're not strong enough to travel!"

"How can you leave your home?"

"I will go with you." Georgiana spoke quietly, but her words seemed to silence all in the room.

"Yes, dear Georgie, you shall go with me. I believe your peril is as great as mine. We shall leave before dawn."

"We shall all go," Mrs. Betz declared. "You know we love you and will stand with you, dear."

"No, I shall need you to remain behind."

"Two young women alone will be much too dangerous," the housekeeper protested.

"We shall not be alone. I have a plan, and it involves all of you."

The servants leaned closer.

"Robert has been gone but two months. I shall allow another four for his return, though two may be enough. Once he arrives in England, I will journey with him on his return trip to America, taking Georgiana with me. The doctor said sea air would be good for me, and Robert's cabin is quite comfortable. Until then, I will go into hiding." She turned to the housekeeper and took her hand.

"You and Mr. Betz will stay here and go about your business in the usual way. All of our neighbors must think I am still here. That will give me time to disappear without anyone following. In four months' time, if Robert hasn't contacted you, close up the house and present yourselves to his solicitor. He will make arrangements for disposing of the house and award you your promised pensions."

Georgiana saw the exchange of glances between the older pair which revealed their relief that they were still to receive their pensions.

"Miss Olivia, your brother charged me to look after you until his return. I work for him." James folded his arms, stubbornly holding his ground.

"Yes, James, and that is why you and Elsa shall accompany Georgie and me to a small village some distance from London where we shall await Robert."

12 ❧

Georgiana felt numb with shock. Coming on top of the long ordeal of Olivia's declining health, the frightening encounter with Sydney left her scarcely able to think. Clearly he had returned from his wedding trip on the continent earlier than expected and had learned that she and Olivia had survived the fire. She shuddered.

Questions and doubts swarmed into her mind. She had been satisfied that Sydney could not have known she was in the theatre the night he set it on fire. In his drunken state, the fire could have been an accident rather than a deliberate attempt to harm Olivia—or her. But was the break-in an attempt to gain access to Olivia, or was it meant to silence someone who knew too much? Was Olivia the intended victim, or was she? If he had seen the newspaper article naming her as Olivia's companion the night of the fire, then she was certain she was the more likely target. Was it reasonable to even hope she could leave Sydney behind and begin a new life far beyond his reach?

Her mind turned to other questions, questions of immediate survival. Olivia was convinced she was in danger and must leave London, but was it really necessary for Olivia to leave her sickbed? It might be that only she, Georgiana, was in real danger. If she left Olivia's house, would Sydney leave Olivia alone? *Not likely. It would be foolish to assume Sydney is only after me.* He would never forget Olivia had rejected him and left him with a scar that invited smirks from other gentlemen. Olivia was right; they must both leave, but how could two women leave London unseen? How would they travel? Did Olivia have sufficient funds? Georgiana's own funds were meager and would scarcely buy a one-way ticket to Liverpool, where she might find work. There was no time to contact Robert's solicitor for more money.

Georgiana knew where to find a fence for stolen goods. There were streets near Madam DuPont's shop where almost anything could be bartered or sold, but did she have time to take one of her jewels to him? And what about the risks involved in making the transaction? She wished she could discuss her concerns with Olivia or James.

"If only Robert were here now." Mrs. Betz fussed with wrapping a shawl about Olivia's shoulders. "He would know what to do."

"He left me a small bag of coins to cover emergency expenses. I think this constitutes an emergency. We will leave tonight while Sydney and his friends are busy seeking a doctor and establishing an alibi," Olivia announced. Her color was better, and though she occasionally coughed, she seemed to have found a renewed energy. "Georgie, Elsa, James, you must each pack just one small bag. Mrs. Betz, you will assist me with my preparations." She sagged back against the chair, her energy spent.

Georgiana hurried to Olivia's side to lend her mistress support. Excitement gripped her. The plan might work, and since Olivia had funds, Georgiana wouldn't have to run the risk of exchanging one of the jewels.

James took charge of the escape plan. "Mr. Betz, I will need you to go to Robert's friend Mr. McDonald and tell him I have need of his assistance. I don't dare go myself in case Miss Samuels has need of me." He then carried Olivia back to her room, and Mrs. Betz followed, wringing her hands.

Elsa and Georgiana looked at each other, reading shock and excitement in each other's eyes, then, as one, they turned toward the servants' stairs. They saw Mr. Betz slip out the kitchen entry, and suddenly they both felt an urgency to hurry.

By the time Mr. Betz returned with Mr. McDonald and the sailor's grown son, Georgiana was packed and ready to leave London. Her bracelet was hidden beneath the tight cuff of her simplest gown, and her coins, except for a few that she'd left in her sewing bag for quick access should she need them, were stitched into the hem of her gown. She wore a sturdy cloak and heavy shoes. In her sewing bag were a change of clothes and the few items she considered essential.

Olivia had ordered the lights extinguished so the inhabitants of the house would appear to be sleeping, but Georgiana's eyes had grown somewhat accustomed to the darkness, and she was able to move about freely. As she made her way down the stairs, she felt a pang for the lovely dresses Miss Olivia had given her and the comfortable bed she was leaving behind. She might not ever own such lovely gowns again or know a home so filled with warmth. This house had been her refuge, and in it, she had known the happiest time of her life. She couldn't help wondering if she would ever know the comfort and pleasant times she'd shared in Olivia's house again in the future.

When Georgiana finally made her way to the kitchen, she discovered Elsa waiting with the other servants and the two seamen. At her feet lay a small bundle wrapped in a cloth. Minutes later, James helped Olivia to the kitchen. Her belongings were in a carpet pull-string bag, only a little larger than the bundles holding the possessions of the other two women.

Tearful farewells were said before the few items the women had prepared for the trip were dumped into three large, canvas seabags.

"In you go," Mr. McDonald instructed Elsa to climb into the bag, which already held her meager belongings.

"Could I not go in the bag you carry?" Elsa asked of James in a hesitant voice.

"Nay, my responsibility is to Miss Samuels." There was regret in his voice, but also a determination to fulfill his duty. "Besides," he argued, "You are the smallest of the women, and it is only right that the older sailor should carry the lightest burden."

Elsa swallowed her disappointment and meekly obeyed by climbing into the bag Mr. McDonald held out to her.

She was followed by Olivia and Georgiana, each in a different bag.

Georgiana found the stifling blackness of the bag claustrophobic, and when she felt herself hoisted to the shoulder of the younger sailor, she stifled a gasp. It was an awkward, undignified position, and she found she wanted to scream and kick in protest. Hearing a slight squawk from close by, she knew she wasn't the only one feeling confused and uncomfortable.

The kitchen door opened, and Georgiana could detect a difference in the air as the men set off down the alley. At first, she felt the bump and jar of each footstep, but in a short time, she became aware of other sounds and smells. The rattle of a coach brought their progress to a halt for a few minutes, and the stench of sour cabbage and ale filled her nostrils. A bawdy ditty erupted from nearby minutes after the sailor began to walk again. She felt the air turn to a damp clamminess and heard the scuttling sound of small animals that she guessed were rats.

After what seemed a long time, she figured they were nearing the Thames, that floating sewer that waited for the change of tides to flush its refuse into the sea. She felt a moment's fear, then recalled that the man carrying her was a trusted friend of Robert's. If Robert trusted him, then she would trust him too. Minutes later, she heard the hollow tread of feet on planks, then felt the sway of a small boat as the bag she was in was lowered until it touched something firm that rocked and swayed beneath her.

Oars dipped into the water, and she felt the boat begin to move. Still in the bag, she found she could sit with her knees brushing her chin and feel somewhat better. Air circulated against her face, and she thought the sailor had loosened the cord that held the bag closed, enabling her to breathe more easily. But since no one spoke or made any motion to release her from her stifling prison, she forced herself to be patient and remain motionless.

In her cramped position, Georgiana sensed that hours passed while the boat moved slowly. The motion of the boat and the claustrophobic closeness of the bag created a slight queasiness in her stomach. She tried to determine whether they were moving upstream or downstream, but she was so disoriented, she couldn't be certain. Sounds seemed to recede, the stench of the water lessened, and the night grew quieter, which encouraged her to believe they were moving inland, away from London and the mouth of the river, which dumped into the sea.

At last she felt a slight bump, which was followed by a whisper, "Let them out now. We're safe here."

The canvas slid down past her face, and she looked around. She was surprised to see almost nothing. It took a few minutes for her eyesight to adjust and to affirm the small boat had been drawn into an inlet sheltered by overhanging trees. She took a deep breath of fresh, sweet air and knew for certain they'd left the city behind. She'd never thought to relish being in the country, but breathing fresh air felt like a luxury greater than any she had previously desired.

"Come." She became aware that the sailor was speaking to her. He took her hand and helped her to feet she could scarcely feel. In minutes, circulation returned to her lower limbs in painful, prickling waves, causing her to grip the sailor's arm tightly until she could bear to take a step. Holding to his arm, she stumbled along beside him. The boat rocked and swayed as each pair left it for a tiny wooden dock and a path that led away from the water. Solid ground beneath Georgiana's feet went far toward restoring her senses.

They didn't have to travel far before they reached a hut hidden in a thick growth of trees. Once inside, someone lit a lantern, and Georgiana rubbed her eyes before being able to see her surroundings clearly. The hut was small, consisting of one bare room, hardly the sort of shelter Olivia deserved or to which she was accustomed. James had already spread his cloak on the floor for Olivia, and she was lying on it with her eyes closed. Georgiana and Elsa hurried across the small space to kneel beside her.

Lifting Olivia's hand, Georgiana asked, "Are you all right?"

"Yes," Olivia whispered. "I'm fine, but terribly tired. I think I shall sleep for a while." Georgiana continued to sit by Olivia as she slept. Olivia was weak from the illness she contracted the night of the fire, and two months of almost constant bed rest had ill-prepared her for the night's adventure. Eventually, Georgiana lowered her head beside Olivia's and slept too.

When she awoke, it was to a bustle of activity. Elsa was tearing chunks of bread from a small loaf and giving them to Olivia, who was washing them down with sips from a tin cup held by James. Her eyes met Olivia's, and she found the bright laughter sparkling there that had been missing for the past two months. Georgiana's heart lifted. She could bear the discomfort as long as dear Olivia was safe and herself again.

"They think I can't feed myself." Olivia laughed.

"You are still weak and must conserve your strength." Elsa pushed another bit of bread into Olivia's mouth.

"Robert would say I am weak from doing nothing." Georgiana was glad to see animation in Olivia's face once more. She wondered if the change was due to danger and excitement or if Olivia was truly on the way to becoming well.

The older sailor brought Georgiana a thick slice of bread covered with freshly churned butter. She wondered where they had obtained the bread but discovered she was too hungry to bother with questions. When she finished eating, James suggested the three ladies wash up at a small pool fed by the stream that emptied into the river. Georgiana led the way.

"Here, Miss Olivia." Elsa handed her mistress a bit of cloth she first dipped in the clear pool. "It will refresh you."

"Thank you." Olivia pressed the damp cloth to her face while Georgiana and Elsa scooped handfuls of water onto their faces and arms.

When they returned to the rest of their party, they were led to the dock where Robert's sailor friends were preparing to cast off. The women were given coats like those worn by the sailors and caps to cover their hair. This time they were allowed to sit up and watch the shore slip by as the boat moved steadily upstream until night descended and all that was visible were dark shadows. Two men rowed at a time, allowing the third short rests. When Olivia grew uncomfortable, James helped her to sit in the bottom of the boat, resting her head in Georgiana's lap. Twice, they halted where small streams emptied into the river to allow the ladies to step ashore for short forays into the trees.

When at last the rowers brought the dinghy to shore well after darkness had fallen, one of the sailors stood, balancing with his legs spread wide, to lift a curtain of willow branches to keep them from slapping against the faces of the boat's occupants as it glided toward the bank. When the branches fell back in place, the little group was safely hidden in a sheltered cove where a medium-size brook ran into the river.

Again, movement was difficult at first, but a hike of some twenty minutes brought the party to a farmhouse. Georgiana looked around. The house wasn't large, but it was a great improvement over the hut where they'd passed the previous night. No lights were visible, but their guides seemed to be familiar with the house. They approached it boldly. Mr. McDonald rapped on the door. This brought an old man who first peered through a window, then he exchanged a few words with the sailors as he dragged the door open.

"Hadley! Richard!" The old man embraced one then the other sailor before motioning for them and those with them to enter the house.

The older sailor introduced the elderly man as his father-in-law, Edward Barlow, and explained that he lived alone in the house and that he would welcome James and the three women's presence in his home until Miss Samuels's brother arrived to take them to America. Georgiana at last sank down on a wooden bench, glad their traveling was finished for a bit.

When introductions were completed, Georgiana looked around, finding herself in a cluttered room that served as both kitchen and great room. A stone fireplace covered one wall of the kitchen area, and a narrow flight of stairs to its right led, presumably, to a sleeping loft. Through an open door at the back of the room, she could see a smaller room with a rumpled bed, doubtless the bed their host had recently vacated. After welcoming them inside, the man busied himself producing a meal of sorts from plum preserves, cheese, and a large, but stale, loaf of bread. They ate ravenously, washing the simple meal down with mugs of hot sugared tea with thick cream.

"You are kind to welcome us into your home," Olivia said to their host. "My brother should return soon and will reward you for sheltering us."

"Many years ago I sailed with Captain Carver's father. He was a good man, who saved my life when I thought all was lost. It is my privilege to serve his son. We'll not be speaking of reward." The man inclined his head as if to say the matter was settled.

Before the women were shown to the space they would share in the loft, James climbed the stairs to make certain it was safe. He returned a short time later to assure them the quarters were safe but filled with dust and the odor of mildew.

"We'll worry about cleaning tomorrow." Olivia took the lead, moving toward the stairs.

"There be aired sheets in the cupboard." The old man pointed toward a heavy, carved piece of furniture. Georgiana detoured to select a stack of sheets and a couple of ragged blankets before following Olivia and Elsa up the stairs. Elsa grappled with a seabag, nearly as large as herself, in which James had placed all three of the women's personal belongings. With difficulty, she dragged it up the narrow flight of steps.

Elsa dropped the bag and sniffed in disapproval upon seeing the thick layer of dust fly about the attic when she reached the top of the stairs. She lost no time pulling back the coverings on the bed closest to the fireplace chimney and tossing them aside. After stripping the bed, she remade it from the sheets Georgiana carried. Together, Elsa and Georgiana helped Olivia out of her gown and into a plain muslin nightgown Elsa unearthed from the seabag. They then urged her into bed before they turned to preparing the other bed for themselves. The last thing Georgiana remembered was how good it felt to remove her heavy shoes and stretch out on the lumpy bed.

When she awoke, it was midday, and her stomach was growling over its neglect. Elsa sneezed, and Georgiana felt her own nose twitch. Dust from the feather bolster was seeping through the bedding. Moving as quietly as possible to avoid awakening Olivia, the two young servants left the bed to quickly dress. When Georgiana finished, she turned to see that Olivia was awake and struggling to dress herself. She took over, completing the fastenings on

Olivia's gown, then arranged her mistress's hair before turning to plait her own in a simple style. Seeing Elsa struggling with her own curly locks more than was usual for the young maid, Georgiana offered assistance, arranging the girl's fiery locks into an attractive but practical arrangement.

When the women were finished with their preparations, they found their way downstairs where they learned that the sailors who had brought them to the farmhouse had already departed on their return trip to London with a promise to notify Robert of Olivia's situation as soon as his ship put in to port. Until then, the refugees would remain in hiding at the farmhouse.

13

The three women sat down that first morning at the farmhouse to a meal that didn't vary much from their repast of the night before. Elsa protested sitting with her mistress at the table, but Olivia assured her that for the time being, they must consider her their equal and do nothing to draw attention to her true identity. With this explanation, Elsa reluctantly sat. When the meal was finished, the trio examined the house more closely and stepped outside to discover that the source of the butter and cheese was a placid cow grazing near the backstep. Olivia checked the pantry, then had a few words with James. She gave him a couple of coins and sent him in search of the village market Mr. Barlow had said was nearby.

Mr. Barlow didn't seem to mind when his guests turned his house inside out in a cleaning frenzy led by Elsa, who seemed to consider each speck of dirt a personal insult. She swept and scrubbed the floors while Georgiana washed the clothes they'd worn for two days. After James returned, Elsa commandeered him and Georgiana to help her haul the feather mattresses down the narrow stairs from the loft and out the door where she beat at them relentlessly before allowing them back in the house.

"Something smells good." James stopped to sniff the air. Georgiana and Elsa followed suit. "I was beginning to think Mr. Barlow lives on nothing but bread and cheese," he whispered, a hopeful note in his voice.

Georgiana thought with longing of the plain but hardy meals Mrs. Betz customarily served.

When they finished with their task and joined forces to haul the mattresses back inside the house, they were surprised to find Olivia, rather than Mr. Barlow, stirring something in a large pot on the stove. James struggled to hide his disappointment, but it was clear he doubted Olivia could be responsible for the tantalizing aromas drifting through the house.

"Sit down," Olivia instructed. James's reluctance to seat himself before Olivia sat was only partially due to the difference in their stations, Georgiana suspected as she hurried to Olivia's side to spoon the stew into thick crockery bowls. Elsa lifted a spoon to her mouth first to take a tentative taste.

"You cooked this?" Elsa gasped, savoring the spoonful of rich beef stew.

"I didn't always have servants." Olivia sounded annoyed. "My mother taught me to cook, and when she and Father passed away, I cooked for Robert whenever we were ashore, until Robert sent me to school on the continent."

Life settled quickly into a pattern with Olivia doing the cooking, Elsa taking charge of keeping the house in order, and James and Georgiana assisting with any task the other two undertook. Elsa even took over milking Mr. Barlow's cow.

Days drifted into weeks, and Georgiana began to feel secure that they had managed to elude Sydney. One day, word came from Edward's son-in-law and grandson in London reporting that someone had been asking about Olivia and that Sydney, after spending three weeks in the country, was back in London and now walked with a slight limp. Georgiana knew Sydney was behind the questions and that he wouldn't easily give up. Olivia had damaged his pride by refusing his attentions, and Georgiana was a threat to his safety and social prestige. She considered sending a letter to the Earl of Dorchester, young Lord Haven's grandfather, telling what she knew of Sydney's highwayman disguise, but she feared the note might be traced to her.

Elsa occasionally accompanied James to the village for supplies, but Georgiana and Olivia agreed not to leave the small farm. The young couple was not apt to be recognized, but it seemed prudent for Olivia and Georgiana to avoid taking the risk of being seen.

Their elderly host appeared to be pleased with having young people around, keeping his house clean and cooking for him. He no longer needed to even milk his cow but was content to sit on a stool in the shade of one of the tall trees that surrounded the house.

At first Georgiana found there was a great deal to do in setting the house to rights and watching that Olivia didn't strain her improving health, but as the household tasks became routine and her fears lessened, she began to feel restless. A stretch of rainy weather, heralding the beginning of autumn, kept her housebound for almost a week. With nothing to do, her spirits plummeted, and she found herself staring out the window at the rain-soaked countryside.

"I wish I had brought just one of my books," Olivia bemoaned. She was bored too.

This elicited a confession from Georgiana that she'd only learned the most basic rudiments of reading and writing. Given enough time, she could read simple stories in a newspaper and decipher plain messages, but she longed to be able to read smoothly like Olivia. "My mother died before she could teach me much, but I promised myself a long time ago that I would learn to read whole books someday." Her voice was filled with wistfulness.

"I shall be your tutor." Olivia pounced on the information. "I know just the place where you can practice your letters. In her excitement, she insisted on leading Georgiana at once to a spot in the woods where the trees formed a shady glen and sand had accumulated near a large fallen log.

Georgiana enjoyed the many hours she spent in the spot with a long stick in hand, practicing her letters under Olivia's tutelage over the next few weeks. Days when the rain streamed down and they were kept indoors seemed long and tedious, but the farmhouse proved cozy, and Olivia continued to grow stronger, much to Georgiana's satisfaction. Soon, her cough and the fragility that had frightened her servants in London were only a memory.

The arrival of a burst of sunshine one afternoon, following a week of rain, enticed Olivia to leave the house for a short stroll toward the river.

"Come with me, Georgie," she pleaded. "We shall stay out of sight and be perfectly safe." Georgiana was quick to accept. She longed to breathe fresh air and stroll beyond the log where they studied on warm afternoons.

When they neared the water's edge, they hung back, wishing to avoid exposure to any passing craft. They watched the water sliding smoothly by for several minutes before Olivia seated herself on a tree stump.

"Are you tired?" Georgiana asked.

"No, I just wish Robert would come and we could be on our way."

"What will you do when we reach America?"

"I suppose I shall keep house for Robert. He has hinted more than once that he would like to make his home in America between voyages. Already he has a small house in Boston. He enjoys his partnership in a shipping company there and would like to take a more active role in the company's affairs."

"Is there an opera house in Boston? And will you continue to sing?" Georgiana hadn't heard Olivia sing since before the fire and missed the music that had been so much a part of the London house.

"I don't think I shall ever sing again." Olivia gazed sadly toward the glimpses of bright water visible through the trees, which were just beginning to lose their leaves.

"You seem to be much better. Are you certain you can no longer sing?" Georgiana suspected Olivia would never be truly happy again without her music, and she very much desired Olivia's happiness. She wondered too if Olivia had truly lost her voice or if she had only lost her faith in her talent. Olivia didn't respond, and Georgiana didn't push. Clouds began to gather, and she was about to suggest they begin making their way back to the farmhouse when Olivia spoke in a voice so low Georgiana wasn't certain her friend even realized she had given voice to her thoughts.

"I'm afraid to try." It was much as Georgiana suspected. Olivia's response filled her with sadness, and she knew no way to help her friend believe in herself again. Placing her arms around Olivia, Georgiana sat close, delaying their return to the house until a cold wind reminded them that another storm was imminent.

They rose to their feet, and with a backward glance toward the river, they began the return walk. A few splatters of rain were beginning to fall as they approached the house. Georgiana began to walk faster. It would never do for Olivia to catch cold again.

"Wait!" Olivia pulled on her arm. "Someone is coming." They drew back behind a low clump of shrubbery. From there, they watched two men in black suits turn in at the farmhouse gate and step toward the front door. Before Georgiana and Olivia could hide properly, one of the men caught sight of them and raised a hand in greeting, leaving Georgiana unsure whether to continue on toward the house or run back the way they had come. A burst of rain seemed to decide the issue, and the women made a dash toward the house. James, who appeared to have been watching for them, opened the door, and they rushed inside. The strangers hesitated until Olivia, taking pity on them, motioned them inside.

"Thank you," the older man said while brushing moisture from a book he held close to his chest. The second
gentleman echoed the first, pausing in the act of wiping
mud from his boots to smile in an engaging manner.
Olivia returned his smile, while Georgiana held back,
eyeing the strangers with suspicion.

Neither man was Sydney, and they appeared to be
harmless, but she wasn't sure of their accent. It didn't
sound like any she had heard before in London, which
relieved her fears somewhat that they had been sent by
Sydney. But one never knew. The first man bowed slightly
and introduced himself as Elder Adams from America and
his companion as Elder Hughes, also from America.

"Did Robert send you?" Olivia smiled and waited
eagerly for the answer as if she knew some marvelous secret.

"Robert?" Both men looked puzzled, and James moved
closer, flexing his powerful muscles in a manner that clearly
stated that the women were not without protection.

"My brother. We are expecting word from him."
Olivia's shoulders slumped in disappointment for just a
moment, then she straightened, becoming the gracious
hostess. She gestured toward a bench beside the fireplace.
"Will you have a seat while you wait for the rain to cease?
Perhaps while your coats dry, you might explain what
brought you here." She took a seat positioned near the fire
and across from the strangers. Elsa rushed forward with a
shawl to place about her shoulders.

"Your hospitality is greatly appreciated," said Elder
Hughes. "We have come from America, with a message
from our elder brother, Jesus Christ."

Georgiana looked at the men with greater suspicion. They didn't look like preachers, and they certainly weren't dressed as the clergymen she had seen in the Anglican churches in London or at the village chapel where Lady Burton and most of her household attended services. She took a step toward the stairs. She wasn't interested in listening to preaching.

Olivia extended her arm, catching Georgiana's arm. "Sit beside me, Georgie," she whispered.

Georgiana hesitated only a moment before seating herself beside the young woman she still considered her mistress, even though Olivia hadn't paid her wages this quarter and she insisted all in the household were equals now. Her tie to Olivia was stronger than that of employee to employer, and if Olivia desired her presence, she would stay. She was happy to see James hovered nearby as well.

Elder Hughes launched into an amazing story about a young boy who saw God and was given golden plates by an angel and how, with heavenly direction, he'd translated the words written on the golden plates into the leather-bound volume Elder Hughes now held in his hands. It was an exciting tale, but Georgiana wasn't sure she believed the man who came all the way from America. It was really a quite preposterous story, but she could see Olivia was enthralled.

"From ancient times to the present, God has called upon the inhabitants of the earth to repent. Through the study of the restored gospel, we learn that faith in the Lord Jesus Christ is the first step to membership in the kingdom of God and that repentance is necessary to prepare for the washing away of our sins through baptism." When the visitor stopped speaking, Olivia peppered him with a dozen questions, which the other American proceeded to answer. Elder Adams was older and not quite so engaging as the first gentleman, but he seemed prepared to take each question seriously and answer it at length. Georgiana found herself so caught up in the answers, she failed to notice that the rain had stopped until Edward Barlow's cow mooed mournfully as a reminder she was in need of milking.

"Goodness!" Olivia jumped to her feet. "The day is quite gone, and there is no dinner on the table. If you would care to join us for a simple meal, I shall prepare it immediately while Elsa milks the cow."

The two gentlemen were agreeable to Olivia's invitation, and Georgiana volunteered to assist by setting the table. She watched Elsa leave by the back door, milk pail in hand. James glanced at the visitors, then at Elsa's back. Making up his mind, he followed Elsa outside. Georgiana could hear the sound of their voices, but not their words. They seemed to be arguing. She wondered if the strange American ministers had upset one or the other. They usually got along so agreeably.

Mr. Barlow continued to sit with the Americans. He introduced one objection after another to the message he'd heard earlier, but the ministers seemed prepared to refute each of his arguments with words from the Bible. Georgiana would have found it humorous if some of their teachings didn't leave her feeling uneasy.

She'd never given much thought to God or religion before, but she'd often had the feeling there was some grand design to life. She'd never quite accepted that people were born, lived, worked, died, and that was all. As the missionaries had told their tale, she'd felt something inside her that whispered she'd heard it all before a long time ago, somewhere far away.

Supper passed more comfortably than she had expected. Elsa came to the table with her eyes bright with unshed tears, and James cast frequent fond glances her way. Each time Mr. Barlow introduced a topic designed to show their visitors they somehow erred, Olivia stepped in to change the subject and ask questions about the land she and Georgiana hoped to soon make their home. The two elders were magnanimous in their praise of dinner and generous with their information about America. It wasn't until the meal was over that they began to share more of the gospel they had traveled so far to teach.

The moon was well into the sky when Edward announced he was turning in for the night and recommended they all do the same. The ministers picked up their hats and books and started for the door.

"Have you a place to stay?" Olivia asked, concern evident in her voice. When she learned the two men were traveling without funds and frequently spent nights sleeping in haystacks, she turned to Edward with a pleading look.

"Oh, all right," he muttered. "You can spend the night here on the floor with James, but you'd best be gone before full light." He turned and stomped to his bedchamber, closing the door behind himself with a little more force than necessary.

Georgiana found sleep difficult that night. The ministers had touched something inside her, causing her troubled thoughts. Her mother had believed in God and frequently asked Him to bless her and Georgiana, but Georgiana hadn't seen that her mother's faith had done her much good when she'd taken ill and become too weak to continue service at Fieldstone House. She'd never considered that her parents might be together somewhere. She found the thought comforting, but she had no illusions about the severity of her own sins. Even without a religious upbringing, she knew certain things were wrong. Stealing the gems ensured that if heaven and hell truly existed, she was doomed to spend eternity in the latter place.

Her mind kept returning to the missionaries' words concerning repentance. They had preached at some length on the topic, and at first she'd felt hopeful. But when Elder Adams said sinners must confess their sins and promise to never sin again, she knew it was a false hope he'd given her. She couldn't tell anyone about the jewels, for if she did, she would be sent to prison, perhaps even to one of the prison colonies she'd heard about. Besides, she really needed the money the jewels would bring. She had her life in America to think about. And she couldn't arrive there penniless.

14

The days grew cooler, and there was little to do while they waited for word of Robert's arrival. Georgiana and Olivia spent hours writing in the sand, then erasing their work to leave behind no trace of their presence. Sometimes Elsa joined them, but she usually preferred to stay near James.

On the few days when there was no rain, Georgiana began taking walks toward the river with Olivia, and alone as well, being careful to stay out of sight of any craft on the water. Seeing the boats and rafts on the river gave them an illusion of contact with the outside world. On this day, she was accompanied by Olivia, and they walked slowly, stopping to view traffic on the river, and then they returned to the log where they frequently sat while Olivia tutored Georgiana. Neither had much to say while they walked. Georgiana had much to think about, and Olivia seemed to have something on her mind as well.

"Look!" Olivia reached into her pocket when they paused beside the log. She drew out a small black book. "Our lessons will be better now that we have a real book you can use to practice reading."

Georgiana's excitement matched Olivia's until she read the title—The Book of Mormon—then a feeling of near panic filled her. The missionaries Olivia had befriended had become frequent visitors to the farmhouse, and their visits continued to trouble Georgiana. At first, she'd attempted to dismiss their words as unimportant, but she was finding it impossible to shut out their teachings. She'd tried to discourage their visits, hoping that if they went away, her troubled feelings would disappear. Now Olivia had a copy of their book and was proposing that Georgiana read from it. She was unable to hide the dismay she felt, and Olivia seized on it.

"Why don't you like the Americans?" Olivia asked, revealing that she had observed that Georgiana was less than friendly to the missionaries.

Georgiana didn't want to offend Olivia, who seemed particularly taken with them, but she couldn't pretend she was pleased with their frequent visits to the farmhouse. "I don't dislike them," she tried to dismiss her reluctance to join in the discussions the missionaries and her friends seemed to enjoy. "I just think it might be dangerous to encourage strangers to spend so much time with us. They might spread word of us to those who, in turn, have Sydney's ear."

"We don't need to worry about that," Olivia said. "They're circumspect concerning all of their contacts. Elder Hughes told me there are many people in England who hate the missionaries and those who join their church, so they don't advertise members' names. He said many members of the Church keep their affiliation quiet until they can raise the funds to emigrate to America."

Georgiana didn't know how to refuse to read from the book. Olivia was so delighted to have a book to use as a text to ease the transition from the sand words to actual reading that Georgiana didn't have the heart to voice her objections.

"Start here." Olivia smoothed her skirt across the log, inviting Georgiana to be seated beside her.

Settling herself on the log, Georgiana opened the book slowly. Holding and touching it made her feel strange. She couldn't help savoring the feel of leather binding and crisp new pages. She skipped a few pages then began to read where the text of the book seemed to begin, "I Nephi, having been born of goodly parents . . ."

Before finishing the first page, she found herself absorbed in the story. Time seemed to fly, and she couldn't help delighting in the improvement her weeks under Olivia's tutelage had brought to her reading skill. She read faster than she'd ever imagined being able to read, and her comprehension seemed to have expanded as well. When shadows began to draw the afternoon to a close, she looked about in confusion. How could she have become so drawn into the story as to forget the time?

Good weather prevailed for almost a week, and each day she and Olivia pored over the book. Georgiana read about the sons of Lehi returning for the plates of Laban and felt encouraged by Nephi's actions in obtaining them. It seemed to her that he'd only done what had to be done to preserve his life and that of his brothers. For a time, she found herself in sympathy with him and viewed Laban as much like Sydney and herself like Nephi, doing what she had to do in order to escape evil designs—until Olivia expressed her admiration for the young man's faith and his willingness to obey God. Faith and obedience hadn't been any part of Georgiana's experience with Sydney, she concluded. Unlike Nephi, she had only been looking after her own interests.

When she reached a paragraph that said God had commanded that man should not steal and those who did would perish, she grew depressed. She'd known since childhood that stealing was wrong, but seeing the words on a page made them seem doubly true. Not just handling the book, but reading its message was causing a kind of misery she couldn't escape. To make matters worse, the season turned rainy again, and Olivia began reading aloud from the book each night at the conclusion of dinner. Sometimes she asked Georgiana to read, but she declined, claiming she was uncomfortable reading aloud to so many people.

One morning, Georgiana took down the book and read the words that troubled her once more, leaving her heart aching. She fled the house in spite of the drizzle that continued to fall from the sky. Her steps took her to a favorite sheltered spot overlooking the river to hide her tears.

Elder Adams was always talking about everyone needing to repent and be baptized, but his words frightened Georgiana because she was beginning to fear the missionaries spoke the truth and their book truly was from God. She regretted all that had happened with Sydney, except she wasn't certain she was really sorry she'd shot him when he'd held up the Earl of Wellington's carriage. *If my aim had been better, I wouldn't be here worrying about it, and Olivia would still be singing at the opera house.* Her thoughts became gloomier. *And I would have been sent to the gallows.*

Her hand caressed the bracelet hidden beneath the long sleeve of her gown. Five gems! Each one different, but equally beautiful and worth a fortune. She'd sacrificed much for the security the gems represented, and should her theft be discovered, she'd be exiled to a penal colony at best. *That is, if Sydney doesn't kill me first.* If she committed herself to joining the Mormons, she would have to give the jewels back and confess what she'd done. She was certain she couldn't do that. *Such an action would seal my fate, and I wouldn't live long enough to be exiled. Sydney would see to that!*

"Georgiana," a voice drifted lightly on the breeze. She turned to see Elsa coming toward her. She hesitated, wiping her eyes, before disclosing her hiding place.

"Over here." Georgiana noticed a glow on the young maid's face. She and James spent almost all of their free time together, and Georgiana suspected the pair planned to marry as soon as it was safe to do so. From the smile on Elsa's face, Georgiana surmised that the young woman was coming to share the news that she and James were officially betrothed.

Elsa came to a stop in front of her. For a moment she fiddled with her apron, then as though she couldn't keep the news to herself any longer, she announced, "James and I are going to be baptized!"

"Baptized?" It wasn't the announcement she expected. She shouldn't be shocked, but somehow she was.

"Yes. Elder Adams and Elder Hughes are holding a baptismal service a short distance up the river Sunday evening. James and I will be among those baptized." Her face was wreathed in happiness.

"But—" Georgiana was at a loss for words. She'd known, of course, that Elsa, and especially James, listened eagerly to the missionaries each time they came, but she'd failed to consider that the message was reaching more hearts than her own.

"James visited the place and found it perfectly secluded. It is safe enough that if you and Miss Olivia should like to witness our baptism, you may do so. Please say you'll come."

"You're already in danger for helping Olivia and me escape Sydney Burton. Aren't you afraid you'll increase that danger by joining a church that is hated by so many people?"

"We don't care about that," Elsa asserted. "As soon as we've saved enough money, we'll go to Zion and live with other people who believe as we do."

"It's a long, dangerous trip, not only the sea voyage, but I've heard there are savages and fierce wild animals in America where the Saints have built their city." Georgiana wasn't sure why she wished to discourage Elsa, but deep inside, she felt something—like jealousy—which brought out her darker side.

That night, as the little group of refugees sat before the fire before retiring for the night, Elsa and James's baptisms were all anyone talked about. Olivia expressed her delight by giving Elsa a hug and shaking James's hand.

"What convinced you?" she asked.

They knew what she meant, and James spoke plainly. "It was listening to Elder Hughes and Elder Adams say things I've always known deep inside were right. When Elder Adams told us about young Joseph kneeling in a private place in the woods and being visited by God the Father and His Son, Jesus Christ, it answered something that has always bothered me. I never had figured out how God could come to earth as a baby and leave heaven empty while He was here. And it never made much sense to me that in the Garden of Gethsemane He prayed to Himself. So when Elder Adams explained how they're separate beings, but one in purpose, I got a warm feeling all over, and I just knew they were right."

"It wasn't so easy for me," Elsa added in a quiet voice. "At first, I was upset because James believed so easily, but the more I listened to the missionaries and to Miss Olivia read the Book of Mormon to us, the more I thought it might be true. It wasn't until I prayed about it that I knew. Warmth and peace filled my heart and, though I didn't hear a voice, inside I felt an assurance that all I'd heard and studied out in my mind was true."

Silence followed the young couple's words, and the ache in Georgiana's heart grew more painful. She wanted to lash out at them, tell them they were fools, but something held her back, and she wondered if she was the one being a fool. She stared at her hands, twisting them in her lap, and wished the missionaries had never come to their door and that Olivia's kind heart hadn't given them refuge from the rain. She glanced over at Olivia and saw tears running down her cheeks.

"Olivia!" She jumped to her feet and hurried to her friend's side. Taking Olivia's hands in hers, she turned back to chastise Elsa and James. "See what you've done," she cried. "You've caused Olivia, who has been so kind to us all, to weep!"

Elsa's face turned pale and James looked torn.

"No, Georgie. Do not scold them." Olivia pulled her hands free and stood, drawing Georgiana to her feet beside her. Then with her arm around Georgiana, she confessed, "My tears are not tears of disappointment or anger because my dear friends have chosen to follow their faith. My only sorrow is that I cannot join them in baptism. I too have received a witness that the Book of Mormon is true and all that the elders have taught us is the real gospel of Jesus Christ. I think I knew it was true before I even met Elder Hughes and Elder Adams. Robert has carried numerous shiploads of Mormons to America and has heard much of their beliefs, many of which he has shared with me. He admires them but is skeptical. When he discovered that he had piqued my interest, we made an agreement that I could study all I wished about the Mormon Church, but I would not be baptized without his consent, though I am of age."

"Why did you not tell us earlier?" Elsa asked.

"I did not know for certain of the gospel's truthfulness until recently. The missionaries appeared seemingly in response to my prayers to find a way to study this new

American religion. The first night they spoke to us filled me with excitement. I do not know when my enthusiasm for learning something new changed to certainty that what I was learning was the truth. Tonight, hearing James and Elsa declare their testimonies, I began to feel that glowing warmth in my bosom, and now I shall never be able to deny the truthfulness of all I have been taught. The true gospel of Jesus Christ has been restored."

Elsa and James rushed to Olivia, and Georgiana found herself standing outside the circle they formed. An awful suspicion that she might find herself standing on the outside of God's circle forever made her heart constrict in pain.

"Eh, young fools." She turned to see old Mr. Barlow glaring at the three people wrapped in a tearful embrace. She thought she had at least one ally until she saw the old man wipe away a traitorous tear that threatened to slip down the side of his nose. He pulled out a large square of cloth from his pocket and blew his nose noisily. Looking flustered, Elsa stepped back, and James followed her lead. All three of them looked toward the old man. Their attention appeared to embarrass him for a moment, then he thrust out his chin as though defying them to contradict him or laugh at his declaration.

"It took ye long enough. At first, I figured those boys was mostly talking nonsense." He harrumphed self-consciously. "Then they said something important what got me to thinking. Remember when Elder Adams said it's God's plan for husbands and wives to be together in heaven like they is here? Well, me and my Martha never

had near enough time together afore she died. I got to
thinkin' 'bout mebbe we could live together again in
them missionaries' heaven, and I started listenin' better,
and I figure they had a lot of things to say that made
sense. I don't know if all they said was true, but it seems
to me, their idea of God is a whole lot more fair than
what I've been hearin' all my life."

"Are you going to be baptized too?" Elsa asked.

"I ain't ready to jump in the water yet, but I'm thinkin'
on it. There's a few more answers I'm lookin' for."

James thumped their host on his shoulder and grinned.
"I'll be praying you find your answers." The old man
seemed pleased with James's gesture.

Panic overwhelmed Georgiana, and she retreated to
the stairs leading to the loft before the attention could
shift to her. Making her way to the mattress she shared
with Elsa, she crawled beneath the quilt, where she shook
with cold for a long time. When Olivia and Elsa made
their way upstairs a little later, she pretended to be asleep.

Over the next couple of days, Georgiana avoided the
overtures made by the others to include her in their
discussions concerning the upcoming baptismal service.
When Olivia read, she pretended not to listen, and when
the missionaries came, she hid in the loft or took a walk.

Even when the sky was dark and rain drizzled, forming
puddles on the saturated ground, she took walks to her
favorite spots near the river to be alone. She tried to
think of all the reasons the Church couldn't be true, but
somehow her thoughts always turned into prayers. Before
meeting the American missionaries, she'd never prayed,

assuming it was a practice reserved for pastors and bishops in churches and cathedrals. Now prayer seemed to be a natural outgrowth of her thoughts. As she prayed though, her heart became heavier, and she didn't know what to do about the dilemma she faced.

The night the baptism was scheduled, Elsa sought Georgiana out again before leaving with the others for a farm almost a mile away where a stream formed a small pond before emptying into the river. She was dressed in her better dress of the two she'd brought with her, and Georgiana had arranged her hair for her earlier, not that her hairstyle really mattered. Being submerged in the pond would undo all of Georgiana's work.

The missionaries had asked those attending the service to arrive in small groups and on foot to avoid drawing attention. Olivia and James meant to depart for the service as soon as the sun set. Edward Barlow and Elsa would make their way to the neighboring farm a little later. Georgiana had heard enough of the plans for the baptism service to know that almost a dozen converts were to be baptized by Elder Hughes that night and that following the baptisms, Elder Adams, Elder Hughes, and two gentlemen who had been baptized earlier would place their hands on each newly baptized person's head to give him or her the gift of the Holy Ghost, a blessing that would guide and help them all of their lives. Again she felt a tug of envy and anger that this blessing would be denied her.

"Georgiana," Elsa began hesitantly, "I know you aren't happy about the decision I have made to be baptized. I wish you felt differently about something that is important to me, but I would still like for you to be there. Will you come?"

"Does this new religion mean so much to you?"

"Yes. I know it is true. I would give my life for it."

"You may have to." Georgiana didn't mean to be harsh, but the words came out that way. "Olivia and the missionaries have spoken of the terrible hatred that drives people to murder Mormons both here in England and in America. And you know some people die on almost every voyage to America. Even after you reach America, you will have to make your way by rail or boat for a great distance, then travel overland to Nauvoo. Some die from the hardships they face. You have chosen an extremely difficult path."

"I know that, but if I die, it will be with the assurance that James and I will be together forever and that our Savior will welcome me into His kingdom." Georgiana looked away to avoid Elsa's pleading face. Didn't they have enough problems hiding from Sydney without getting mixed up with some strange American religion?

After a few moments, Elsa made her way back to the house, but Georgiana continued to sit, staring at the river until voices intruded on her thoughts.

"I don't like it," she heard Olivia say. "I don't think it is wise for our group to be separated."

"You and I will look like a young couple merely walking out," James explained. "And Elsa in those old clothes Edward found for her looks like a farmer's daughter. No one will suspect anything of a daughter helping her elderly father visit a nearby farm."

"But what about Georgiana? She will be alone."

"It is her decision to remain behind," James reminded Olivia. "She will be quite safe, and should any strangers come looking for you, she knows to hide in the hayrick." Georgiana wondered that James would place Olivia in any danger but felt somewhat reassured when she learned the two pairs planned to remain within shouting distance of each other. Until James made mention of it, she hadn't considered that she would be alone and without protection.

The prospect of Sydney finding her alone and unprotected had her moving deeper into the thick woods that separated the farmhouse from the river. She found a fallen log and sat with up-drawn knees. Her arms gathered her heavy skirt against her knees, clasping them tightly. Georgiana stayed on the log until the sun began to fade, and she shivered with the cooling night air. She thought of James and Elsa being submerged beneath the cold water of a farm pond and shuddered.

Holly grew in profusion from the large trees around her, and some type of evergreen shrub provided a barrier between her and the river. She could see patches of water but was invisible to anyone passing by. She considered returning to the house. Elsa and James would be chilled when they returned and would welcome a warm fire. She continued to sit.

A raft floated by. It was large with a tent in the center. The owner's flag flew from a pole, letting Georgiana know it belonged to a person of some importance. Several swift crafts, manned by eight or more rowers, flew by, and a similar long boat nosed its way upstream. Seeing the way the boat traveling upstream hugged the shore and paused at the mouth of the nearby smaller stream that emptied into the river, her senses sharpened, and she slipped behind a thick tree trunk where she could see better and still remain out of sight. She held her breath, fearing the boat would slide beneath the willow branches, which were now nearly devoid of leaves, and discover the crumbling dock.

Hearing voices, she crouched lower, not wanting to risk being seen. The men manning the small boat sounded angry. She counted a full complement of eight rowers, though not all of the men appeared to be supplying an equal amount of exertion. Several long guns rested beside some of the men, and she caught the flash of pistols tucked into the belts of others.

"This one ain't deep enough!" The shout was followed by a string of curses.

"Quiet! You want them to hear us?" a hoarse voice attempted to whisper a warning to be silent.

His warning sent a frisson of fear tingling along Georgiana's spine. Thieves had been known to raid houses located near the river. Sydney's scouts were no doubt searching for her. Or the men could be the enemies the missionaries had spoken of, men so filled with hatred for the gospel that their only wish was to disrupt and destroy gatherings of the Saints.

"Careful," someone cautioned. "The stream is getting narrower."

Georgiana could no longer see the boat, but the voices were getting louder, telling her its occupants were attempting to row up the narrow stream that passed near the farmhouse. She considered running for the hayrick but was unable to move. She was probably as safe staying where she was as she would be in the pile of hay anyway. At least she hadn't heard Sydney's voice! That was something for which to be grateful.

Another string of curses assaulted her ears. It seemed the boat had run aground. A loud splash was heard, then another, accompanied by complaints concerning the temperature of the water. She could no longer see the boat or its occupants, but she surmised several men had leaped overboard to lighten the load or to pry it loose from a sandbar.

"There's a farmhouse over there!" The shout filled her heart with dread.

"You think we should check it out?"

Georgiana cringed, waiting for the answer. She was glad the others had gone. Hopefully, whoever these men were, they would soon discover the farmhouse empty and conclude that all of the house's occupants were away. If the men conducted a search and found her, she didn't know what harm they might inflict on her. It was possible they might even kill her.

"We ain't lookin' for a house, you dolt!" the angry voice she'd heard first shouted, and the slight slur to his words hinted that the owner of the voice had been drinking. "Them Mormons are baptizin' a bunch of fools tonight, and I heerd them say they'd meet at a pond close by the river. There ain't no pond here!" His angry words were followed by a larger splash and a hoot of laughter.

"You gettin' baptized tonight too, Sam?" Someone guffawed at his own cleverness.

"No, I ain't, and you'd best get in this water and help get this boat floatin' again or someone might mistake you for a Mormon lover and pepper your lazy behind with buckshot afore this night is through!"

Georgiana rocked backward, sprawling in the damp leaves. Sydney hadn't sent the louts in the boat looking for her and Olivia, and the men weren't river rats looking for homes to loot, but they certainly meant harm to Olivia. Elsa and James too. Even old Edward Barlow was at risk. And the missionaries. She knew what she had to do. She must warn her friends.

She stayed out of sight until the raiders regained the river, then using the trees as cover, she worked her way toward the lane that led to the nearby farm where the baptismal service was taking place. Gathering up her skirts, she walked quickly down the lane to the road. She wasn't too concerned about the men on the river hearing her. She was some distance away now, and if they were making as much noise as they'd been making when they found the stream leading to Edward Barlow's farmhouse, they weren't likely to hear the faint sound of running feet some distance from the river.

She'd never been beyond the lane, but she'd heard the directions the missionaries had given Elsa and James for finding the meeting place. Once she reached the road, she ran as quickly as she dared, all the while listening for anyone else who might be on the road. She ran until she got a stitch in her side, then slowed to a walk. Hearing a cart, she darted behind a hedge to wait until it passed by.

Too tired to run, she trudged on, watching for three yew trees growing close together beside a narrow bridge. When she found them, she turned to follow the stream toward the river until a second trickle of water joined the one she followed. This combined stream led to the pool she sought. In spite of the darkness, she picked out a small crowd of people waiting by the shore.

She started toward the group just as James waded to shore and held out his hand to Elsa. Georgiana moved closer as James led Elsa to the spot where Elder Hughes waited in water that reached his waist. She paused at the edge of the water, drawn to the sight before her. Silence hung over the small congregation as Elder Hughes raised his hand, then after saying a few words he lowered Elsa beneath the surface of the water.

When he brought her back up, Georgiana thought her heart would stop. In spite of the darkness, a light seemed to hover over the scene before her, and she could almost feel Elsa's joy. She had never experienced anything like the emotions that swept over her. There was something perfect and beautiful in this little gathering. She half expected to hear angel voices give shouts of exultation. Her eyes grew damp, and she longed with all her heart to be part of the scene that held her spellbound. Elsa was right. She said she would give her life for this church, and Georgiana's heart told her that she too must be willing to make the sacrifice of her life if need be. She bowed her head, knowing what she must do to be worthy of the joy she felt all around her. Then she remembered her errand.

Moving swiftly forward, she raced toward the group. Elsa saw her coming and detached herself from the others to meet her.

"I'm glad you changed your mind." She smiled and reached for Georgiana's hand.

"I didn't change my mind," Georgiana gasped. "Someone is coming. I came to warn you." By this time the others had noticed her. She raised her voice.

"A group of men are coming up the river in a boat. They're looking for you, and they're carrying guns. I think they have been drinking spirits."

"You saw them?" someone asked.

"Yes, they pulled into the stream by Edward Barlow's house by mistake and grounded their boat. I heard them making threats against the Mormons. They mean to cause you harm."

15

"We must act quickly." Elder Adams took charge. "Ben," he addressed a young lad, "work your way down to the river, but stay out of sight. Come running if they turn up this stream." He sent the boy scurrying toward the river.

"James, sit on this rock." James complied, and a group of men gathered around him. He didn't seem to be bothered by his wet clothing, but Georgiana caught sight of Olivia placing her cloak around Elsa's shivering form.

Time seemed to stand outside the realm of reality as one person after another took his or her turn sitting on the rock and receiving a blessing Georgiana couldn't quite hear. In spite of the threat hanging over the group, there was also an air of expectancy and hope. By the light of a bright moon, she saw joy on each face replace the fear she'd brought with her announcement. When each brief blessing was finished, the recipient melted into the trees, sometimes alone, sometimes with a small group who had waited for him or her. At last, only Elsa was left standing with Olivia, Edward, and James. Georgiana stood nearby, but a little apart.

"They're coming!" The boy who had been sent to watch charged into the clearing. Instead of running toward the trees, Elsa rushed to take her place on the rock. There was a look of determination on her face. Elder Adams hesitated only a second, then he began to speak almost before the other men's hands rested on the maid's sodden curls. Georgiana was torn between lingering with Elsa and diving for cover. The sound of boisterous laughter, crackling branches, and pounding feet met her ears. She began to ease her way back toward the trees, grasping Olivia's hand and dragging her along. Edward began shifting backward too.

None of the blessings, or confirmations as they were called, had taken long, but Elder Adams cut Elsa's particularly short. The moment he said, "Amen," James grabbed her hand, pulling her into the trees where Georgiana and the rest of their party had taken refuge.

"Get down," James ordered in a barely audible whisper, and they all crouched low. It wouldn't do for the Mormon haters to hear the sound of breaking branches and fleeing feet. Hopefully, the intruders would find the clearing empty and leave.

The missionaries and the two men who had remained with them followed young Ben into another stand of trees. The clamor of their running footsteps died at the same time as a group of men burst into the clearing from the path that led from the river.

"They're gone," one man bellowed.

"Mebbe they're hidin' in the bushes!" the voice Georgiana remembered from earlier that evening shouted just before the firing of the old blunderbuss he carried sounded, sending shot crashing into the trees near where

Georgiana and her friends crouched. She felt a sharp sting on the tip of her ear and wondered if she'd been shot or bitten by an insect. Remaining motionless seemed more imperative than investigating her stinging ear. Since she didn't seem to be in imminent peril from the wound, she did her best to ignore her discomfort.

Minutes later, as the invaders discovered the path and charged up it, James urged their little group deeper into the trees. Once they were a considerable distance from the pond, Edward took over, showing them to a path that he said would lead them back to his farmhouse and safety. James placed himself between Elsa and Olivia. No one spoke as they hurried down the faint path after the old man. All seemed to be in agreement that they should make as little sound as possible.

Feeling something wet on her cheek, Georgiana lifted her hand to her face. The sticky wetness needed no explanation. She was bleeding, but it was just a small amount, and she would wait until they reached the farmhouse to tell the others. Using her apron, she wiped away the trickle of blood but soon felt the tickle of a new stream making its way down her cheek.

"James." Elsa's voice was so low, the others barely heard her. It was followed by a slight sound, and Elsa crumpled at James's feet. Olivia barely caught herself before stumbling over the prostate form.

Instantly, James dropped to his knees beside Elsa. "What is it?" he hissed. There was no answer. "She's unconscious," James whispered, and there was fear in his voice. He rose a moment later with Elsa in his arms. "Her cape is soaked. I don't believe it is from her baptismal dress. She seems to be bleeding. I fear that fool's blunderbuss didn't miss us all as I had supposed."

"This way." Edward began a blistering pace, and they all fell in behind him. Georgiana thought she would never forgive the Mormons for exposing Elsa to such terrible danger. She touched her ear. Why had she received a superficial wound, while sweet, believing Elsa had received the brunt of the blast?

Their entire party was panting and short of breath before they reached the farmhouse. When Georgiana saw its familiar silhouette a short distance ahead, she once more lifted her skirts and raced ahead of Edward to light a lantern and throw a chunk of firewood on the fireplace coals.

"Put her on the bench by the fireplace," Edward told James as James carried Elsa through the door. There was just enough spark from the banked coals to ignite the fire, and Georgiana was aghast at what the light revealed. Blood indeed soaked Elsa's cloak, and her cheeks were porcelain pale. Olivia scurried to place her folded cloak on the wooden bench before James lowered the unconscious girl to it. Georgiana rushed forward with the lantern. She lifted it high, illuminating the bench where Elsa lay.

The wound, located just above the girl's hip on her left side, was small, but blood continued to seep from it to drip on the floor. Elsa was ghostly white. For a moment they all seemed frozen by what they saw.

"Hold her up," Olivia instructed James, and he lifted her carefully while Olivia checked for an exit wound. When she didn't find one, her features turned grim. "The lead didn't go all the way through," she announced in a trembling voice.

"Just a minute." Edward stopped James before he could lower Elsa again. His old hand shook as he reached forward and felt the wet material of her dress to press against a small lump on Elsa's back. "I think the lead almost passed through. If this is the ball, and I think it is, it will be easier to reach from the back than the front."

"Have you ever . . ." Olivia and James both turned eagerly toward him.

"Nay, that I haven't." He shook his head and held out his hands which trembled visibly. "Even had I experience, these hands would forbid such a delicate labor."

"Miss . . ." James turned imploringly to Olivia.

"No." She shook her head to emphasize her lack of experience. "I've heard that the lead must be removed or the patient will die, but I don't know how it is done."

"I've seen it done." Georgiana stepped forward. She wasn't sure what made her volunteer, but she felt driven to do all she could. In some way she didn't understand, she felt responsible for Elsa's injury. "I'll need a thin, flat knife with a sharp tip, not too large, and my sewing bag." A collective sigh greeted her words and everyone scrambled to do her bidding.

"You might be needin' this." Edward held out a jug he unearthed from the bottom of a cupboard. She wasn't sure if he was offering it to her to bolster her courage or if he thought she would pour it down the unconscious maid's throat. She remembered washing Lord Wellington's wound with the contents of his flask because it was all she had at hand for the task. His valet had also used a small flask of brandy to wash the wound after his arrival, even though Wellington's daughters had fetched water by the time he arrived. Perhaps there was something medicinal in the liquor. The valet had acted as though he knew what he was doing. She reached for the jug. It would do until there was warm water anyway.

She plunged the knife Olivia brought her into the jug, swirling it about a few times to make certain it was clean. Elsa abhorred dirt, and it didn't seem right to use a utensil that didn't meet the maid's high standard of cleanliness. Then Georgiana rinsed the blood from her own small wound off her hands with the potent-smelling brew before approaching Elsa. She cut a larger hole in Elsa's dress and bloomers, tearing it to where she could feel with her fingers for the tiny spot Edward had pointed out.

Feeling the slight lump, she took a deep breath and hoped the old man was right. "Please Father, guide my hands." The quick prayer was an unconscious gesture she would analyze later.

"Edward, there may be more blood. Could you find cloths that can be torn up for bandages—and a basin? And James, you'll need to hold her steady. She may wake and jerk about." They hurried to do her bidding. James especially appeared grateful to have something to do. At last Georgiana was ready to begin.

Placing the tip of the knife against Elsa's skin, she was suddenly afraid. It had looked easy when Wellington's valet had performed the procedure, but actually pressing a blade into her friend's back was harder than she'd expected. Nevertheless, it had to be done; and Georgiana had never been one to shy away from what needed to be done. Her knuckles turned white, and she was conscious of the agony on James's face, then James, the room, and all else receded to some distant place as she focused on the patch of skin before her and the knife in her hand.

She pressed slightly and a thin, red line appeared. She felt the flesh beneath her fingers quiver, but Elsa didn't awaken. A roll of moisture slid down the side of Georgiana's own face. She neither knew nor cared whether it was more blood from her nicked ear or perspiration. Using the tip of the knife as a probe, she pressed deeper and felt something hard. As though she could see through the knife in her hand, she recognized the lump as metallic. Next she maneuvered to place the knife beneath the lump. Drawing the iron pebble back through the incision she'd made wasn't as easy as it had looked when Wellington's valet had done it. Twice it rolled away from the blade. But at last the small pellet was drawn from the incision. It rolled from the blade and bounced to the floor.

A trickle of blood filled the incision. Setting down the knife, Georgiana took a bit of wool from Edward. She dunked it in the basin he had filled with warm water, then pressed it to the wound she'd made. Elsa flinched and Georgiana took that as a positive sign. Removing the wool, she proceeded to close the wound with small, neat stitches. Elsa moaned once or twice, but did not awaken.

"Turn her over again," Georgiana said to James. He did so with great tenderness, and she prepared a second sop of wool. She pressed it into the entry wound and held it there while trying to decide the best way to bandage the two wounds. Olivia sent the men outside for more firewood while she helped Georgiana remove what remained of Elsa's dress. Olivia handed her a long strip of bed linen, and the two women wound it around Elsa's thin form and tied it in place with a narrower length of the same cloth. Olivia fetched Elsa's nightgown, a cushion, and a blanket. When James and Edward returned, Elsa was properly attired and appeared to be merely sleeping. No red seeped through the bandage, and Olivia speculated that the bleeding had stopped. Georgiana fervently prayed it was so.

Convincing James to get some sleep that night was difficult, but Olivia finally told him he would be of no use to Elsa or to the rest of them if he didn't get some rest. She ordered him to his bed, and reluctantly he rolled out his bedding beneath the table, where he would be close at hand. Georgiana wondered how much he would actually sleep.

Olivia and Georgiana took turns sitting with Elsa through the night. Georgiana insisted on the first watch, and James crawled from his blankets to gaze at his love each time the two women changed positions. Elsa's condition didn't change, and Georgiana consoled herself by noting that it didn't deteriorate either.

Light was just creeping into the house when a tap sounded on the farmhouse door. James left his blanket and moved stealthily toward the window with his pistol in his hand. At some time during the night, he had retrieved it from its hiding place. Allowing as little of his face as possible to show, he peered outside. After a moment, he pocketed the gun and stepped to the door to lift the heavy bar.

"Come in." He motioned for someone to enter. Georgiana was surprised to see Elder Hughes and Elder Adams step across the threshold. She wanted to scream at them to go away, but something held her tongue. As much as she wanted to blame them for Elsa being shot, she knew she was being unreasonable. They hadn't forced Elsa to be baptized, and she'd seen nothing in their actions or their teachings that advocated violence.

She busied herself with placing cold cloths on Elsa's brow. Her patient had seemed flushed when Georgiana had relieved Olivia a short time ago, and she'd begun cooling Elsa's face and neck with a damp cloth. She remembered her mother cooling a childhood fever in the same way a long time ago and that Olivia had responded to the treatment better than to the doctors' treatments. She wished she knew more about healing. She made up her mind to learn more at the first opportunity.

She was aware of the whispered conversation between James and the missionaries as he told the visitors about Elsa. The elders' exclamations of sorrow sounded genuine.

"She never said she had been hit, and she walked some distance before she collapsed," James told them. "I picked her up, and I could feel the warm stickiness of her blood. We hurried as much as we could and saw no more of the villains who attacked us. When we got her here, Miss Fenwick, who had been nicked on her ear a bit herself, removed the lead and patched her up, but she hasn't awakened yet."

Georgiana was surprised to learn James had noticed her own slight wound. No one had mentioned her bleeding ear, and she'd taken advantage of the first opportunity afforded her to wipe away the trickle of blood that had dried behind her ear and down her neck. Compared to Elsa's injury, her own was of no consequence.

"Sister Fenwick, is Elsa any better?" She couldn't muster enough antagonism to refute the address. Whether Elder Hughes addressed her as "sister" or "miss" no longer mattered. Elsa hadn't responded to the cool cloths, and her skin now seemed to burn. Georgiana didn't think she could bear it if Elsa died.

"She needs a doctor," she spoke sharply.

"There is no doctor in the village." She hadn't heard Edward enter the kitchen. His words filled her with despair. Had she done something wrong? She'd tried so hard to remember everything Wellington's valet had done for the earl, and she knew nothing more to do.

"What about your own wound?" There was concern in Elder Hughes's voice.

"It's nothing." She shrugged aside the matter. "Only the tip of my right ear was scratched. It bled profusely at first, but now I'm scarcely aware of it."

"Would you give Elsa a blessing?" James's voice betrayed his struggle to combat his fear for the life of the woman with whom he'd fallen in love. "Elsa took comfort in the stories you told of the Prophet Joseph healing people dying of the influenza and ague."

"Yes, the Lord has promised succor to those of the household of faith. If it is the Lord's will that she should recover, the maid shall be made well according to her faith." Elder Adams approached the bench where Elsa lay.

"You know her faith is strong." James bowed his head.

Elder Adams placed his hands on Elsa's head just as Georgiana, seated beside Elsa, wrung out a cloth and draped it across the girl's brow. Their hands touched, and Georgiana withdrew hers as quickly as if she had touched a hot flame. Elder Hughes, who stood near Georgiana, reached over her seated form to join his hands with his companion's.

Georgiana felt a moment's panic. She was trapped beneath the missionaries' arms with Elsa. *They know you won't leave Elsa's side*, a voice seemed to whisper in her ear, and she felt a calmness come over her until she remembered Elder Adams had said "household of faith." Could her presence prove an obstacle to a healing blessing for Elsa? *It probably doesn't matter. Mere words can't help her.* Negative thoughts came unbidden. Her sense of calm began to fade until a passage of scripture the missionaries had read only a few days earlier from the Bible sprang to her mind. A father was pleading for Jesus to heal his son, and Jesus told him that all things were possible to him that believed. The father had sworn he believed, then prayed, "Help thou mine unbelief." She found herself echoing those words as Elder Adams began to pray.

The prayer was both peaceful and commanding. Tears seeped from Georgiana's eyes as Elsa was promised her strength would be an inspiration to many, and though much would be required of her, the day would come when her descendants would revere her name. "Thy trials will be many, but thy days on earth will not end until thy mission is complete. Look to the Lord and walk in faith." Georgiana felt almost as if the words were somehow meant for her too, and she trembled with both joy and fear. When Elder Adams ceased speaking, there was silence for a moment, then Georgiana heard James's fervent amen and she was scarcely aware she echoed the word. She knew. There could be no more pretending the gospel wasn't true. Tears streamed down her face.

While she was scrambling in her pocket for a hand-kerchief to wipe her wet cheeks, she heard Elder Adams speak again. "Elsa. Elsa, it is time to rise." Georgiana lifted her head in time to see Elsa's lashes flutter. Elsa blinked several times, and Georgiana stared in astonishment through eyes that remained misted with tears.

"Elsa!" James was suddenly on his knees. He cradled her head in his arms, nearly overcome with emotion.

"James." His name was little more than a sigh. Elsa shifted as though seeking a more comfortable position. For just a moment, pain forced her to open her eyes wide, then her expression softened. She smiled wearily, then drifted back to sleep. Georgiana listened to Elsa's rhythmic breaths and knew she was no longer unconscious, but merely sleeping.

Georgiana backed away from the makeshift bed. She flexed her tired shoulders, but she didn't turn toward the sleeping loft. Instead, she gathered up her cloak and opened the door. The sun was shining with an unusual brightness, but a chill wind swept inland from the river. She hesitated only a moment before setting out for the spot she'd come to think of as her own. Finding a dry spot beside the tree she'd hidden behind the night before, she knelt.

She had prayed before, but not the way she prayed now. She poured out her heart, pleading for forgiveness and direction. At last, the peace Elsa and Olivia had described burned in her heart, and she knew she wasn't a lost and forgotten soul. She was loved, and He would welcome her home should she be required to pay the ultimate price for her sins. She knew what she must do. She must repent and be baptized.

In time, she regained her feet. She stood absently stroking the familiar ridges beneath the sleeve of her gown as she pondered the steps she must now take.

"Miss Fenwick," Elder Adams's voice came from behind her. She wasn't surprised that he had sought her out. Slowly she sank back onto the log where Olivia had helped her learn to read, where she had studied the Book of Mormon. It was all true. She thought maybe she'd known it was true all along. It was her fear and a lifetime of insecurity that had made her hesitate to accept what she'd known deep in her soul. She felt a strange reluctance to turn toward the missionary.

Lifting one well-worn boot to the log, Elder Adams looked down at her and waited for her to speak. She looked at the water shining beyond the trees and at her hands, slowly twisting in her lap. Then she told him everything, making no excuses. When Georgiana stopped speaking, she still didn't look at the missionary. She merely waited.

"Though your sins be as scarlet, they shall be as white as snow; though they be red like crimson, they shall be as wool," the missionary quoted in a soft voice.

The words were familiar, she'd heard them sometime before but hadn't known then what they meant.

"The Lord forgives where there is true repentance, and I can see your soul is wracked with sorrow for your sins.

My companion and I have talked much about repentance, but it seems to come as a surprise to each individual when he learns for himself that God will remember his sin no more when he accepts our Savior's atoning sacrifice. He gave His life that our transgressions might be taken from our shoulders. All you have spoken of will be wiped away when you have repented and turned your life to serving Him. Repentance is the first step. When you've done all you can do, the Atonement takes over, and our Savior will shoulder the rest."

"It seems so unfair that He should pay for the terrible things I have done, when it was my own pride and vanity that led me to sin."

"He has already paid the price. If you don't repent and accept His gift, then you will compound the sin, causing Him greater pain and cutting yourself off from the blessings He wishes to give you. Do you understand this?"

"Yes, I think it will require following Him all my life to compensate for the wrong I have done. Out of anger, fear, and hurt pride, I took what wasn't mine. The gems are of great worth, and I still have them. I must return them. In my heart, I know God will forgive me when I do all I can to restore them to the rightful owners." She paused, and when she spoke again, it was with the anguish of one who faces death but longs to live. "The Burtons will never forgive me. When Sydney learns what I have done, he will kill me."

"I don't believe the Lord requires that you should sacrifice your life in order to return the jewels. Even shooting young Sydney is not an offense requiring a sacrifice of your life since you did it in an attempt to save the Countess's life and perhaps your own. That's no different from the wound James inflicted on the same man while performing his duty to protect Miss Olivia."

"I stole from the Earl of Wellington, and he had done me no harm. Out of spite, I took that which Sydney stood to inherit." She lowered her head in shame, waiting to hear the pronouncement that she deserved to die.

Elder Adams was silent for a time, then he said, "I think we should think on this and, with the Lord's help, devise a plan for returning the jewels to the Earl of Wellington with a full explanation. You might consider also whether you have a duty to inform the Earl of Dorchester of the identities of the highwaymen you encountered. Wellington can then return to the Burtons the gems that are theirs by right and bring charges against his son-in-law if he sees fit. Dorchester can pursue the information you give him to determine if Sydney was also responsible for the death of his heir."

"What shall I tell the others—Olivia, Elsa, and James? I cannot deny the gospel any longer and once they learn I have had a change of heart, they won't understand why I do not seek immediate baptism."

"Would it be so hard to tell them the truth?"

"Harder than you can imagine," she whispered. She'd once believed the jewels would bring her happiness; now she knew Olivia, Elsa, and the others had enriched her life far more than any bits of stone ever could.

Confession was a penance she knew she must pay, but it was unbearable to think of. Olivia, James, Elsa, and Edward had become her family. Anguish filled her soul as she considered the probability of losing their friendship. Olivia knew something of her problems with Sydney but not the full extent of her situation. She didn't know Georgiana had been a thief. It was unfair to enjoy the association of her dear friends without being honest with them, she acknowledged in her heart. They had a right to know with what kind of person they were sharing a roof.

"You're right," she said without enthusiasm. "I must tell them."

"I'll stay with you while you tell them. Perhaps I can help," he offered.

She didn't see how anyone could help her, but she appreciated his offer.

"Would you like me to pray with you before we return to the house?" She nodded her head and led him to the spot beneath the large tree where they could kneel without getting their clothing muddy. Clasping her hands together, she listened to the words Elder Adams spoke and added her silent plea to his for forgiveness and understanding. When he finished praying, they stood, and Georgiana wiped her eyes with the corner of her apron. She squared her shoulders and told herself this wasn't the first time she'd faced a difficult task. She could do it.

Taking one last look through the trees at the river, much like a prisoner saying good-bye before facing the executioner, she reeled with shock. Someone was coming. A light skiff, manned by two men, was gliding directly toward the willow tree that hung over the dock.

"Look!" She pointed. Elder Adams raised his head in time to see the boat disappear beneath the hanging branches. "We've got to warn the others." She whirled about and fled toward the house with Elder Adams at her heels.

16

Flinging open the farmhouse door, Georgiana stood on the threshold, gasping for breath. James looked up then reached for his pistol. Jumping to his feet, he asked, "Is it the mobbers?"

"I don't know," Georgiana managed to say. "We saw a skiff bearing two men pull into the stream and disappear beneath the willow tree."

James dashed to the window to peer out. "Two men are coming this way," he announced in a worried voice. Elder Adams dropped the bar in place to secure the door. Olivia left Elsa's side, where she had been spooning broth into the girl's mouth. She made her way to James's side to peek through the window at the approaching men.

"There's time to leave by the back door. We can hide in the woods until they're gone." Edward rose to his feet, ready to lead the way.

"No! I won't leave Elsa, and she's not strong enough to move." Georgiana rushed across the room to where Elsa was reclining against a stack of pillows that must have been gathered from every bed in the house while Georgiana was away. "The rest of you may go, and perhaps when those men only see two helpless women, they will continue on their way."

"I can carry her." James turned from the window and was beside the bed in a few strides. He made a move as though to lift Elsa.

"No, James. We mustn't risk reopening her wound." Georgiana held out her arm to restrain him.

"I won't leave her."

"Wait, I think that . . ." Edward was cut off by a shriek from Olivia.

"Robert!" Olivia dashed from the window to the door. She fumbled with the beam barring it until James assisted her in moving it out of the way. Then flinging open the door, she ran down the path with her arms flung wide.

"Robert! Oh, Robert!" It was impossible to tell if she was laughing or crying.

Robert lengthened his stride, leaving his sailor friend behind. He swooped his sister into his arms, then twirled her about. All but Elsa watched from the doorway, smiles lighting their faces.

A flutter in her chest that only seemed to appear when Robert was around had Georgiana envying Olivia and Robert's exuberant welcome for each other. She couldn't help wishing she might receive such a welcome from him as well, but knew it couldn't be. Turning away, she retreated to check on Elsa.

Olivia is fortunate to have a brother so resourceful and handsome as Robert, Georgiana thought, though honesty compelled her to admit she didn't wish Robert were her brother. Just seeing him coming up the path brightened her day, until she remembered the confession she had to make. She didn't know if she could confess in front of Robert. After learning she was a thief, he might not want her to accompany Olivia to America. He certainly wouldn't consider her a woman he might come to care about. It was vain and foolish of her to dream of Robert caring about her anyway.

The house seemed smaller from the moment Robert ducked his head and entered through the door. He looked about, seeing Elsa lying in her makeshift bed and a pile of bloodstained clothing lying beside a washtub. He turned to James and merely raised an eyebrow on seeing the pistol still gripped in his hand. His eyes seemed to seek Georgiana out, and she felt heat rise in her face as he took his time studying her, making her conscious of the dark streaks on the dress she hadn't taken time to change and the untidy curls falling from the severe bun she'd pulled her hair into before the impromptu surgery. She suspected her eyes were red from the tears she'd shed, and they were, no doubt, surrounded by deep shadows from an almost sleepless night. He scowled and looked to Olivia. Clearly he wasn't satisfied with her appearance either. His sister was almost as disheveled as Georgiana.

"James, what is going on here?" He demanded an accounting of the man he'd hired to protect Olivia and her household during his absence.

"Robert, your manners!" Olivia chided, drawing her arm through his. "James will explain everything, but first I must introduce you to our guests. This is Elder Adams." She touched the older missionary's sleeve, then turned to Elder Hughes.

Georgiana was startled by the faint flush on Olivia's cheeks as she introduced the younger missionary. Why hadn't she noticed before that Olivia's interest in the missionaries extended beyond her interest in the message they brought? Her curiosity aroused, Georgiana studied Elder Hughes a bit more closely. The tips of his ears were red. Other than that, he was quite a handsome man. She wondered why she hadn't noticed that earlier either. It would seem he returned Olivia's regard. She turned her attention back to Robert and didn't wonder anymore, since being in the same room with Robert absorbed almost all of her attention.

Robert seemed annoyed to find Olivia entertaining American missionaries, but he extended his hand and was gracious in acknowledging the introductions. Georgiana suspected he had questions concerning the Americans but decided to explore the threat that had sent his sister into hiding before pursuing the reasons surrounding the missionaries' presence in the farmhouse. He turned once more to James, who immediately launched into a history of all that had brought them to Edward Barlow's farm, finishing with an account of the previous night's adventure. Robert didn't interrupt James's narrative, but he did raise an eyebrow more than once.

Georgiana listened while checking on Elsa. She felt her cheeks flush when James described her part in preventing Sydney from entering the bedroom where Olivia lay, not yet recovered from the illness that followed her long tramp in the rain following the theatre fire.

Elsa's bandages were still dry and wouldn't need changing for another day, she decided. What the young woman needed was nourishment to build her strength. Georgiana picked up the spoon and bowl Olivia had set down and continued feeding her patient. Elsa didn't speak, but her eyes expressed gratitude, and she ate eagerly, which went far to assure Georgiana that the young maid would recover.

Olivia, too, found something to keep her busy while James reported to Robert. Soon the aroma of griddlecakes and stewing apples filled the room. When James finished speaking, she summoned them all to the table.

"Come," she called. "None of us have eaten yet this morning, and I don't suppose either you, Robert, or your friend took time for breakfast either. We can talk more while we eat." All but Elsa found a seat around the table.

Robert appeared thoughtful while he ate, but he didn't comment on the events James had related to him, nor did he appear surprised to find his sister serving as cook. It was a quiet meal with everyone concentrating on their food rather than conversing, yet there was a sense of expectancy in the silence, highlighting their awareness that their lives were about to undergo another upheaval. Once the meal was finished, Robert pushed his plate back as did Edward's grandson.

The young man excused himself, saying, "The *Nightingale* is due to sail in little more than a week. I shall return in five days' time with my father and a larger boat to convey your party back to London, sir." Edward followed his grandson to the door where the two spoke softly before the sailor disappeared beneath the willow tree's trailing fronds.

* * *

Robert stood beside the fireplace and the group looked expectantly toward him. When he had all their attention, he addressed his first remarks to James.

"It's a shame your aim wasn't more true," he said, glaring at the guard. "Still, had you killed Burton, the scandal would have reflected on Olivia I suppose. I appreciate your quick wit in getting her out of London. I did some checking when McDonald informed me of your situation and found that young Burton and his bride returned to London but a day before the attack and traveled on the next day to a remote estate assigned to Sydney in their marriage settlement. A little more than a fortnight later, Burton returned to London, leaving Daphne, who is rumored to be increasing, alone at the long-neglected estate."

Georgiana thought of Daphne with a tinge of sorrow. The young girl was shy and quiet, accustomed to obeying her mother and spending her time surrounded by her sisters. She was not at all the sort to enjoy a long sojourn at a remote estate far from her family. *At least she won't have to endure the gossip that will inevitably surround her husband's escapades or hear of his string of mistresses at every turn.*

"And my thanks to you, sir." Robert turned to address Edward. "For providing shelter for my sister and those she brought with her."

"They are welcome guests, and I enjoy their company." The old man who still sat at the table looked down at his plate, piled high for the second time.

"Though I am well aware of your expertise in the kitchen," Robert turned to Olivia, "I never expected to see you serving as a cook."

"Nor I," she answered with a giggle. "Cook was left behind, and neither of my maids were trained in the culinary arts. Since I would not starve, the task fell to me."

"And a right fine job she has done." Edward inclined his head in her direction. He appeared sad, as though he'd just realized the meals he had been enjoying were about to disappear.

"We shall talk more in private concerning this obsession Sydney Burton has for you," Robert turned again to address his sister.

"I have not encouraged him."

"She has avoided him at every opportunity," Georgiana defended her friend. "She is innocent of any sort of provocation."

"He has been indulged all of his life and assumes anything he desires is his by right." Olivia's voice was filled with contempt for the man she despised.

"If you would speak of it now, then we shall." Robert looked around the table, raising a questioning eyebrow as his gaze stopped on the two missionaries. It was clear he felt reluctant to discuss a personal matter before strangers. Before they could explain their presence or excuse themselves, James spoke up.

"Sir, these gentlemen are here out of concern for Elsa. They are missionaries, representing the Church of Jesus Christ of Latter-day Saints, or the Mormons as they are more popularly called. Elsa and I were baptized members of the Church last evening. Before the service was finished, mobbers arrived with muskets, which they fired indiscriminately into the shrubs where we had taken refuge. Elsa was struck, and we feared for her life. This morning, the missionaries called to ascertain we had arrived here safely, and they stayed to give her a healing blessing." Robert's face darkened as the young man spoke. Georgiana feared he disapproved of the baptism of two of Olivia's servants. His anger would likely increase when he learned of Olivia's desire to become a Mormon.

"Georgie was struck by shot as well," Olivia added before Robert could say anything. "Though her wound was minor and seems to be causing her little discomfort." She cast her brother a look that seemed to Georgiana to be some kind of challenge.

"You were injured?" Robert turned to Georgiana. The concern on his face was impossible to miss and cheered her somewhat. When she nodded self-consciously, he added, "Were you baptized as well?"

"No," Elder Adams answered for her before she could speak. "But I think she may have saved all of our lives. She discovered the attackers' intent when they stopped here by mistake. At great risk to herself, she carried a warning to us at the place where we were holding the baptismal service. I have been told she is also the one who removed the piece of lead from Miss Elsa's back."

Robert didn't comment on this information, but there was a hint of approval in the glance he sent her, which warmed her greatly.

"I've kept the promise I made you, Robert," Olivia spoke up. "Though I feel to tell you, I was there last night at the baptismal service. There is much on that score I mean to discuss with you privately when the opportunity comes." She directed a determined look his way.

"The maid will recover?" Robert asked, looking to Georgiana for an answer.

"Yes, I believe she will," Georgiana said.

"Olivia is wise to put off discussion of religion for the present, though I certainly mean to get to the bottom of all that has occurred here. It seems this attack had nothing to do with the events in London, and that is what I wish to discuss first." Robert returned to the table, where the others had resumed their seats. He rested his forearms on the table and leaned toward those seated down the length of the sturdy wooden table. "Something needs to be done about young Burton."

"It would be futile to complain to a magistrate," Olivia pointed out. "The word of an opera singer carries little weight against the son of a viscount. And the only witnesses would be dismissed as mere servants. It appears that my only recourse is to emigrate, taking my witnesses with me."

"That is true," Robert conceded with a sigh. "As long as justice can be bought and sold in her majesty's corrupt courts, the rich and titled will prevail. I am certain it will not always be so, but being realistic, there is little option save removing you to Boston. Still, I would like to expose Sydney's part in this. I do business with his father-in-law and believe him to be an honest man who might exert pressure to curb Sydney's excesses if he knows what the boy is about."

Georgiana tried to stifle the voice inside her head telling her the time was now to reveal what she knew of

Sydney's perfidy and of her own sins, but the voice would not be silenced. It was not fair to Olivia, nor to any of the people she loved, to withhold information concerning Sydney. They all believed that Sydney's obsession for a woman who had rejected him was the sole reason for his attempt to enter Olivia's home. She suspected none of them understood the lengths to which Sydney would go in order to silence anyone who might know of his extracurricular and highly illegal activities. Stalling for time, she made herself question whether the prompting to speak out was motivated by a desire for revenge or a desire to repent and be baptized.

"Physical assault, burning down the theatre, and attempting to invade my home are not boyish pranks to be curbed. They are crimes," Olivia stressed. "Sydney should be punished, not slapped on the hand. It is morally indefensible that I must be the one to flee my home and abandon my career. But I, too, have a practical side. Any attempt made by persons of our social ranking to press for justice will only place us in greater danger. Being a frail female further reduces my standing in court." Olivia's indignation turned to painful resignation. "How soon can we sail?"

"There's something I need to tell all of you." Georgiana began in a soft voice, but it seemed to command everyone's attention. There was an expectant stillness around the table. Taking a deep breath, she stood, bracing her hands on the back of her chair. Avoiding eye contact, she began, "Olivia is not the only target of Sydney Burton's quest for vengeance. When he retired to the country to recuperate from the wound to his throat Olivia gave him, I was at that time employed by his mother as a hairdresser." She went on to detail her relationship with Sydney and his betrayal of her, learning of his plan to dispose of her, then she went on to admit to stealing jewels before fleeing from Burton House. She told them of coming upon the Wellington carriage and the theft of two more jewels, along with the wounding of the highwayman and her discovery that the highwayman was Sydney Burton. This brought a collective gasp from the group gathered around the table.

"Though I don't know how he could have known I was in the theatre, he may have found out I was there and set it on fire to punish me," she speculated. "Or it might have been an accident resulting from too much drink that night. But I feel certain he learned of my whereabouts from reading the papers following the fire." She took a deep breath and stared at a spot on the floor, painfully aware of the silence that filled the room following her confession. She wanted to run away, never to face these people again, but she wasn't through. She had to go on. Then if they wished for her to leave, she would go.

"There may be some desire for revenge that prompts me to tell you about Sydney holding up his bride-to-be's coach and shooting her father, but there is more to my reason for speaking of a matter I would prefer to hide, particularly from you, the people I care about more than any others. I desire your forgiveness for the danger in which I have placed you and my failure to be honest concerning my past. I have come to know that the Book of Mormon and all I have been taught about the Church of Jesus Christ of Latter-day Saints is true. I am not worthy of baptism, though I desire it with all my heart."

There was an audible gasp from behind her, and she knew Elsa had heard her words.

"Robert and Olivia have both pointed out that Sydney must be stopped. By making my story known, there may be a chance that his father and father-in-law will bring him to account. I am truly sorry for my part in placing you at risk and for misrepresenting myself to you. If it is your desire, I will gather my belongings and leave at once."

Olivia's chair flew over with a resounding crash as she jumped to her feet. In seconds, her arms were wrapped around Georgiana. "You are a good person, and I don't blame you for anything. Sydney had no knowledge of your presence in the theatre that night. I was his prey. You saved me from his clutches when you hid me, and when you prevented me from throwing myself from the window, you saved my life. I won't hear of your leaving."

Georgiana wiped at the tears brought by Olivia's words.

"I'm glad you have decided to be baptized." Elsa's soft voice joined Olivia's. "You have done nothing to require my forgiveness, only my thanks. I owe you my life."

"No, 'twas the Lord's blessing that spared your life," Georgiana responded to Elsa in a choked voice.

"I suppose I have some repenting to do as well." Olivia wiped away a few tears of her own. "In my heart, I cheered when you described shooting Sydney."

"Good for you." Edward suddenly erupted in a cackle. "The bounder deserved a bit of lead."

"Then my shot was the second bullet he took," James spoke slowly. "I know the type. He won't be satisfied now until he finds revenge against all of us, not just Olivia and Georgiana. He'll think he has cause to come after me because I also shot him and Elsa because he will suspect she knows too much of his perfidy."

Robert's head came up. Georgiana hadn't been aware she was waiting intently for his reaction. His face was inscrutable, but he spoke directly to her. "Are you certain he knows it was you who shot him during the holdup?"

"He recognized me, I'm certain, though none of the Wellingtons indicated they had discovered my identity.

"And the jewels? What became of them?" Robert peered at her closely. Shame caused her to duck her head, unable to meet his eyes. In a fumbling motion, she loosed the band that held her left sleeve closed, pushed the fabric back, and held out her arm for all to see.

A shaft of sunlight, finding its way through the window caught the gems' refractions, sending a kaleidoscope of color bouncing across the table. James whistled softly through his teeth, and everyone stared at the five sparkling jewels.

"They aren't mine." Georgiana drew the sleeve of her dress over the bracelet once more. "I must return them before I can be baptized."

"Return them?" Edward was aghast. "Those little rocks are worth a fortune. They're enough to keep you and your friends fed and warm while you start new lives in America. Seems to me you have a right to claim them after all that rapscallion has done to you and Miss Olivia."

"If you return them, Sydney will have you hanged or, at best, sent to the penal colony in Australia," James added his concern. "If he didn't already think he has cause, once he finds out about the gems, he'll come after you. He'll not be content until you lie dead."

"That is part of the reason she chose to speak to all of you," Elder Adams put in. "She needs your help in finding a way to return the jewels to their rightful owners without exposing herself or any of you to an evil man's revenge."

"If I am transported, I will somehow accept my lot, but I cannot bear it if my actions bring harm to any of you." Georgiana twisted the bracelet on her wrist and kept her eyes lowered. "I have already made up my mind to write a letter to the Earl of Wellington, confessing all I have done. I will arrange to meet him to return the gems and throw myself upon his mercy."

"There is too much risk involved in such a plan." Robert's voice was brisk. "Our first concern must be getting you all safely aboard the *Nightingale*." Seeing the surprise on James's face, he added. "None of you are safe here, and you and Elsa have earned a chance to start over in a new land. All four of you will travel as my guests." He turned back to the discussion of the gems. "I shall arrange for the return of the jewels after we have put to sea."

"But I must apologize . . ."

"Not at the risk of your life and perhaps the lives of these others." Robert waved his hand, encompassing all those who sat at Edward's table.

"You mentioned a small, silver pistol," James said thoughtfully.

"It is a match to the one you found in the garden following the attempt to break into Olivia's house. If you wish to see it yourself to determine that it is a match, it is in the bottom of my sewing bag."

"The Earl of Dorchester reported a pair of silver dueling pistols missing when his grandson was beset by highwaymen," James spoke in a musing tone. "I wonder if he might be able to identify them."

"Contact with either of the gentlemen before we are safely on our way is too dangerous to consider," Robert warned. Speaking to Georgiana, he continued, "You might write letters to Wellington and Dorchester, explaining all, but instead of posting the letters, I will give them to my solicitor to hold until we have embarked. I will also make arrangements for the transfer of the jewels."

Georgiana bowed her head in acquiescence. Robert's stern voice didn't invite argument, and Georgiana wondered if she was being cowardly to accept his plan. It held out hope for her future, but she wasn't certain it would satisfy the steps she must take to fully repent of her wrongdoing.

"Very well," she whispered. "How soon shall we depart?"

"As soon as Elsa is ready to travel." Robert pushed back his chair without meeting Georgiana's eyes. He rose to his feet, signaling the discussion was at an end. Turning his back, he strode from the house.

17 ～

For two days, Georgiana, with Olivia's assistance, alternated between composing letters and tending to Elsa. Though she felt self-conscious knowing her friends were aware of her theft, she was grateful they didn't shy away from her. Instead, they continued to treat her with complete deference. All except Robert, that is. He wasn't unkind; he simply ignored her.

On the third morning, Elsa left her bed and made her way slowly about the house. By evening, she appeared to be much improved, and they began making plans to leave the farm two days hence as originally scheduled. "Elsa's recovery is nothing short of miraculous," Olivia spoke quietly to Georgiana. "I am sure it is the fruits the scriptures say will follow the believers of Christ. It has strengthened my resolve to attain baptism."

Olivia's words seemed to haunt Georgiana as she pitched in to scrub the house so that they might leave it spotless for Edward. When they finished, Olivia dispatched James to the village to purchase provisions that they might leave the old man with full cupboards, and Robert escorted Elsa on a short walk to satisfy himself of her readiness for the journey.

Seeing Elsa and Robert moving slowly along the lane as dusk descended, Georgiana clutched her cloak tightly about her and fled in the opposite direction. When she reached her favorite log, she seated herself upon it. At first, she tried to keep her mind perfectly blank, but the murmur of flowing water and the appearance of a nearly full moon shimmering through the trees served to relax the tight hold she'd maintained on her emotions for the past three days.

Sorrow and regret were the first thoughts to crowd out the blank emptiness. If only she'd known about God's goodness, surely she would have trusted Him to take heed of her instead of resorting to stealing the gems. *But I did know it was wrong. The Spirit whispered to me, and I denied the voice because I did not want to hear it.* Shame and remorse weighed heavily on her bent shoulders, and she felt an overpowering need to pray.

Darkness swirled about her, twisting and tearing at her heart. Doubt overshadowed Elder Adams's promises, making her question that God could ever forgive her. Never in her life had she felt so worthless.

When an urge to throw herself into the river to end the misery that nearly consumed her began to be overwhelming, she prayed with greater desperation. Overriding the darkness came the memory of the cleanliness that had permeated the scene when Elsa was baptized, filling even Georgiana's unclean soul with joy and hope.

"Father!" She fell to her knees beside the log, and with tears streaming down her face, begged to experience that cleanness again. "I'm sorry, so sorry." She wept. Creeping as slowly and quietly as the fog drifting off the river, peace entered her heart. After doing all she could do, the Master would forgive. She regretted the weakness that had made her doubt and vowed she would not allow her faith to falter again. Even if it took months or years to gain God's forgiveness, she would continue to seek it with all her heart.

"Georgiana." She heard her name.

Brushing at her tears, she straightened and looked around, sensing the hour had grown late and she had been missed.

"Georgiana," came the call again.

"Over here." Regaining her seat on the log, she smoothed her gown and waited, her heart pounding. It was Robert who had come searching for her. Olivia may have grown concerned and sent him to find her.

When Robert reached her side, he stood watching her for several minutes before he asked, "May I join you?" His voice was stiff and formal, not that of the companion she'd known in London.

She swept her skirt aside, making room for him on the log. She felt awkward, not knowing what to say.

He sat, leaving an arm's length between them. He didn't speak for several minutes more, and she guessed he felt as awkward as she did. It was the first they'd been alone since his return, and her confession had changed the bright hope she'd harbored all the months they'd been apart.

"Did you love him very much?" She knew he meant Sydney. A stab of disappointment caused a momentary ache. She did not wish to speak of Sydney, but something inside her suggested Robert had a right to know more than she'd told the others.

"No. At first, I thought I loved him, but when I learned of his duplicity, my heart wasn't broken. My pride suffered far more than my heart. And though I feared for my life, anger, spite, revenge, a desire to hurt as I had been hurt were stronger motivators in the action I took than was any lingering sentiment." She would tell Robert all this once, then she wished to never speak again of her infatuation for a man she now despised.

"He was handsome and charming. He made me laugh and forget I was his mother's servant. His mother clung to the ways of society she had known as a young girl during the Regency, but I thought Sydney was anxious to join a more enlightened age and that he placed less importance on inherited wealth and class than she did. As much as it shames me to admit it, Sydney wasn't the only one at fault. I longed for fine clothes and to see places of which I'd only dreamed. I was vain, believing my looks entitled me to a greater position in life than other servants, and I looked down on them as less deserving. Sydney saw me only as another conquest, but I was no better. He was to be my ticket to a better station in life. I feel nothing but contempt for him now—and for myself."

"He certainly deserves your contempt, but you should not judge yourself so harshly." Robert stretched out his long legs. Shifting brought him a little nearer Georgiana, and he spoke as though he'd considered the matter at great length. "It is one of our nation's great faults that we have only allowed a privileged few to succeed in bettering themselves and have assumed the masses are content serving those few. I don't subscribe to this view, and I understand your desire for something better than a servant's lot."

"Olivia said you had become American in your views."

"I'm not certain my views are as much American as stemming from a sermon a Mr. Woodruff preached aboard my ship one Sunday. He spoke of God not being a respecter of persons. According to him, we are all the same before God, both master and servant. The more I thought on it, the more comfortable I became with that view. I talked with him at length, following his discourse, and concluded God just might have a higher opinion of those who work to better themselves and others than He does of those who consider themselves superior by reason of birth and who spend their days in idleness."

"Elder Adams often speaks in the same vein, but English law doesn't share that view. If the Honorable Sydney Burton had found me the night of his engagement ball, he would have turned me over to his gypsy friend, and I would have been without any defense or recourse. Had his shot been more true than mine when he held up the Wellington coach, no charge would have been brought against him for killing a mere female servant."

"There are great inequities in the law for people of the lower classes, and you have more reason to fear him now than you did then. If he learns of the jewels, he'll not stop his attacks until you are dead." Robert clasped his hands and leaned forward as if to dissuade her from revealing her theft of the gems. "I understand your desire to be truthful with those you consider your friends, but none of us wish to see you risk falling into Sydney's hands. It is not too late to reconsider."

"If your solicitor agrees to hold my letter until after my departure for America, will I not be safe?"

"For a time. But if Daphne's father dismisses your accusations as nothing more than the spite of a spurned lover—and a thief at that—Sydney may seek revenge against you. He could send someone to America to seek you out and silence you." Robert leaned closer, placing a hand on her shoulder.

"I know his reputation for seeking redress for even minor slights." She attempted to appear calm, but she hadn't considered the possibility that Sydney's spite might reach even to America.

"I think he may be more dangerous than you know." Robert's eyes filled with sadness. "I checked on his whereabouts after I learned from McDonald that Olivia and part of her staff had fled the city following an attack on her home. It seems Sydney and Daphne returned early from Europe and Sydney left Daphne with a handful of servants at a remote estate, expecting her to stay there alone until their child is born, but Daphne escaped to London and her father. It is rumored that she arrived covered in bruises bestowed by her husband."

"Daphne? But she's such a mouse, how would she dare to defy Sydney?" Georgiana couldn't imagine circumstances that would bring shy, sweet Daphne to take such a step.

"Rumor has it, too, that there's more of Daphne's mother in her than anyone had supposed. She discovered a fine piece of horseflesh hidden in some out-of-the-way spot and mounted it to make her way to the Wellington estate, thus escaping a staff that were more jailors than servants. The countess has put it about that her daughter was much abused by her husband."

"Unfortunately, that is his right." Georgiana sighed. "Have they since reconciled?"

"They are living under one roof, but have naught to do with each other. The earl has suffered several bouts of illness over recent months. The Countess of Wellington moved her household to the family townhouse in London to be near him, and the earl insisted both Sydney and Daphne take up residence with the family since Sydney stands to inherit the management of the Wellington estate until such time as their child, if male, is of age. He has made it clear he will not countenance their living apart."

"Poor Daphne. Sydney will find a way to rid himself of an uncomfortable wife."

"She's not in as great danger as you are," Robert pointed out. "As long as they live in the Wellington household, she will be safe from him."

"Not if her child is a male. He'll have no further use for her after the inheritance is secured. There will be nothing to prevent him from killing her at the first opportunity, just as he will kill me if he can, when he learns of the jewels. His rage has no limits."

"Perhaps Dorchester will launch an inquiry." Robert endeavored to sound hopeful. "And have you considered that if you must rid yourself of the bracelet before you can be baptized a Mormon, would it not serve your interests better to donate the gems to a charity or send them to Wellington anonymously?"

"I must do all I can to seek forgiveness. Neither Wellington nor Lord Burton can forgive if they do not know they have been sinned against. Lady Burton's maid told me of a strange incident that resulted in the death of Gerald Burton's son who, had he lived, would have replaced Sydney as Gerald's heir. For a long time I told myself I didn't know for certain that Sydney was responsible for Gerald and Elizabeth's baby's death. It might have been a coincidence as well that Sydney owned a set of dueling pistols like those stolen from young Lord Haven at the time he was murdered by highwaymen, and he could have attempted to enter Olivia's home only to try to persuade her to be his mistress, but I have been lying to myself. I know he is a thief and a murderer. I ignored his callous treatment of Lord Wellington, and I closed my eyes to the attempt on my life made by his henchman, Raul, after Sydney took Daphne to Europe. I can't pretend anymore. I have to do what I can to prevent him from taking other innocent lives. Now that I know my Savior died for me, I have to do my part to deserve the sacrifice He made for me."

"Even if it costs you your life?" It was almost more statement than question.

"Yes, it is better that I should die trying to prevent further attacks than that I should live with my silence condemning others."

"I see you are quite set on becoming a Mormon," Robert said, resignation in his voice.

"Yes, at first I thought James and Elsa were being foolish, but when I prayed, I knew the missionaries spoke the truth. The answer to that prayer is burned so deeply in my bosom that I would be courting a fate far worse than Sydney has planned for me were I to deny it."

"I envy you that conviction." Robert's voice held a note of wistfulness. "I admit I am intrigued by what I know of the Mormons, but for me, there has been no undeniable witness."

* * *

That night, Georgiana sat on her bed with her legs folded beneath her. She removed the bracelet from her wrist and examined it closely. It had come to mean more to her than a valuable means to purchase a new life, or even a reminder that she had bested Sydney and his greedy family. The weight on her arm had grown familiar and just removing the bracelet to view it closely one last time left her arm feeling naked. The light caress of her fingers over the stones had given her comfort and courage for more than a year. She would miss it. With a sigh she clasped it once more around her wrist, choosing to keep it close until the last possible moment, not from any lingering desire to own the jewels but because of a sense of personal responsibility to keep the bracelet safe until she could turn it over to the Earl of Wellington.

She reread the letters she'd written, then placed them on the table near her bed and opened the Book of Mormon that lay there. As she read, her fears vanished.

Elsa was right. Becoming a member of God's church was worth every sacrifice she might be called on to make in order to be baptized.

* * *

It was early morning when they bid good-bye to Edward Barlow and began the return trip to London. The river voyage passed far more quickly than their upstream voyage had, and by rowing on into the night, they hoped to reach the *Nightingale* without an overnight stop. Robert constructed a shade to protect the ladies from both rain and the curiosity of other travelers on the busy waterway, and the voyage passed without incident, save for a pervasive dampness. Georgiana listened for a return of Olivia's cough, fearing the damp air would invite a return of the malady that had inflicted her earlier, but Olivia appeared unaffected by the dampness and cold.

Elsa slept through much of the journey, and both Georgiana and Olivia were at pains to ensure she stayed warm. It seemed far too soon for the girl to leave her bed, but she had been adamant that she was on the mend and that their journey should not be delayed on her account. A continuous drizzle of rain reduced visibility toward evening, thus protecting them from curious onlookers as they approached the city.

On reaching the quay where the *Nightingale* was anchored, Robert assisted Olivia from the boat to the wooden wharf. James followed carrying Elsa, and Georgiana and Edward's grandson brought up the rear.

Stiff from long hours in their cramped positions and chilled from the wet, cold air, the little group staggered as they made their way toward the ship. Without the assistance of torches, they made their way up the gangplank to the deck. Though Georgiana's balance was off and she found herself stumbling, she pushed on. Robert led the way to a cabin that she surmised from its roominess and fine appointments was his own. When she asked where he would stay, he assured her he would be comfortable bunking with the first mate for the length of one voyage.

"Put her here," Olivia instructed James as she pulled back the blankets covering the lower bunk to accommodate Elsa. He hesitated, and she insisted that Elsa claim the lower bunk while she would share the upper one with Georgiana. He looked to Robert, who nodded his head, before placing Elsa on the bunk. Olivia pulled the blanket to the maid's chin. The exhausted young woman was asleep at once.

Robert left, taking James with him, but James returned a short time later with a tray laden with bread, cheese, and a thick stew. James attempted to wake Elsa to coax a few spoonfuls of the stew into her mouth, but she was exhausted and soon fell back asleep. Georgiana touched her forehead and was reassured the fever hadn't returned.

"Captain Carver has given me leave to place my pallet just beyond your door," James informed the women when they had finished their late supper. "Until the *Nightingale* sails, I shall be close at hand at all times. You can rest assured that no one shall find access to you while you are asleep."

Georgiana and Olivia felt a greater need to move about after their long confinement than to sleep, so Olivia suggested they stroll about the deck for a short time.

"Robert has posted two sailors on deck to guard against unauthorized persons gaining access to the ship, so you shall be perfectly safe," James agreed to their plan. "I shall stay just outside your cabin door, should Elsa awake and need anything."

Georgiana had never been aboard a ship before and found herself quite dependant on Olivia to lead the way. Once they reached the ship's deck, Olivia didn't walk far, only to the railing where they could see little but the dark shadow of the wharf and the stark outlines of several nearby ships with their bare masts pointing toward the sky. Georgiana had heard about the invigorating qualities of sea air but found the slight breeze blowing from the land less than pleasant. It seemed laden with the stench prevalent in the worst neighborhoods of London.

"Not ready to turn in?" It was Robert's voice coming from behind them. She turned, but he was mostly in shadow, and she couldn't see his face.

"We were feeling cramped from the long day on the river and thought a stroll on the deck might enable us to sleep better," Olivia said.

"I meant to speak with you concerning being seen on deck. It will be at least a week before passengers begin to board and several days after that before we can sail. As much as I would like, I cannot change our departure date. It would be best if you do not show yourselves on deck during daylight hours before we sail."

"Do you think Sydney has spies watching for us on outgoing vessels?" Olivia sounded alarmed.

"I have no reason to think he has hired spies, but I would prefer not to take chances. If he knows of my relationship to Olivia, he could very well set someone to watching my ship and movements."

"We shall stay below deck during the day and only walk at night," Olivia promised.

"Do I have your word as well, Miss Fenwick?" Georgiana was surprised when he addressed her directly. They had only spoken once since her confession. And that conversation had hinged on his concern that returning the jewels might invite retribution by Sydney on all their heads. She had also noted his formal address of her.

"Yes, Captain. I would not endanger your sister." She followed James's earlier example in reverting to the use of his title now that they were on board his ship.

"Tomorrow I will call on my solicitor. I shall drop by your cabin for your letter following breakfast." His manner was stiff, and Georgiana mourned for the loss of his friendship. When he'd sought her out a few nights earlier, she'd hoped they could be friends again, but it seemed that wasn't to be. He paused as though he wished to say more, then settled for, "Good night, ladies."

18

Robert appeared promptly after their breakfast dishes were removed to collect Georgiana's letters to the Earl of Wellington and Lord Haven's grandfather, the Earl of Dorchester. He tucked them into an inside pocket with precise care, relieving Georgiana's concern that the letters might somehow be misplaced.

"Do you wish to take the jewels now too?" she asked, though she much preferred to keep them on her wrist for the present. She couldn't explain why she believed them to be safer on her person than in the solicitor's safe.

"No, if they should be seen by some of the clerks, they might incite talk," Robert said. "The morning of our departure, I will carry them to Mr. Ethinbridge. I will be checking with the royal mail for last minute packets destined for Boston and New York near his office that morning, and it will be no trouble to deliver the jewels into his keeping at that time."

"If only you could stop by my house to collect a trunk of gowns, linens, and books." Olivia sighed. She was unaccustomed to having but two gowns—and those two showing signs of wear.

"It would not be wise to do so," he told her with regret in his voice. "I thought it best for the Betzes to remove to their son's home when I first learned of your situation. I feared they might be in some danger should they remain in the house. They were given instructions to ready all of your personal effects, along with any belongings of Elsa, James, and Georgiana, to be delivered to the company warehouse after we're gone for me to transport on my next voyage. Ethinbridge will handle the sale of the house once we have departed. I don't think we should draw attention to the house, since any activity there might lead to the *Nightingale* while she is still in the harbor."

"You're right, of course," Olivia acknowledged. "It's just that . . . It doesn't matter. Gowns are of small import compared to our safety."

Robert smiled, kissed her cheek, then turned to leave.

There was little for the three women to do that first day aboard the *Nightingale*. They read from the Book of Mormon and said their prayers. They mended their clothing and cleaned Robert's cabin. James called on Elsa and joined them for both breakfast and lunch, which were brought to them by Robert's cabin boy. Enticing sounds came from above, and Georgiana found herself wishing she could be topside to observe the stowing of cargo and the preparations for more than two months at sea. With winter coming on and the possibility of storms on the North Atlantic, Robert prepared for the possibility of delays.

The afternoon of that same day, Robert ended their boredom when he knocked on their door, laden with parcels, which he deposited on the table where on other journeys he had kept maps and charts.

"What is this?" Olivia asked, pulling on the string securing one of the bundles. Out tumbled a roll of fabric, then another. She clapped her hands with joy. Robert had purchased an array of fabrics and a pattern book. "Look, Georgiana." She pointed to the fabric and the essential notions for dressmaking as she pulled Georgiana closer to examine the treasure. Georgiana fingered the fabric with appreciation, her mind already whirling with possibilities for a new wardrobe for Olivia.

"Open these next." Robert presented a hatbox to each of the women. Along with stylish hats were parasols and gloves.

"Thank you," Georgiana gasped. She'd never owned anything so fine. While admiring her hat, she heard Elsa burst into tears.

"I can't accept this." Elsa sniffed and wiped at her eyes. "This hat was designed for a lady."

"Then who better to wear it?" Robert's big chest rumbled with merriment. "In America, any woman can be a lady."

James rushed to Elsa's side and insisted she try the hat on, and Olivia fetched Robert's shaving mirror. Elsa peered one way then the other in apparent surprise at seeing a fashionable young lady staring back at her from the glass.

After the ladies had all tried on their hats, Robert handed Olivia one more package. Her eyes grew bright as she tugged impatiently at the string. When she got the package open, Georgiana shared Olivia's excitement on seeing three small leather-bound books. Olivia examined the first, then handed it to Georgiana. Reverently she ran her fingers across gold letters that read *A Christmas Carol* by Charles Dickens. Next came *Retrospect of Western Travel* by Harriet Martineau, and the third book was an anthology of birds with delightful watercolor illustrations.

Olivia embraced her brother, thanking him repeatedly for his generosity. When she drew back, she held a roll of fabric before Elsa and closed one eye to better study the effect. She then draped a length of the fabric around her own neck, preening as though attired in the grandest ball gown. Laughter met her play.

"Thank you, Robert." Olivia giggled. "We shall be the grandest ladies at sea. I couldn't bring myself to ask for one more thing, but I am so glad I will not have to appear before the Americans in New York in one of the only two gowns I was able to carry away with me when we departed my home so precipitously. And Elsa has but one gown, since her best one was ruined the night she was shot."

"I was assured that a clever seamstress might concoct an entire wardrobe for three ladies from that lot." He waved a hand toward the packages. "And it is my understanding that Georgiana is an accomplished seamstress." His unexpected attention and use of her first name brought a blush to Georgiana's cheeks.

Robert looked directly at her and suggested she walk with him for a moment. Georgiana felt a flutter of nervousness as she followed Robert out the door to a long corridor that led to a stairway to the ship's deck. Robert paused a short distance from the cabin door. He looked at her and, for a moment, seemed about to speak. Then, changing his mind, he offered his arm before walking on.

He led her up the stairway, and she was surprised to see dusk had fallen and a few lights could be seen both on the other ships tied to the wharf and from the doorways of businesses crowded along the quay. Robert halted at the rail on the waterside of the ship. With his back to the water, he faced her.

"I tendered your missive to Charles Ethinbridge, my solicitor, as we had planned. He promised to keep it in his safe until the day following our departure, then to deliver it at once to Wellington. The missive for the Earl of Dorchester will be posted the same day. I informed Ethinbridge I would have a package for him the day of our departure, and I warned him not to deliver the package, but to retain it in his safe until the earl presents himself in person to collect it. For the present, you would do well to keep the bracelet out of sight."

"Thank you." She worried the bracelet with restless fingers and found it difficult to meet Robert's eyes. She wondered what had possessed her to steal the gems. Her lapse in judgment had surely cost her the kind esteem of a man she admired more than any other. "I shall be glad when I no longer have the responsibility of the jewels," she whispered, then forced herself to look up. "I do not know how I shall ever repay your kindness, nor that of your sister."

"Keep Olivia entertained and out of trouble." His statement was dry, and she did not miss a slight twinkle in his eyes. She smiled hesitantly in turn. They stood looking at each other for what seemed a long time before Robert excused himself and hurried toward a group of sailors standing at the far end of the ship. Georgiana remained on deck, gazing out over the water for some time.

Her hands gripped the rail, and she thought there had been something in Robert's eyes that told her he felt at least a little affection for her. At length, she returned to the cabin, and her heart felt a small amount lighter as she joined Olivia and Elsa in unwrapping the lengths of fabric and exclaiming over the designs in the pattern book. She felt as overwhelmed as Elsa at the prospect of a new wardrobe, thanks to Robert and Olivia's generosity in sharing the fabric.

It was decided that Elsa should have the first dress, and she chose a plain navy gingham. A large piece of gray wool would be turned into cloaks for each of them. Olivia chose red silk for a lining for her cloak, and Georgiana chose a bit of Scottish plaid, while Elsa insisted plain black was the only suitable choice for herself. Olivia was taken with a length of pale blue linen, and Georgiana was persuaded to fashion a length of deep hunter green wool into a fashionable day dress for herself.

Georgiana found her time much occupied in cutting and stitching their new wardrobes during their wait. She set both Olivia and Elsa to stitching the straight seams while she concentrated on completing the more intricate details. As they stitched, they talked and made plans for the lives they would lead in America. Once, Georgiana caught the faint sound of humming, and a smile tugged at her lips. Wisely, she said nothing. Time passed quickly until the evening James interrupted their stroll on deck with a request for Elsa to accompany him for a short distance alone.

Olivia took Georgiana's arm as they leaned against the rail, watching until the young couple was out of sight. A chill wind swept across the water, and they agreed that though it was much colder blowing from the water than from the city, it brought a freshness to the air and was more pleasant to smell.

"We must be on our way soon, else winter storms will catch us on the Atlantic and make the crossing more difficult." They turned to see Robert step out of the shadows to stand beside them. "Tomorrow morning, passengers will begin boarding. With a sufficient number of passengers aboard, Olivia, you and your friends will no longer stand out to observers along the dock. If you wish to mingle with the passengers on deck, you have my permission to do so. By evening, we shall withdraw a short distance from the quay to allow the *Carolina* to take our berth and begin loading her passengers and goods. We shall be tethered to the *Carolina* to allow us access to shore for another day, then we shall sail." A shiver of excitement slid down Georgiana's spine.

Olivia and Robert talked for several minutes while Georgiana remained silent, listening to their light banter. How she envied Olivia's ease in discussing matters large and small with Robert.

A gust of night air fluttered the women's skirts and sent a ripple chasing across the bay.

"We must hurry with our cloaks." Olivia hugged herself in an effort to stave off the chill wind. "The nights are becoming too cold for walking. I think I shall retire to our cabin and a warm blanket."

When Georgiana would have followed, Robert held out a hand, catching her arm. "Stay a moment," he said.

She hesitated, then resumed her position beside the rail.

"I have business tomorrow that will keep me from visiting my solicitor, but there will be time the following morning before we depart. I shall seek you out early that day to obtain the bracelet. We do not sail until the evening tide, and I will return in plenty of time to make preparations for casting off."

"I'm sorry that you must take time from your duties to assist me. If I knew your solicitor's direction, I could perhaps take the bracelet there myself," Georgiana suggested.

"No. You must not consider leaving this ship." Robert touched her arm in a gentle gesture. "Sydney is not the only danger to a pretty woman along the waterfront. You must stay here and allow me to handle this business for you."

Her heart thrilled to hear Robert call her a pretty woman, but she felt some annoyance that he didn't consider her capable of attending to what was her responsibility, not his.

A soft feminine laugh sounded from the deep shadows near the ship's stern, followed by the deeper chuckle of a man's voice. She recognized the voices of Elsa and James.

"The maid seems to have recovered," Robert said in the droll voice he sometimes used when he found something to be humorous.

Georgiana smiled. "She is young and very much in love with James," she said.

"They have asked me to wed them once we have passed Land's End."

Georgiana clapped her hands in delight. "It will be great fun to have a wedding. Elsa has chosen only the simplest cloth and styles from the selection you provided, but I will make certain she has a suitable gown for her marriage dress."

"I thought you might." Robert's laugh was a deep rumble that brought warmth to Georgiana's heart. "James tells me that after our arrival in New York, he and Elsa shall depart for a Mormon village in Illinois as soon as arrangements can be made."

"Yes, Elsa has mentioned her desire to go to Nauvoo and meet the Prophet Joseph Smith."

"Is that where you wish to settle as well?" She sensed an underlying question behind the one he asked.

"I wish to become a member of the Church as soon as possible, and Nauvoo is the only place I know to go to find someone who can baptize me, but I may have to find work in Boston and wait until I have saved enough to make the trip."

"You'll not stay with Olivia?"

"Olivia says you have a small cottage in Boston and she expects to keep house for you there. She will have little need for a hairdresser or a seamstress." Georgiana turned away to stare out at the open sea. "Besides, I do not think you approve of me as a companion for your sister."

"Don't approve? Olivia keep house?" He sounded genuinely confused. "Why shouldn't Olivia resume her career? Boston and New York both have opera houses. I made arrangements for Ethinbridge to sell her London house, and I shall reinvest the funds for her in a home in whichever city she desires."

"You don't know?" Georgiana hesitated. Why hadn't Olivia told Robert, and would she be angry for Robert to hear it from someone else? But Robert should know, she decided. Her voice dropped, and a note of sadness crept in. "She cannot sing. She lost her voice following the fire. Whether it was the smoke or the terrible cold that turned to pneumonia, the doctor did not know, but he was definite that she would never sing again."

"Lost her voice! But why didn't she tell me?" He sounded confused and perhaps somewhat hurt. Georgiana placed a sympathetic hand on his sleeve.

"I think she did not want to cause you further concern."

"But Olivia without music is not Olivia." He straightened, and his voice turned stern. "I shall see that she has the best physicians. I will take her to Vienna if necessary. But whatever the result, she shall not become my housekeeper. I have funds enough to ensure her an income and a home of her own."

"She may wish to settle in Nauvoo." Georgiana spoke softly, fearing her words would further disturb Robert.

"Ah, yes," he sounded troubled. "She has spoken to me of her desire to become a Mormon."

"And you are opposed to this?"

"Not exactly opposed, but I fear for her safety if she takes such an action. The Mormons have been driven from state to state, and there is an order for their extermination should they return to Missouri. Even their city of refuge in Illinois incites great controversy. I fear they shall be driven from there before long and forced into the wilderness west of the Mississippi. I do not want Olivia subjected to such danger, nor do I want her to be far from the kind of music halls where her talent can be appreciated."

"If the Mormons are forced to flee again, they shall turn the wilderness into homes and farms, and Elder Hughes said culture and arts are promoted by Joseph Smith. He greatly encourages all of the arts."

"Yes, they are an enterprising people, and many are cultured. I have spoken much with both their missionaries and the converts who feel a mandate to gather to the Mormon Zion. I make few voyages that the decks of the *Nightingale* are void of Mormons either journeying to Nauvoo or expecting to proselytize among the peoples of Britain's isles. I hear much of their philosophy and of their persecution."

"Have none of the missionaries touched your heart and made you wonder if their message is true?" Georgiana wondered how a man as kind and good as Captain Robert Carver could fail to accept the gospel.

"Aye, I have wondered," he admitted. "But I am not much for churches. My mother attended services regularly, but they brought her little comfort, and when she remarried, her new husband was a devout Christian, who found much to fault in the views of the village vicar. These differences resulted in many heated conversations between my stepfather and the vicar. I had almost decided to ignore God—until I went to sea, then I found Him in the rolling waves by day and in the brilliance of stars that hold their places at night. One of your apostles," he said this as though she were already a member of the Church, "a Mr. Woodruff, said many things that convinced me the God I have come to know and respect is closer to the God his people worship than the one most religions have constructed as an amalgamation of Bible truths and man's expediency."

"Captain!" A voice halted their discussion before Georgiana could respond.

Robert excused himself and turned away, only to pause and turn back. He lifted Georgiana's hands from the rail where they rested and held them clasped between his. "I would not have you believe I disapprove of your friendship with my sister. Quite the opposite is true. I admire you greatly and deem it an honor to share your acquaintance. You must forgive me for the jealousy I allowed to overtake reason when I learned you had accepted another man's proposal of marriage. I fear that while I weighed the facts in my mind and worried over whether you still harbored a tenderness for Burton, I led you to believe I held you in disdain. Quite the opposite is nearer the truth. It is my hope that when you are prepared to trust again, it shall be me to whom you look." He released her hands and stepped away, disappearing into the darkness before her stunned disbelief could be replaced by the joy that made her steps light as she hurried toward the cabin she shared with Olivia and Elsa.

* * *

By mid-morning the following day, several parties had boarded the *Nightingale*, most of whom found space on a level lower than the officers and first-class passengers, who were assigned to cabins. Barrels and crates filled the holds and overflowed into the space where families were arranging their belongings. Seeing them, Georgiana felt gratitude to Olivia and Robert, for without them, the best she could have managed was steerage. It was much later in the day when she and the other two young women decided there was a sufficient number of women on deck for their presence to go unnoticed. James cautioned them to stay near the rail on the side away from the dock, then escorted them to the stairs, where he moved quickly ahead of them to be certain all was safe.

Linking arms, the women stepped onto the deck and began a casual stroll. James followed a short distance behind. Utter confusion seemed to have taken over the deck where just the evening before they had strolled in peace. Georgiana experienced a kind of shock to hear so many voices, both men and women conversing and sometimes shouting. Knots of men gathered in various places and a steady stream of porters hustled from carriages parked on the dock, up the gangplank that stretched from the dock to the ship's deck, and back again. Piles of luggage impeded their steps at every turn. Children ran about, weaving their way around people and bags, their voices high as they played their games or cried when they became separated from their mothers.

"It's the excitement," Olivia tried to explain. "It's all so new."

"I feel a little giddy myself." Georgiana laughed as a small boy dashed between them with another chasing behind him. They stepped aside to allow a porter to wheel a trolley loaded with trunks past them.

They paused beside two women who were discussing various remedies for seasickness, and Elsa spoke in alarm. "Do you think we shall become seasick?"

"When Robert took me to Paris, I didn't feel the slightest illness, but on the return, the channel was rough and I felt some queasiness," Olivia told her. "There's no way to tell in advance who will be sick and who won't, though those in first class usually fare better than those in steerage. With a cabin to ourselves, I feel certain any illness we feel will be of short duration."

"Oh, look! That must be the *Carolina*." Georgiana pointed toward a ship that was swaying at anchor some distance away. With sails furled and her sleek lines gleaming in the morning light, the ship appeared to be a twin of the one the women stood upon.

James squinted his eyes, attempting to peer more closely at the other ship. "It is the *Carolina*. Robert said they are sister ships, belonging to the same investors with which he has affiliated himself. The *Carolina* is fresh from

Scandinavia with passengers bound for America. They will put in here but a day to take on more passengers and supplies. Her captain wishes to depart on the same tide that carries us onto the North Sea."

Georgiana glanced behind her toward the dock. The long line of carriages and drays and the bustle of people made her uneasy. What if Sydney had guessed she was leaving the country and had set spies to watch for her and Olivia? Several well-dressed idlers lounged against the buildings, watching the activity. Boys and men in nondescript clothing were in abundance, and there were even a few brazen women flirting with the sailors. A dark shadow seemed to blight her enjoyment of being on deck in the bright sunlight.

"I think I shall return to the cabin," she told her companions and began at once making her way through the throng.

"Perhaps we should all go." Olivia caught up to her. She seemed about to say something more, then stopped. Georgiana suspected she too had felt some evil presence watching from the shadows.

19

Georgiana and Olivia moved toward the stairs, keeping their steps casual in order to avoid drawing attention to themselves. They hadn't gone far when snatches of conversation reached their ears. "Joseph Smith" and "Nauvoo" were two words that stood out. Taken by surprise, they drew closer to the small group of men standing in a tight cluster.

"The missionaries received word less than a fortnight ago that they should not delay their return to Nauvoo," a tall man in a too-small coat spoke in an earnest manner.

"Elder Adams attempted to gain passage on this ship, but found it full. He was forced to book passage on another ship, carrying Scandinavian converts, or make his way to Liverpool," a second man added.

"I understand that both ships will depart at almost the same time tomorrow night, and since there are several persons scheduled for the second ship who have faced recent difficulties, it is well that he shall be with them," the third man spoke with an American accent.

Georgiana and Olivia looked at each other, then back at the group of neat but poorly dressed men gathered near the head of the stairs.

"Are you Mormons?" Olivia blurted out. The men turned to look at her, and several pulled caps from their heads. Some shuffled their feet and glanced about as though seeking assistance.

"We are," one declared boldly.

"Are Elder Adams and Elder Hughes really boarding the *Carolina* tomorrow?"

"And who might you be?" one of the men asked, suspicion in his voice. His eyes traveled over Olivia who was attired in one of her new gowns and looking elegantly fashionable. A look of fear came into his eyes.

"We are friends of the missionaries," Olivia said. She introduced herself and her companion.

"We have hope of being baptized when we reach America," Georgiana added. The men appeared to relax, but there was still a hint of concern in a few eyes as their leader introduced himself as Elder White. Seeing Olivia bite her lips, Georgiana suspected her friend wanted to ask if Elder Hughes was accompanying his companion on the *Carolina* but was afraid to show her interest in the younger missionary. Sympathizing with her friend's dilemma, she asked, "When we met Elder Adams, he was traveling with a younger man. Is he also returning to America?"

"Yes, since the Prophet Joseph's assassination, the Twelve have taken over the management of the Church's affairs. Brother Brigham sent word to Elder Adams to return at once with his companion and as many of the English Saints as were prepared to gather to Zion."

"There is a great deal of turmoil with Brother Rigdon wishing to assume guardianship for the Church and some desiring one and some desiring another of the brethren to lead the Church. The murder of Brother Joseph has not brought an end to the harassment and persecution of the Saints by the mobbers, and should the Church be forced to leave Nauvoo, many of the leaders wish every able-bodied brother to be present to aid in the exodus." This man's accent was also American, suggesting he too might be a missionary.

"Brother Joseph was murdered?" Elsa had caught up to Olivia and Georgiana. She looked around at the solemn-faced men and began to cry. Olivia stared at the men in shocked dismay, and Georgiana felt as though something inside her had burst.

James rushed forward and placed an arm around Elsa. "What is going on here?" He glared at the gathering.

"James," Georgiana hastened to explain. "These gentlemen did not offend Elsa in any way. They are merely the bearers of bad news." She turned back to the men who stood, shifting their feet uneasily. "We had not heard of Brother Joseph's death. Perhaps you could give us the details?"

"We know little ourselves," the first man with the American accent explained. "Almost a month ago, a letter arrived for Elder Adams, who is in charge of the mission-aries in this part of England. It arrived while he was away attending to a baptismal service some distance from London. He was further delayed by yet a second group seeking baptism. When he returned and read the letter, he immediately contacted us all and advised us to meet him here today, and he would arrange for our passage home.

The only details he could pass on was that on June 27, scarcely more than three months past, the Prophet was jailed in Carthage awaiting trial when a mob broke into the jail, killing both him and his brother Hyrum."

James's head snapped back as though he had taken a hard punch. "What shall become of the Church? Who will lead us?"

"Jesus Christ Himself will continue to lead us as He always has," Elder White said. "But who will be His mouthpiece? I am not certain. I recall hearing Joseph say the Twelve as a united body hold all the keys, so perhaps they will continue to lead us until they receive further direction."

They conversed further with the group of saints and learned that Elder White was not sailing with them on the *Nightingale* but would be sailing on the *Carolina*. He had come aboard at the invitation of the small group of converts who had booked passage earlier on the *Nightingale*.

After discussing the situation at length, Georgiana again grew uneasy. Her eyes met Olivia's, and they excused themselves to continue on to their cabin.

They picked at their dinner that night and were much subdued. After James left, the women readied themselves for bed and spent a longer time than was usual reading from the Book of Mormon and saying their prayers.

Long after she could hear Elsa's gentle breathing turn to soft snores, Georgiana continued to lie awake. It saddened her that she would not be able to meet the Prophet in person, but her faith did not waver as to the truthfulness of the Church. She felt confident the Lord would make His wishes known about the next leader.

"Georgie?" Olivia revealed she was also unable to sleep.

"I'm not asleep."

"Robert gave me permission to be baptized. He said he talked to you and you helped him understand why it is so important to me. Thank you. But I wish I could be baptized before we begin our journey. Do you think we might go aboard the *Carolina* tomorrow and speak with Elder Adams and Elder Hughes? Perhaps there is some way to be baptized before we sail."

"Robert is taking my bracelet to his solicitor in the morning. Once that is accomplished, I will ask Elder Adams how much longer I must wait before I can be baptized." Her voice turned wistful. "I too desire to be washed clean before going further." She ran her fingers over the large gems at her wrist.

Just one more night, then the stolen jewels would be gone. They would be on their way back to their rightful owners and no matter what temptation came her way in the future, she would never steal again. With the return of the jewels, she expected a burden would be lifted from her shoulders, but how much longer would it take to know if she had been forgiven by her Heavenly Father?

* * *

Georgiana awoke to pronounced movement. Her bunk was swaying, and she could see that items that had been left on the table the previous night now rested on the floor. When she crawled to the ladder and tried to climb down from the upper bunk, she had difficulty maintaining her balance. She dressed quickly, though she found tasks such as buttoning her shoes difficult with the swaying motion of the ship. Hearing a giggle behind her, she turned to see Olivia making her way down the ladder from the upper bunk they shared.

"Oops!" Elsa clasped the bedpost for support. She, too, had been awakened by the moving ship. By the time all three were dressed, the ship had settled to the easy rocking motion they had become familiar with over the past week, signaling that the task of switching positions with the *Carolina* was complete.

A tap on the door heralded the arrival of breakfast, and James arrived a few minutes later. Over breakfast, he suggested that they go aboard the *Carolina* to search out the missionaries who had taught them the gospel. Olivia voiced immediate approval of the plan, and Elsa agreed it would be good to see the elders again and to meet some of the other members of the Church who were headed for America. Perhaps they would journey together all the way to Nauvoo.

"Robert said he would stop by to get my bracelet this morning. I think I should stay here until he arrives," Georgiana said, expressing regret.

"We shall wait then," Olivia declared, but it was obvious to Georgiana that her friend was disappointed at the delay. If her suspicions were correct concerning her friend's interest in the younger missionary who had taught them the gospel, waiting would be torture for her.

"No, you go ahead. I'm sure Robert won't be long." She insisted the others should not change their plans. "Since Robert will have to board the *Carolina* to reach the wharf after he collects my bracelet, perhaps he will allow me to accompany him as far as the sister ship, and I can meet up with you there."

"I'm certain he will be pleased to escort you." Olivia dabbed at her mouth and stood, anxious to be on her way. James and Elsa rose to their feet as well, and Olivia scurried to fetch the hats and parasols Robert had bought them to aid in their disguise as much as to complement their new attire.

"Keep the door locked until Robert gets here," James cautioned.

Once the others were gone, Georgiana returned their dishes to the tray and set it outside the door for the cabin boy to retrieve, then locked the door. Once that was done, she busied herself picking up the hairbrushes and small items that had been left scattered about the cabin by its various occupants. When she could find no more tasks to fill her time, she sat with the Book of Mormon in her lap. She tried to read but found herself unable to concentrate. After several futile attempts, she set the book down and paced the length of the room and back. Once she thought she heard hurried footsteps outside her door, but no knock followed, so she continued to pace and worry. It was unlike Robert to be late or to forget his promise.

He had said he would arrive early to collect the bracelet, as it was a considerable distance from the port area to the city proper, where his solicitor had offices. The return journey would be faster, but he wished to be aboard his ship well ahead of the time set for their departure. She unclasped the bracelet and looked at the jewels one last time. They were beautiful and seemed to beckon to her, but she refused to allow herself to be swayed.

Hurrying to the cupboard where she kept her few belongings, she searched until she found her sewing bag and in it the small cloth bag she had made for carrying the square of soap she used to keep her needles sharp. She pulled out the soap and dropped the bracelet inside the bag. She wondered if it might be better to remove the jewels from their settings and send just the stones on to Lord Wellington, but she wanted Lord Wellington to see the cheap bracelet and to confront Sydney with it. Besides, she wanted no reminders of Sydney Burton's perfidy and her own weakness about her.

That reminded her she still had Sydney's small silver pistol. Once more, she retrieved her sewing bag and this time removed the gun she'd hidden in the lining. It was too large to fit in the bag with the bracelet, so she dropped it in her pocket. She'd ask Robert to send it on to the Earl of Dorchester with the letter she'd written to him.

She wished Robert would arrive. Not only did she want to put Sydney and the jewels behind her, but she was anxious to see Robert this morning. She'd remained awake a long time last night savoring his words, and now she needed to be certain she hadn't imagined his kindness and words of admiration.

At last, the rap of knuckles on the door sent her scurrying to answer it. As she reached for the key, something made her hesitate.

"Robert?" she called softly. There was no answer. She waited with her ear pressed against the door, then she called his name in a slightly louder tone. When there was still no answer, she began to move away from the door. If Robert had knocked, he would have called her name, she reasoned, and he would have knocked again. With her head down, she stepped back, and that is when she saw that a piece of cream-colored stationery had been pressed beneath the heavy door.

Stooping, she retrieved the missive. On the outside of the folded paper was her name, Miss Georgiana Fenwick. With shaking fingers, she opened the sheet to discover a short note. She read it slowly. *Dear Miss Fenwick, I have been detained and will be unable to reach the Nightingale this morning. I must attend to business in the city. I have retained a boy to deliver the aforementioned item to my solicitor's office. Please meet him on the wharf at half past eleven sharp.* It was signed, *Captain Robert Carver.*

A wave of disappointment assailed her. She'd been looking forward to seeing Robert. She felt disappointment, too, that his brief note was so formal. It was as if last night had never happened. Perhaps it hadn't. Perhaps it was all a dream she had deluded herself into believing was real.

With her spirits somewhat dampened, she tied her bonnet in place and donned her newly completed cloak. She looked at her parasol and decided against carrying it.

Yesterday there had been a stiff breeze, and the weather was likely much the same today. Her bonnet would protect her face from prying eyes.

Opening the cabin door, she stepped into the hall and was struck by an almost eerie silence. Save for the creaking sounds the ship made, it was as though the vessel had been abandoned. The voices and bustle of the previous day were gone. The sound of her footsteps on the polished floor seemed particularly loud to her ears. They produced an echo, sounding like someone else's footsteps pursuing her. Feeling a sudden urgency to be around other people, she rushed up the steps and burst onto the deck.

At first she saw no one. Even the sailors she'd become accustomed to seeing rush about on deck were absent. The *Nightingale*'s ghostly silence was unnerving. To distract herself, she counted a large number of ships bobbing at anchor near the mouth of the river. Feeling calmer, she turned toward shore and was amazed by how close the *Nightingale* was to the *Carolina*. Other ships were anchored along the narrow wharf too, where the water was deep enough to allow them to hug the quay while loading or unloading. A person could almost leap from one ship to the next and in several instances a rough bridge made of rope and planks spanned the gap between two vessels. Such a bridge linked the *Nightingale* to the *Carolina*. A sailor stood on the near side of the bridge, watching the activity on the other ship.

The *Carolina*'s decks swarmed with activity. Voices called out in several different languages, little boys leaned over the rail, while clusters of people and luggage gathered in various spots, impeding the baggage carts. The sight chased away her case of nerves, and she searched the *Carolina's* deck for familiar faces. She caught a glimpse of a gray cloak and wondered if she might be lucky enough to locate her friends on her own. If so, James would surely accompany her to the rendezvous with Robert's messenger.

Georgiana approached the link between the ships with a great deal of trepidation. She could see the lashed planks lurch and bob in motion with each sway of the ships. She stepped closer and nearly swooned, though she had never swooned in her life. The bridge swung from side to side and there were gaps between the planks. Through the gaps, she could see brackish water far below. It lapped at the sides of the ships, and she could see numerous objects floating in the water, one of which appeared to be a small dead animal. She wrinkled her nose in disgust.

"Hold onto this rope, miss." The sailor nearest her extended a thick hemp rope toward her, and she clasped it gratefully in her gloved hands. Looking up, she saw a sailor on the other ship holding the other end of the rope, who was smiling encouragingly at her.

"Don't look down," the sailor beside her advised. "The other passengers, even the children, crossed without mishap, and you can do it too."

Taking a deep breath, she placed a foot on the first plank. Hand over hand, she clung to the lifeline as she placed one hesitant foot before the other. Without the rope, she feared she would have fallen into the filthy, cold water between the ships. Her progress was slow, but at last she caught sight of a hand extended toward her. She reached for it, and a grinning sailor guided her safely aboard the *Carolina*.

She looked around for a moment while catching her breath and willed her trembling limbs to cease their shaking. Once she'd gotten her bearings, she made her way toward two gray cloaks she thought might belong to Olivia and Elsa.

"Out of the way," a voice roared, and she barely managed to step aside for a cart laden with baggage.

A commotion behind had her turning to see a lad rolling a barrel across the deck. A woman screamed indignantly as it swiped too close to her skirt, and two gentlemen, shouting in some foreign tongue, chased after the boy. From the tone of their voices, she assumed they were berating the child for his carelessness.

From the corner of her eye, she saw someone else crossing the bridge between the two ships. She hadn't been the only passenger still aboard the ship after all. Reaching the *Carolina*, the man leaped from the end of the bridge and disappeared into the crowd. Georgiana felt her heart race. He had looked more than a little bit like Sydney. Horror almost brought her to her knees. Was it possible she hadn't been alone on the *Nightingale?* Had Sydney been that close to her? She tried to reason with herself. The person she'd seen couldn't be Sydney. Her imagination was playing strange tricks on her because she was nervous about the change in Robert's plans. Nevertheless, she ducked behind a portly gentleman and followed him until he stopped to converse with another gentleman.

After a few moments, her courage reasserted itself. She must hurry. Since she had no idea where her friends might be, she would have to make her way to the gangplank by herself. The sooner she turned the bracelet over to Robert's messenger, the sooner she could reboard the *Carolina* to search out her friends.

It took longer than she expected to worm her way through the crowd. She was almost to the gangplank when she saw Sydney. This time there was no mistake. He had just reached the bottom of the ramp leading from the *Carolina* to the wharf. He hurried across the wooden dock, dodging carriages and wagons. He stopped near an alley and beckoned to someone Georgiana could not see. A few moments later a boy emerged from the alley. They spoke together, then Sydney handed the boy something.

It was a trick! Somehow Sydney had learned about the jewels and discovered she was aboard the *Nightingale*. He had sent the note. She shivered, recalling the rap on her door. Her subconscious had been trying to tell her Robert no longer addressed her as Miss Fenwick and he wouldn't sign a note addressed to her with his title. She began to back away. She'd had a narrow escape.

Just then, Sydney looked up. She knew the moment he discovered her standing near the gangplank. Her mind screamed for her to run, but her feet were slow to respond. She saw him dash across the quay and leap toward the heavy planks that separated them. Suddenly she was moving, darting between people and circling luggage. She had to find James or even one of the sailors from the *Nightingale*.

Seeing a group of men in dark suits, she dashed toward them, hoping they were some of the missionaries and would give her shelter. Her foot brushed against something soft and a cry erupted as an infant rolled free of a ragged blanket and tumbled into her path. Teetering, she struggled to avoid stepping on the baby, only to trip, falling to her knees. Throwing out her arms to catch herself, she grasped the baby and rolled with it. Coming to a stop beside a tall coil of rope, she struggled to stand with the child in her arms.

Her mind seemed to freeze, and she was barely aware of the squirming infant. Soon, a realization of her predicament descended on her, and she frantically looked around for a place to hide. The baby screamed and flailed her tiny arms. Georgiana had no idea what to do with an infant at the best of times. Now she feared the child's cries would attract attention to herself. She couldn't abandon it to its own devices on the crowded deck. Someone might step on it or knock it into the water. But how could she escape Sydney while encumbered with an infant?

She placed the baby against her shoulder and patted her back as she had seen other women do with fussy children. To her surprise, the baby quieted. But now, what to do with her?

Her eyes darted every which way, searching for Sydney. She spotted a determined young woman with a coil of yellow braids atop her head attempting to push her way through the crowd. The baby's mother! She was starting toward the woman to hand over the child when an idea flashed into her mind. Sydney might catch her, but he must not find the jewels. She needed to hide them. But where? The answer was in her arms. No man would think to look in an infant's nappy! It took but a second to hide the small drawstring bag, then she was thrusting the infant into the startled young woman's arms.

The woman clasped the infant to her and said something Georgiana could not understand, but Georgiana didn't dare stay to find out what it was she said. She darted away into a cluster of families making their way below deck.

James, Elsa, and Olivia were nowhere to be seen. Sydney was aboard, but she had no idea where. Could her friends have returned to the *Nightingale?* She began weaving her way toward the connecting bridge.

As she passed a companionway that led to the ship's first-class cabins, something hard dug into her back, and Sidney's voice hissed in her ear. "Well, well, well. We meet again." He wrapped his arm around her neck and dragged her toward the stairs. Her hands tore at his arm as she tried to break his hold. Unable to breathe or keep herself upright, she fell more than walked, and she felt the stinging pain of first her hip, then a knee striking against the sharp edge of the stairs he forced her down. Her elbow struck a wall, sending shooting pains to her shoulder as Sydney pulled her into a dark recess beneath the steps. She continued struggling to free herself but could not break his hold. His arm was cutting off her air, and she was beginning to see spots before her eyes. She would die without being baptized—or seeing Robert again.

20

Sydney's hold suddenly lessened, and she drew in a deep gulp of air. She wanted to cry for help, but before she could draw sufficient air into her lungs, he grabbed her hair and pulled her face close to his.

"If you scream or try to run, I'll shoot you and toss your body overboard," he growled. "Give me the jewels, and I'll let you live."

"How—" She gasped, unable to even complete the question.

He laughed. "Wellington is dead. The old fool died two days ago, leaving all his assets, including the title, to his expected grandson. As the brat's father and guardian, it will all fall to me, including the jewels you stole." He chuckled without mirth, revealing a dark, cruel streak. "Imagine my delight when a messenger brought your letter last night just as I was leaving for my father-in-law's club— mine now. Foolishly, I set it aside until my return early this morning, else this would have already been settled."

He grabbed her arm, twisting it up behind her back. When she whimpered, he laughed.

"The jewels?"

"I—I don't have them."

He jerked harder on her arm. She screamed, and he clamped a hand over her mouth. Her hat tipped sideways, falling over one eye.

"Where are they? I know you haven't given them to Captain Carver because I arranged for him to be somewhat delayed this morning."

His words sent a fresh stab of fear to her breast.

"Here now, what's going on?" A shabby fellow with a rural accent peered through the stairs at them.

"Be about your business. A man can punish his wife as he sees fit," Sydney snarled.

Georgiana gasped and spoke the first name that popped into her mind. "Hughes." It came out as almost a moan. The man looked at her oddly, then turned back to the stairs and was soon gone.

"*He's?* Were you trying to say *he's* not my husband? What a fool you are. No man will take the word of a woman over that of a man, particularly a gentleman." Sydney delivered a vicious slap to her face and quickly covered her mouth to prevent her scream from attracting attention.

A young woman in a maid's attire, carrying a toddler and trailed by three little girls, started down the steps. The girls whined and protested returning to their cabin. "Your Papa said we shall sail late this evening and he wants you rested so you can join him on deck to bid England farewell."

Sydney drew Georgiana deeper into the shadows. She felt her hat fall and scarcely noted when her foot landed on its wide brim. When the children and their nursemaid disappeared into one of the cabins, Sydney scanned the stairs and the hall before dragging her to first one cabin door, then another, until he found one that had been left unlocked. He shoved her inside the room and turned the key, barring anyone else from entering.

His unexpected shove sent her stumbling forward. She barely managed to catch herself before striking her head against a post that supported one end of the cabin's two-tiered bunks. A soft thud against the wooden post reminded her of the small pistol in her pocket. She had shot him once, and she would do so again if it became necessary. She fumbled for the weapon, and as her fingers, made awkward by the gloves she wore, grasped the hard metal, the gun slipped from her fingers, sliding soundlessly between the blankets and the footboard of the bunk. The disappointment brought tears to her eyes.

"Hand it over!"

For a moment, she thought Sydney meant the dueling pistol.

"Those jewels are mine, and I mean to have them."

Relief swept through her. It was the bracelet he wanted. He didn't know about the gun, and if he didn't know, she might still find an opportunity to retrieve it. "Your interference cost me the Wellington jewels once, forcing me into marriage with a fool."

"You gave me the bracelet," she stalled for time. "You swore the stones were precious jewels, and you have no right to take it back."

"You're very clever—and beautiful too." He fingered a long curl that had come loose from her coiffure. "I quite admire your cleverness in discovering the faux gems and replacing them with some of the most valuable jewels in England outside of the royal treasury. It's too bad we couldn't have made a real match."

"I would sooner be dead than paired with you." Impulse rather than wisdom compelled her to repudiate his sly suggestion.

"You'll have your wish, but first the jewels!" He grasped her shoulders and shook her.

"I don't have them! Do you think me such a fool, I would carry them about on my person?" She struggled to free herself. One violent twist sent her sprawling before the cabin door. Before she could regain her feet, he grasped the back of her cloak, ripping it from her shoulders. He tossed it aside and reached for her again. She trembled with fear that he meant to search her person.

On her feet now, she backed away. "Had you waited but a few hours, Captain Carver would have delivered the jewels to his solicitor, and you would have only needed to present yourself at his office to claim them."

His eyes blazed with fury, giving him a demonic look that suggested he wasn't quite sane.

"Daphne thinks she has been clever, but she shall pay for planting doubts about me in her father's mind. She persuaded him to make her son his heir, and Wellington's solicitor refuses to advance me funds before it is known if the child is a male. He considers it his duty to dole out only that which he deems necessary to the upkeep of the estate until Daphne's child reaches his majority, but I cannot wait that long. I need those jewels now."

Georgiana understood more than Sydney knew. Should Daphne deliver a daughter, the estate would remain out of Sydney's reach until she produced a son and he reached adulthood. Sydney was a gambler and desperate for funds to finance his high life, and he would never tolerate less than complete control of the Wellington fortune. Suddenly she feared for Daphne. Sydney would find a way to punish her and obtain what he desired.

Leaping aside, she dashed away from Sydney, stripping off her gloves and screaming for help as she ran. She didn't expect anyone would hear her cries through the solid oak door of the cabin, but if she got another chance to shoot Sydney, she didn't want gloves to hamper her touch. Instinct told her Sydney would kill her if he discovered the jewels. He might kill a helpless baby and the child's mother as well if he discovered where she had hidden the bracelet.

Pounding sounded on the door, followed by the scrape of a key. Perhaps she had been heard and was about to be rescued. She opened her mouth to scream again. Sydney reacted quickly, grabbing her and placing his hand over her mouth as he dragged her behind the door, which abruptly shoved open. Sydney was prepared. He thrust her aside, and his gun came down on the head of a hapless porter whose only fault was delivering a large trunk to the cabin.

Georgiana watched in horror as the porter sprawled at her feet. Before she could climb over the prostate man, Sydney blocked her access to the open door, which he kicked shut and locked. Seeing him pocket the porter's key increased her fear. There seemed to be nothing she could do for herself, but seeing the man on the floor was bleeding profusely and in need of aid, she attempted to go to him. Sydney shoved her away.

He removed a length of rope that held the trunk fast to the porter's cart and used it to tie the unconscious man's hands. His eyes searched the room until he spotted a ball of fabric, lying kicked to one side. He reached for it, and Georgiana feared he would guess why she had abandoned her gloves. To her relief, he didn't comment on the gloves but used them to stuff the porter's mouth.

Catching a glint of silver peeking from beneath a quilt trailing from the bunk to the polished wood floor, she dashed toward it. Sydney caught her shoulder, twirling her toward him. His fist struck hard, and she felt herself falling into a sea of blackness.

* * *

When Georgiana awoke, it was to find herself contorted into a small, dark space with a terrible headache. At first, she was conscious only of her discomfort, then she remembered Sydney and all that had happened. She suspected she was inside the trunk the porter had delivered, which thought filled her with despair. She tried to think rationally, to plan an escape, but how could she escape from a sea trunk? She pounded on the sides of the trunk until her hands ached. Deciding the action was useless, she ceased hammering to think.

She had no idea how long she had been unconscious. She didn't even know if she were still aboard the *Carolina*. It seemed logical to assume Sydney had placed her in the trunk in order to transport her to some other place for questioning, and since she couldn't feel the gentle rocking she'd grown accustomed to on the *Nightingale*, it was probably also safe to assume she was on land.

She wondered if the *Carolina* had already sailed, taking the bracelet with it, and if the *Nightingale* had also put to sea, carrying her friends far away. And what about Robert? Was he even alive? Sydney had boasted of preventing his return for the bracelet. The prospect of never seeing Robert again brought tears to her eyes and pain to her heart. Closing her eyes, she began to pray that Robert was safe. She wondered if she had been missed and if her friends had launched a search for her. She prayed again, mostly for strength to endure the terror that awaited her.

After what seemed a long time, she heard footsteps, followed by a grating sound, alerting her the trunk was about to open. She braced herself to fling herself at Sydney. Perhaps she could catch him off guard and make her escape. The lid opened slowly, and Georgiana pushed her way upward, not in the dramatic gesture she had planned, but in an awkward tumble that left her sprawled across rough cobblestones. She looked up, bracing herself for a confrontation with Sydney. Instead of Sydney, she found herself staring up at his wife, Lady Daphne Burton.

"Who?" Daphne appeared every bit as shocked as Georgiana.

Georgiana had no idea what Daphne had expected to find in the trunk, but clearly she wasn't it.

"Who are you?" Daphne finally asked. She hesitated, then a smile spread across her face and she answered her own question. "You're Georgiana, the girl who sent the letter to Papa. Quick, you must be away before Sydney returns." She rushed toward Georgiana, who was struggling to regain her feet, and offered her assistance.

When they stood facing each other, Georgiana asked, "You read the letter?"

"Yes. I will explain later, but now we must leave this place." Taking Georgiana's arm, Daphne urged her toward an open door that let light into what Georgiana could see was a rough gardener's shed. Feeling numb and somewhat confused, she followed Daphne into sunlight coming from low in the west. As she looked about her, her confusion grew. Olivia's house could be glimpsed a short distance away beyond a familiar garden. She turned toward it.

"This way," Daphne clutched at her arm, turning her toward the path that led away from the house and to a gate that opened onto a narrow lane. Georgiana heard its familiar squeak as Daphne thrust it open.

"Your baby," Georgiana protested, seeing Daphne's awkward gait, but Daphne didn't slow her steps.

"There's no time to delay," Daphne gasped, holding her stomach with one hand while urging Georgiana to hurry with the other. In minutes, they came to a pony cart, and Daphne urged Georgiana to climb inside. Daphne took the reins, and the pony began to move at a brisk clip down the narrow lane that connected the carriage-house-turned-garden-shed to a slightly wider but familiar street.

"My friends . . . The *Nightingale*." Georgiana stopped in confusion. Was Daphne helping her or was she obeying the bidding of her husband? It could be a mistake to trust Sydney's wife.

"Don't speak," Daphne warned. There was a strange glitter in the young woman's eyes that made Georgiana wonder if she were as mad as her husband. "I know you are anxious to sail with Captain Carver, and I will do my best to get you to the quay before his ship departs. It is a considerable distance, and we must hurry." Slapping the reins across the pony's back, she urged it to a trot. The lane gave way to a busy street, and Daphne became occupied with threading her way through traffic. At length, she turned onto a less-traveled byway that followed the river.

"You may well wonder why I am helping you instead of my husband," the fashionably dressed young woman began. "I will do my best to explain." She slapped the reins across the pony's back, urging it to greater speed.

The rocking, bumpy ride brought a new worry to Georgiana's mind. She'd heard of such rides bringing on premature labor. She certainly didn't wish to be delayed by the birth of a baby. She did some quick calculations in her head and concluded the babe's arrival couldn't be expected before the new year, so perhaps all would be well.

"At first I thought my husband was merely young and had not yet learned responsibility," Daphne began to speak.

Georgiana sat up straighter, hoping to gain information that might enable her to discover whether she was being rescued or if she should jump from the cart and endeavor to make her own way to the wharf.

"He left me alone for days and weeks at a time on our wedding trip, and he sulked and was impatient when we were together. Wishing only to spend his time in gaming halls, he became angry because of my desire to visit cathedrals and view paintings I had heard so much about. He slapped me when I displeased him, then came frequent beatings."

Georgiana gasped. Robert had mentioned rumors of her mistreatment, but hearing Daphne speak of Sydney's abusive behavior made it more real, especially when she touched the tender spot on her own jaw where Sydney's fist had rendered her unconscious.

"Sydney cut our trip short. I'm certain it was because he ran short of funds due to his gambling. Upon returning to England, we stayed one night in London, but he refused to let me see my mother or sisters. The next morning, we traveled to one of the estates Papa had turned over to us as part of my dowry. Sydney was excessively cranky on the journey, and I discovered he had sustained some sort of injury that pained him when he walked."

Georgiana considered explaining about the wound James had given Sydney, then decided remaining silent might be the better course to pursue. And for the present, she'd remain in the pony cart. It was headed in the right direction and moving faster than she would be able to travel on her own.

"I quickly learned the extent of his cruelty." The flat tone Daphne had been using disappeared and her tone turned bitter. "Sydney returned to London without telling me of his intentions to do so, though he beat me thoroughly before departing. I soon discovered the handful of servants left to attend me to be rude and dis-respectful and that I was a prisoner in a long unused castle that had been in my father's family for centuries. One day, I was able to slip past the old dragon who watched my every move. Because I had visited the estate as a child, I knew of a secret passage leading to a monk's hole and from there to an abandoned folly in the garden. I made my way through the tunnel, though I am deathly fearful of spiders. From the folly, I slipped into the woods and made a discovery that changed everything." Daphne glanced sideways at Georgiana, then urged the pony to greater speed.

"In a new stable, some distance from the manor, I came upon a magnificent gray gelding. I share my mother's passion for prime horseflesh, and I recognized the animal almost immediately. It was the animal the assailant who held up father's coach the morning after my betrothal ball had ridden. Poking around the stable, I discovered a black suit of clothing and a mask."

Georgiana felt sympathy for the girl. What a terrible discovery for a new bride to make.

"I wasn't as surprised as you might think," Daphne said. "I was already familiar with my husband's cruelty and his need for money because of his gaming habit, so seeing him as the thief who shot Papa wasn't a great leap."

"Someone is coming!" Georgiana whispered, becoming aware the pony cart wasn't the only conveyance on the quiet road they traveled. Daphne expertly turned the pony toward an opening in the trees. Once out of sight, she climbed down from the cart and stood at the pony's head with her hand on the animal's nose to keep him from whinnying a greeting to the pair pulling the fast-approaching conveyance.

After but a few moments, a carriage flashed by, traveling too fast for Georgiana to tell whether it was a private or public vehicle. They waited until the sound of the passing carriage died away before resuming their journey. A slender moon had risen, a signal she had heard sailors aboard the *Nightingale* speak of as their warning to man their posts, for it was the hour the tide would change. Georgiana's agitation increased. The *Nightingale* would soon be on its way, without her if they didn't soon reach the wharf.

"At that moment, I made a decision," Daphne went on as though there had been no interruption. "Sydney had almost killed Papa once and shown he had no regard for me. I feared he would kill Papa to obtain the Wellington fortune and with Papa out of the way, he would rid himself of me as well. Not even our child would be safe once Sydney gained control of Papa's fortune. Fearing someone might stop me before I could warn Papa, I donned Sydney's clothes, save for the mask, and covered myself with my cloak. It took four days and three nights spent sleeping in the woods to reach London. I went to Papa, but he could do little, though he insisted on our removal to his London home when he discovered I was with child."

The cart left the country lane and bounced more precariously on a cobbled street. Georgiana caught a whiff of the rank air that constantly hovered over the docks, near where the river widened into the bay. She clung to the sides of the cart and prayed the pony would move faster. Daphne was still talking, and Georgiana had long since gotten over her shock at the change in the previously quiet young woman.

"While returning from a visit with his man of business, Papa was injured when another carriage forced his off an embankment into a canal. He was ill for some time but appeared to be much better the past fortnight. Then two days ago, he died quite abruptly. His valet suspects he was smothered, and Mama agrees. Sydney has already informed Mama that she and my sisters must retire to a small estate owned by her brother, which shall eventually fall to our second son should we have one. "

"Oh no!" Georgiana hesitated. "I am sorry for the loss of your father. I hesitate to say, I already knew of your father's demise and that Sydney shared that information in such a way as to raise my suspicions that he had a hand in it. Do you know where he was at the time of the earl's death?"

"Well you might ask." Daphne sounded bitter. "He claimed he was visiting his mistress, the opera singer, Olivia Samuels, at the town house we just left. He frequently boasts of their relationship to taunt me and has spent much of his time of late at that house."

"Olivia and her staff left that house two months ago. She is not his mistress and never has been," Georgiana stated in no uncertain terms. "She despises him."

"You are certain? Sydney is not the only one who has suggested to me that they have a relationship of long standing." Daphne looked uncertain, and Georgiana hastened to explain.

"Olivia Samuels is Captain Carver's sister, a most respectable young woman who is being forced to leave England due to Sydney's harassment—which almost resulted in her death by fire. She has never been any man's mistress, and though Sydney is obsessed with her, she detests him." Georgiana glanced sideways at Daphne, wondering if she had said too much.

The hollow sound of wooden planks replaced the clatter of a cobbled street. "We shall reach the place where a number of ships are anchored in a few moments. Will you be able to ascertain which ship is Captain Carver's?" Daphne asked.

"Indeed I shall." Georgiana began peering through the gloom, searching for the *Carolina* and hoping the *Nightingale* was still nearby. Daphne began speaking faster, anxious to complete her story.

"Sydney left in a fury this morning just after returning from a night on the town. In his hurry, he dropped a letter near the foot of the stairs where a maid discovered it and carried it to me. I learned the young woman who gave my family aid and possibly saved my parents' lives the day following my betrothal ball was not a governess as we had assumed, but a servant fleeing for her life from Burton

House. I find it worth the price of a few jewels to know the name of our savior that day. I plan to use your letter once you are safely away to convince a magistrate to name my mother's brother, instead of Sydney, my child's guardian."

"But how did you find me?" Georgiana asked.

"Your letter said you were leaving England, so I expected Sydney would attempt to intercept you before you could leave. I sent my father's valet, Charles, to enquire concerning which ships were expected to sail today. Learning Captain Carver's ship was among those expecting to depart this evening, he hid himself to watch for Sydney. He saw him board the ship then leave it a short time later with a large trunk. He followed Sydney to the opera singer's house, where he left the trunk before rushing away again. Charles then reported to me. The strongest impression came over me that I should find out for myself what the trunk contained."

"When Sydney found I didn't have the jewels, he must have returned to search my cabin," Georgiana mused. "Oh, please hurry. If he finds Olivia, he will kill her." Georgiana leaned forward as though she would leap to the ground and race the pony to the wharf. Shadows were lengthening, and businesses appeared shabbier. An awful stench filled the air, and loud laughter erupted from a nearby pub. She felt sudden concern for Daphne. "You aren't safe here," she warned the woman who had rescued her. "Let me down and return quickly to your mother."

"I'm safer than you think." A dark shape loomed out of an alley and caught the bridle of Daphne's pony.

Georgiana shrank back before she recognized the Earl of Wellington's valet.

"You must hurry," the former soldier told her. "Sailors are removing the gangplank linking the *Carolina* to shore."

21

Georgiana took Charles's hand and leaped to the ground. "Thank you," she hurled the words in Daphne's direction as she sprinted away. Clutching her skirt high lest she stumble, she raced for the ramp leading to the *Carolina*.

"Wait!" she called as she ran toward an ever-widening gap between shore and the gangplank that was being drawn toward the deck of the ship. "I must get aboard." *I can't be this close and fail!* She ran as she'd never run before. "Please wait!" she screamed once more.

"You're too late," one of the sailors shouted back, but the plank stopped its movement. A gap yawned between its end and the shore. The sailors held the gangplank steady, seemingly waiting for orders from someone higher in command.

"Jump!" someone shouted. She didn't think to wonder who, though it may have been Daphne or Charles. Without taking time to think the action through, she clasped her skirt tighter and launched herself from shore toward the plank hovering over the water, landing in a heap against the gangplank boards. With both hands, she scrabbled for a hold, ignoring her smarting knees and the undignified spectacle she made with her skirts whipping around her legs and her hair falling across her face. Grasping the edge of the plank with her fingers, she gripped with all her might and felt for a foothold with her toes, only to become aware that her feet dangled over the water. Perhaps she could crawl. If the sailors continued to hold the gangplank steady, she could make it. She struggled to draw up her knees beneath her then began inching one hand forward for a new handhold.

A loud report she recognized as a gunshot rang out, and splinters of wood struck her face. The unexpected attack nearly cost her the precarious hold she had on the heavy plank. It dipped and swayed beneath her. Flattening herself against the boards, she lay still, almost frozen with fear. Screams echoed from aboard the *Carolina*, followed by angry howls. It became evident the passengers lining the ship's rail were outraged that someone had shot at her. She felt a jolt, then rapid, steady movement as the sailors pulled at the plank to which she clung. Another shot sounded, sending most of the passengers running for the stairs. The bullet whizzed past Georgiana's face, then fell harmlessly to the water below. She cringed, knowing a third shot could come at any moment and might be more carefully aimed.

She closed her eyes and prayed. When she opened them again, she saw hands extended toward her, mere inches from where she gripped the plank. She also heard voices shouting for those drawing in the gangplank to hurry. She reached forth one hand, and at last her fingers touched a calloused sailor's hand, then she was crawling from the plank to the deck of the *Carolina*. A dozen sailors and bystanders encircled her, offering her safety.

"This way, miss." A sailor hustled her toward a companionway. "You'll be safe . . ."

"With me." Sydney stepped in front of her, a triumphant light in his eyes and a pistol pointing at her heart. He held out his free hand toward her. The sailor shifted, offering her partial protection with his body.

Sydney would kill her if she went with him, but if she did not, he would shoot the sailor who was attempting to protect her. She could not further endanger the sailor, and she would prefer death to revealing the location of the jewels. Though the jewels were worth a considerable fortune, she knew turning them over to Sydney would not secure her freedom. Whether he got the jewels or not, he meant to kill her. She sensed that in his twisted mind, his grievances against her had multiplied. He had assigned blame to her for their thwarted affair, for running away, for interfering with his theft of the Wellington jewels, for outwitting him in substituting valuable jewels in place of the colored lumps of glass in the bracelet he had given her, and even for Olivia's repudiation of him. Even though she was a woman, he couldn't risk having her identify him as a highwayman and possibly a murderer. No matter what she did, he would kill her. Better it should be in a public place where there were witnesses.

"No," she backed away. Not expecting her refusal, Sydney hesitated, appearing uncertain. Those seconds gave her a chance to put a small distance between them.

"Put the gun down," a stern voice commanded, and Georgiana halted to stare past Sydney at Robert, who was emerging from the companionway with a tiny derringer in his hand, one she knew well. Her heart leaped, not just at his timely intervention, but because the silver pistol was evidence he had gone looking for her.

Sydney whirled, firing prematurely, then twisted back to launch himself toward Georgiana. Startled into a response, Robert fired too, and a small hole appeared in Sydney's coat, slowing, but not stopping him.

"Run, Georgie! Run!" Robert shouted.

Georgiana's feet flew. She lost a shoe as she darted behind a mast and crouched behind a furled sail. If she could reach the bridge between the boats, she would have a chance. Taking advantage of lowered sails and coils of rope as well as cargo lashed to the deck, she worked her way toward the walkway linking the two ships. Recognizing at last the spot where she'd stepped aboard the *Carolina*, she made a dash for the rail. Grasping it, she stared across the gap that separated the ships. The terrible reality left her mind almost numb. There was no break in the rail and the bridge was gone!

Raising her eyes, she saw Olivia, James, and Elsa leaning over the rail of the *Nightingale*. They waved and shouted, but she couldn't make out their words. James made frantic signals she couldn't understand, then he turned away, running toward a group of sailors. He waved his arms and shouted, but the sailors merely shook their heads. One pointed to something she couldn't see. Then both James and the sailor disappeared in the opposite direction from the place where she stood.

A cold chill ran up her spine as she realized the ships were farther apart than they had been that morning and no sailor stood ready to help her across. Where all the sails had been down since their arrival aboard the ship, now a few were slowly filling with wind. Suddenly she understood what James had tried to tell her. The *Nightingale* was drifting toward the open sea. But that made no sense. How could the *Nightingale* leave without her captain?

Hearing shots behind her and the sound of pounding feet, she looked from side to side, searching for a place to hide. Seeing Robert running toward her, she felt a moment's joy and took a step in his direction, then Sydney appeared behind him. He was swaying as he ran, but coming fast with a gun in his hand, which he was attempting to aim at Robert.

"Jump!" Robert shouted when he saw her. Before she could react, his arm was around her waist. She clung tightly, circling both arms around his chest. Together, they flew high over the rail. She dug her fingers into his coat. The shock of cold as they struck the water almost forced her to inhale. They seemed to go down forever, but at last Robert reversed direction, pulling them upward with powerful kicks. Her head broke the surface of the water, and she clung to Robert, gasping for air and sputtering with shock. Water streamed from her eyes, obscuring her vision.

"Are you all right?" Robert asked, concern in his voice.

"Yes," she whispered, though she really couldn't be certain. She was bruised, shaken, and remembering too clearly the filth she and Olivia had held their noses at in the river earlier as they'd gazed down at the water from the deck of the *Nightingale*, but she was glad to be alive and to feel Robert's arms around her.

"Can you swim?" Robert asked.

"No," she whimpered. A ripple of water caught them unexpectedly. It closed over their heads and she feared she would drown. Her grip tightened on Robert, and she struggled to climb above the water. Feeling her head above the water again, she spluttered and spit to make certain she hadn't swallowed any of the foul river water.

"You're safe," Robert assured her, "but you'll drown us both if you grip my neck any tighter." Ashamed, she eased her hold.

A shot rang out, and a small splash was heard nearby. It served as a frightening reminder that Sydney was trying to kill them. Raised voices came from the ship above them, followed by more gunfire, some of which landed much too close.

"We're going to have to swim." Robert kicked backward toward the deeper shadows near the ship.

"But, I can't . . ."

"Hold on to my shoulders," Robert instructed. "You won't hurt me, I promise. Whatever you do, don't panic and grip my neck. We'll stay in the shadow of the *Carolina* as long as possible. Sydney won't be able to see us in the blackness of the ship's shadow."

At first, it felt strange to float through the water, just above Robert's back, clinging tightly to his shoulders. Each ripple of water seemed higher than the last, colder too, and they left her gasping for breath. She wondered that the water could be so cold when the past few days had been almost warm.

The turmoil on the ship seemed to subside as Robert made even breaststrokes following the *Carolina*'s length to her bow. It may have been the cold, settling deep inside

Georgiana, that made the sounds aboard the ship seem to fade away. Lethargy crept over her, and she was no longer certain she was still clutching Robert's muscular shoulders. Perhaps drowning wouldn't be so bad and she would be at peace.

"Georgie! Georgiana!" Robert's voice was stern, calling her back to an awareness of their situation.

"So cold . . ." Her mind began to drift again.

"Just a few more minutes," Robert pleaded. He drew her around to face him, treading water to support them both. From somewhere close by came a creaking sound.

"Sydney! He's coming." She jerked to full awareness.

"No. Everything is all right."

A black shape loomed before them, and Georgiana cringed, expecting the sharp bite of a bullet.

"Over here," Robert called just above a whisper. The shape came closer, and she nearly collapsed when she saw a dinghy materialize before her.

"Captain?" a voice she recognized as belonging to Robert's second mate queried as the rowboat pulled even with them.

Her hands refused to cooperate as she attempted to haul herself aboard the small boat. Numb with cold, her hands were useless. Other hands reached to pull her over the side, where she collapsed on the bottom of the small wooden boat. Someone wrapped a blanket around her. A breeze picked up, further lowering the temperature and adding to her misery.

She was vaguely aware of two people pulling and shoving to drag Robert into the boat. She wanted to help, but she couldn't move. Robert landed beside her, and her foggy brain told her she should share her blanket with him, but before she could gain her frozen limbs' cooperation to lift it toward him, someone else wrapped a blanket around him. Almost as though they had planned it, their exhausted, cold bodies, wrapped in scratchy, wool blankets, slumped toward each other.

Georgiana and Robert huddled together while their rescuers rowed toward the *Nightingale*. The part of her that was still conscious braced for the impact of a bullet as the boat left the ship's dark shadow, but none came.

She was never to remember her actual arrival aboard the *Nightingale*. Her first real awareness came as Elsa and Olivia removed her sodden gown and eased her into a half barrel filled with steamy water. Elsa scrubbed her hair twice, and Olivia poured a pitcher of warm water laced with perfume over her head to rinse away the last of the smelly river water. They toweled her dry and helped her into her sleeping robe before Olivia handed her a warm mug of creamy, rich chocolate. Her friends watched her closely until she drained the last drop of it. She drifted asleep, feeling warm and safe and loved.

When she awoke, it was to an awareness that something was different. She noticed first that she was lying in the lower bunk where Elsa had slept since their arrival aboard the *Nightingale*. Then she felt the rocking motion of the ship. They were at sea. Something else had changed as well. She could hear singing. The melody was soft and not quite familiar. Then she recognized a tune Elsa had sung on occasion since her baptism, but the singer was not Elsa. Olivia sat on the floor a short distance away. Her voice was soft, but filled with a vibrancy and joy Elsa could never manage. She appeared absorbed in thought, oblivious to the lovely sound coming from her throat.

"You're awake!"

Georgiana must have moved or made some sound that caught Olivia's attention.

"Are you feeling better? Is there anything you need?"

"Robert?" she asked.

"He's fine. After but a short rest, he insisted on claiming the helm. He prefers to guide his ship personally until it passes Land's End. He sent a messenger a short time ago asking after your condition," she added with a grin.

Georgiana sat up, a happy glow filling her heart, then she remembered. The jewels were gone. She had no way to reclaim them or return them to their rightful owners. She had failed. Tears came to her eyes.

"What is it, Georgie?" Olivia scrambled to her knees, then sat beside her on the bunk. "Are you in pain? Did Sydney hurt you?"

"No, I am fine, but I wish to be baptized. I felt certain the Holy Spirit was protecting me and that it was Heavenly Father who sent Daphne to rescue me, but without the jewels, which I hid aboard the *Carolina*, I can never make restitution."

"Perhaps you can reclaim them when we reach Boston, but if not, I'm not certain it matters. Elsa, James, and I spoke at great length with the elders about baptism. I think Elder Adams may have had you in mind when he said the first step to membership in the Church is faith in the Lord Jesus Christ. He said it is that faith which gives us the determination to repent, which is the next step."

"He explained that to me when we first discussed my desire to be baptized." Tears continued to stream down her cheeks.

"But then, he looked right at me, to say, 'sometimes it is not possible to correct our mistakes and return all as it was. Then our Savior steps in to carry the burden for us. He is not as concerned about the details of restitution, if we have done all in our power to make right our sins, as He is about our broken hearts and contrite spirits.'"

"Elder Hughes said I needed to return the jewels. They are lost now, and if I work the rest of my life, I will never earn enough to repay their true owners."

"Did you do all you could to return them?" Olivia reached for her hands and looked into her eyes."

"I'm not certain. When I returned to the *Carolina* after Sydney took me away, my only thought was to reach the *Nightingale*."

"You nearly paid with your life for attempting to return the jewels. Now I believe it is between you and the Lord to decide whether your efforts to make restitution were enough. If you truly believe all you have been taught, then you must pray, and only God can tell you whether you are ready for baptism."

Olivia's words brought calmness to Georgiana's heart. She would pray, and she would not give up. God knew better than anyone else her intentions and her desires. One day He would accept her offering and allow her entrance into His kingdom. Until then, she would work at proving her worthiness.

When you've done all that you can, the Savior steps in to do the rest. That is the meaning of the Atonement. Elder Adams's words came to mind and brought comfort.

"Come now, you must eat and dress. A turn on deck will help to clear away any lingering ill effects from your misadventure." Olivia smiled encouragingly, and Georgiana shoved back the covers. An overpowering urge to seek out Robert to assure herself that he was safe sent her scrambling for her clothes.

* * *

Stepping on deck, Georgiana looked around in amazement. The ship's sails billowed above her like clouds, and a stiff breeze ruffled her hair. A number of people strolled on the deck, and sailors could be seen attending to a variety of tasks. One sailor, perched at a dizzying height above deck, kept watch with a spyglass. The deck beneath her feet dipped, and she felt herself sliding toward the railing that circled the ship. Reaching out, she used the rail to steady herself, then watched in fascination the steady sheet of water flying backward from where the bow of the ship cut through the water. It was a magnificent sight.

Clinging to the rail, she made her way to the place where Robert stood, braced in a wide stance, behind the ship's wheel, his powerful hands resting on the polished wood. There was something exhilarating about flying before the wind across the water, hearing the cry of sea birds, and feeling a faint spray of seawater on her face. Most exciting was seeing Robert's broad shoulders and knowing his strength and character. He turned, as though sensing her presence. He beckoned her closer, then before returning his hand to the spokes of the great wheel before him, he drew her within the circle formed by his hands on the wheel.

She stood within his arms, enjoying the fresh, tangy breeze on her face and the warmth of Robert's bulk behind her. Then he spoke as though reading the questions that still crowded into her mind.

"I learned early yesterday morning that Lord Wellington had died and that his wife had requested an investigation into his death." Robert seemed anxious to explain his failure to keep their appointment to transfer the jewels to his safekeeping that morning. "I hurried on to London to stop the delivery of your letter, fearing it might fall into Sydney's hands. When I reached my solicitor's office, I learned my fears were well grounded as a new clerk had acted precipitously. Fearing the turn of events had placed you in danger, I was anxious to return to my ship. Leaving Ethinbridge's office, I was stopped by a gentleman who claimed to be an investigator. He questioned my interest in Wellington and insisted I accompany him or be placed under arrest. At length, I became convinced he had no connection to the Watch but had been set to delay my return to the *Nightingale*. When I confronted him with my suspicions, he became belligerent and a fight ensued. Though I beat him handily, it further delayed my return."

"Sydney hinted that he had arranged for you to be delayed," Georgiana confirmed his suspicion.

"I rushed back to the *Nightingale* to learn you were not in your cabin, nor were you with Olivia. Immediately, I launched a search. One of the missionaries, an Elder Hughes, approached me with a story of a farmer convert coming upon a man who was beating his wife. The farmer was concerned that the woman had called out for Hughes. Sensing something was amiss, Hughes went in search of my sister and found me. We proceeded to the place where the altercation supposedly took place and discovered your hat, at which we both became alarmed. With the cooperation of the *Carolina's* captain, a search of the cabins followed and a porter was found bound and gagged in one. Your cloak was there and a small pistol such as you had described to me earlier was found under a quilt."

"I wanted to use it to threaten him, but I dropped it."

"The porter said the man who hit him, leaving him stunned and unable to move, knocked you out and stuffed your body into the trunk he had delivered earlier. I despaired of ever seeing you again."

Was it her imagination or had Robert pressed his lips to her hair? "Daphne helped me escape." She related Daphne's role in her rescue and return to the ship.

The wind turned cold, filling the sails as it carried them westward, leaving Land's End far behind. Georgiana stood between Robert's arms and scarcely noticed the chill air. He pointed to something large, a fish of some kind that rose out of the water then slid back beneath the waves.

"When I thought I had lost you, I was filled with rage and fear, but I couldn't give up. Something inside me urged me to continue searching. Elder Hughes said that was the Holy Spirit telling me not to lose heart. That was when I determined to remain in England and pursue Sydney until I found you. I gave the first mate orders to sail on schedule, should I not return before the tide turned. And as I began making my way toward the gangplank, I saw you leap toward it. I began running to assist you aboard, but there were so many other willing rescuers, I couldn't get close." He was silent for several minutes, and she placed a hand on his arm, feeling him tremble with emotion.

"I heard gunshots," he continued at length. "The crowd, who had been on deck to observe the ship's departure, ran for cover, shoving me backward. I struggled my way back to the deck to find you being held at gunpoint." He lifted one arm from the wheel and drew her close. His voice murmured in her ear. "On one of my voyages, the Mormon elders said a temple was being built in Nauvoo and that when it is finished, a man will be able to marry his wife forever, not just until death separates them. I've been thinking about that and have concluded that is what I want, to be with you for eternity. Do you think you might consider marrying a seafaring man?"

"Only if that seafaring man is you." Tears crept down her cheeks to be tossed away by the wind.

"I know of your desire to be baptized a Mormon. I'll not stand in your way. I promise you that, not because I love you, which I do, but because I have thought on the

Mormon faith and it has become apparent to me that I am more than a little interested in studying more about the Church myself. There are missionaries aboard this ship, and by the time we reach Boston, there may be three of us waiting to be baptized."

* * *

In the days to come, Georgiana frequently stood between Robert's arms as he piloted the tall ship closer to America. He had declared his love for her, and they had yet to discuss whether she would accompany him to sea in the years to come or if she should remain behind to welcome him at the end of each journey. This day, she stared pensively to the west. Somewhere out there, the *Carolina* moved westward too, carrying a bracelet worth a fortune. She had learned the sister ship was bound for New Orleans while the *Nightingale* would land in New York. There had been no sign of the *Carolina* since they had departed England, and the farther they traveled, the less chance there would be of their meeting again.

Someone who had watched from the *Nightingale's* crow's nest the night of their departure had reported that shots were fired after she and Robert took to the water and that Sydney had fallen on deck. Robert had speculated that removing Sydney from the ship and answering a magistrate's questions had delayed the *Carolina's* departure and placed considerable distance between the two vessels. He'd also attempted to assure her of Daphne's safety. Even if Sydney had survived, there was still the post sent to the Earl of Dorchester and a whole ship full of witnesses to Sydney's attempted murder of her and the *Nightingale's* captain.

A sound carried on the ocean air, above the rush of the wind and flapping of sails. It was Olivia in full voice. A sailor stopped. He gazed toward the place where the singer with arms flung wide stood near the ship's prow as though he were witnessing an angel's song. Georgiana's eyes met Robert's and they both smiled. Free of Sydney, Olivia's voice had returned and was growing in strength each day. Meeting with Elder Hughes before they departed and giving him her promise to meet him in Nauvoo by Christmas could have played a part in the return of her voice as well.

Georgiana's gaze caught a sparkle on the water, reminding her of the jewels she'd worn on her wrist for more than a year. She wondered if she would ever see the bracelet again or what would become of it. It could go to the bottom of the ocean for all she cared. It wasn't hers, and she'd done all she could to return the jewels to their rightful owners. She had all she wanted—Robert, dear friends, and a quiet assurance from a still, small voice that she could be baptized when the opportunity arose. Deep in her heart, she felt the love and warmth of her Heavenly Father's forgiveness.

She snuggled closer to Robert and wondered who officiated at a shipboard wedding when the captain was the groom—and how long it would take to finish that temple in Nauvoo.